BY BRIAN CALLISON

A Flock of Ships
A Plague of Sailors
The Dawn Attack
A Web of Salvage
Trapp's War
A Ship is Dying
A Frenzy of Merchantmen
The Judas Ship
Trapp's Peace
The Auriga Madness
The Sextant
Spearfish
The Bone Collectors
A Thunder of Crude
Trapp and World War Three
The Trojan Horse
Crocodile Trapp
Ferry Down
The Stollenberg Legacy

BRIAN CALLISON

THE STOLLENBERG LEGACY

HarperCollins_Publishers_

HarperCollins*Publishers*
77–85 Fulham Palace Road,
Hammersmith, London W6 8JB

www.**fire**and**water**.com

This paperback edition 2001
1 3 5 7 9 8 6 4 2

First published in Great Britain by
HarperCollins*Publishers* 2000

ISBN 0 00 651392 1

Set in Meridien by
Palimpsest Book Production Limited, Polmont, Stirlingshire

Printed and bound in Great Britain by
Omnia Books Limited, Glasgow

CHAPTER ONE

His features had hardly been marked at all. In fact he'd changed very little in the nine months since Kyle had last seen him. Apart, that was, from his being dead this time.

'Are you able, sir, to confirm that it . . . he . . . is Mister David Wallace McDonald?'

'Doctor McDonald,' Kyle heard himself correct dully. 'Not medical. A doctorate in military history. From King's College?'

That the constable should fully appreciate David's achievement seemed terribly important, somehow.

'*Doctor* David Wallace McDonald,' the officer standing beside Kyle at the mortuary viewing window amended uncomfortably. But then he was young: far too young, Kyle would have thought, to be charged with conducting such grim ceremonial. Too young to be a proper policeman, come to that, and patently ill at ease. Though bemused by the pace with which this utterly harrowing duty had overtaken him, Kyle had hardly failed to register that his chaperon appeared to be undergoing a considerable degree of stress himself. A degree seemingly at odds with his vocation.

Could it be, Kyle speculated listlessly, *that our joint pilgrimage to this doleful place – unarguably a nightmare for me – also represents his maiden voyage into bureaucratic waters disturbed by sudden death?*

A surge of envy, almost of resentment briefly claimed priority. *Either way he's still more fortunate than I. Merely enduring for the first time one of the least pleasant aspects of a policeman's profession. A theoretically impersonal observer on behalf of the State – that's all he is. Here only to witness, not to actually* make *identification of just another provisionally tagged corpse following its unscheduled conversion to that unhappy state.*

'Please, sir – can you?' the young officer pressed. 'Identify the deceased as Doctor David Wallace McDon . . . ?'

'Yes,' Kyle said, unable to deny David's waxen counterfeit behind glass any longer. 'He . . . it is. *Was*.'

Kyle thought he'd signed some sort of official form then. He couldn't really remember. An awkward eternity followed before the boy in man's uniform concluded the initiative was his once more and nodded tentatively to the other exhibit behind the window: the one wearing the faded green dustcoat and clinically sombre expression.

'Thank you,' he called into the intercom; encompassing and dismissing both living and dead with unconscious economy before eyeing Kyle sideways. He appeared hugely relieved that his charge hadn't broken down, embarrassed everybody by rushing sobbing through the little hospital chapel's connecting door to prostrate himself across the husk of a very dear friend now officially catalogued as the late David Wallace McDonald.

'That's . . . well – *it* then, sir,' he hazarded.

Trouble was, in his nervousness, the youngster forgot to close the viewing curtain specifically intended to provide release from Kyle's statutory trauma, so Kyle didn't respond. Couldn't bring himself to simply turn away and squander those extra seconds of precious finality. Instead he found himself still concentrating with almost masochistic determination on the fluorescent-cold tableau before him.

The mortuary attendant looked a bit perplexed on seeing his audience apparently refusing to budge, then, obviously deciding to play the somewhat irregular encore by ear, inclined his head in brief condolence and drew the shroud discreetly to cover dead eyes which had shared so many horizons with Kyle's own. He waited a further few seconds for the final curtain then, in the continuing absence of any cue from their unpractised director, frowned, offered Kyle a slightly apologetic shrug and, for want of further inspiration, began to push David firmly from the sterile room bound for some interim resting-place the like of which Kyle dared not contemplate.

As he did so Kyle's hands convulsed, fingernails bearing savagely into horror-damp palms: a futile act of self-castigation but he so desperately needed to experience pain – experience *something*, dammit! Until that moment of absolute parting he'd been conscious only of an irrational guilt at having felt so detached – so damnably remote from grief during the course of this most awful event. Only after the ritual was complete might he begin to confront the reality that he would never, ever see him again.

. . . see David, that was. Not the attendant.

Kyle became dimly aware of a fly buzzing sporadically in one corner of the chapel. A house fly . . . a *charnel* house fly? Resist as he might, he couldn't help falling prey to the diversion. *Your proper place, Fly, is with The Dead on the other side of that glass*, he found himself remonstrating absently. *Come to that, you shouldn't be here at all if you're going to behave so inconsiderately. Just buzzing aimlessly? I mean, buzzing during what should properly be a time for silence and solemn reflection betrays a quite inexcusable lack of –*

The service door closed smoothly, remorselessly behind the green man and the no-longer man, and David was gone. Kyle continued to gaze fixedly at nothing, listening to the fly and trying to reconcile himself with the irreconcilable. To accept that the man who'd been his best friend – no, much more than that – had been his brother in all but blood, had abruptly ceased to be, well . . . anything at all.

Not that grief would come as a complete stranger to him, as it happened.

*   *   *

They'd been closer than many actual siblings for most of their lives, Michael Kyle and David McDonald.

Admittedly it had been an enforced childhood collusion at first. An alliance of unhappiness between two otherwise dissimilar little boys because they shared a common suffering. Their respective parents had died long before any child's parents should be called upon to die – Kyle's as a result of an air crash when his mother accompanied his father in flying out to Korea to take command of a new passenger ship; David's less than one week later, while driving between offices of his dad's architectural practice. It seemed their car had left a clear road at seventy miles an hour and exploded against a tree.

During their ensuing years spent together in foster care David, always more academically able, had cruised with distinction through school examinations, presenting mountains of anxiety to Kyle, desperate to attain the standards required to follow in his father's wake and pursue a career at sea. McDonald had helped him unselfishly: spending hours coaching him into stumbling response to questions that he, David, considered elementary. Kyle, on the other hand, had managed to square the debt a little by encouraging, sometimes goading David with the caustic brutality of youth into attaining the level of athletic achievement so necessary to fulfil *his* dearest ambition. That of joining the army.

Disappointingly for McDonald, that was not to be. During his entry medical some congenital defect was detected which, while minor, effectively precluded him from taking up a service life. Kyle remembered his response.

'Oh well,' he'd sniffed, trying hard to sound dismissive. 'They may be able to stop me making military history, Mike, but I'm jolly sure they won't stop me writing it.'

He'd grinned then, and eyed Kyle triumphantly. 'No more than *you'll* ever be able to taunt me into playing another game of bloody rugby!'

By the time Kyle joined his first ship, David had won a place at King's College, London. He'd gained his doctorate in military history at about the time Kyle scraped through to acquire his Foreign-Going Master's ticket. McDonald had then moved roughly two miles across the Thames to take up a research appointment with the Imperial War Museum while Kyle moved a hundred thousand to criss-cross the world's oceans, first as a deck cadet, then junior mate and eventually to his current berth as chief officer of a Kuwaiti-owned container ship.

Kyle's roots had long ceased to be, yet because of their enduring relationship he could still delight in the anticipation of returning home between voyages: home being a flat they shared in the Bayswater district of London. David McDonald was Kyle's family, and Kyle was his. Their hopes, their fears, their achievements and their failures were shared by both, and concerned or delighted them equally.

In the interim David had never aspired to marriage; content to settle for a succession of attractive if – in Kyle's jaundiced worldly view – somewhat bookish girlfriends while Kyle, for his part, fell deeply in love in many ports but never met any woman he cared little enough for to inflict upon her the long separations demanded by a career at sea.

So family had always been just the two of them.

Until that bleak November morning.

Even the fly had wearied with buzzing by the time the constable finally replaced his brand new helmet with tongue-protruding precision, confirmed to himself that the unfamiliar object was seated properly by screwing it tentatively between both sets of fingertips, then cleared his throat.

'It's over. All finished now, sir,' he reiterated with firming resolution. Kyle changed focus just in time to catch the young man's reflection in the glass of the viewing window. It was looking wistfully for the way out.

Helpfully he reached up and closed the curtain himself. His beardless guardian whirled, mortified. 'Oh, *Jesus*, but I'm sorry!'

'It doesn't matter. I'm sure you'll remember next time,' Kyle comforted him, turning at last from the window while indicating vaguely that the constable should reassume his role of pilot from that scrupulously antiseptic necropolis.

For the first time he became aware of a fierce desire to blink. As had proved the case in his communion with the fly, he found that concentrating on peripheral irrelevancies – like the neatly trimmed hairline under the pristine blue helmet now forging thankfully ahead – helped a little to counter the emptiness suddenly crowding in on him. It seemed imperative to maintain some pretence of being a rugged seafarer home from the sea. A bucko ship's mate.

Not that Kyle harboured any illusions about the pain to come. He had learned, following the loss of his parents, that only when the judicial processes demanded by sudden death were complete would he truly begin to confront the reality that he would never, ever see his friend again. And now he was an adult even that ritual would require careful orchestration. The rules of being British said he must wait until he could take himself to a less public place where he could cry freely and without shame for David, before addressing a suspicion unthinkable only hours before, yet persistent enough to imbue the already abominable with an extra dimension of horror.

According to the police, McDonald had been the victim of a London Underground accident. Specifically, David died as a result of having fallen in front of the 7.53 morning service as it entered Lancaster Gate, the tube station most convenient to their Bayswater flat. The driver hadn't noticed anything untoward while routinely applying his brakes and didn't even realize someone was under the train until he'd brought it to a halt.

'Still to be formally established at the inquest, sir, but as my inspector told you, it seems there was some jostling for boarding positions on that section of platform when it happened. Just, well, unlucky, I suppose,' Kyle's callow guardian had opined with a professional certainty born of almost a week on the streets.

Kyle didn't – couldn't – accept that, the police version, at face value. Not even though fully aware that any gut feeling he, a novice in the study of locomotive slaughter, might harbour counted for little against the opinion of experienced accident investigators.

Admittedly his alternative thesis was tenuous in the extreme – and infinitely more chilling. But nevertheless Kyle couldn't divorce himself from a growing suspicion that David McDonald, the kindest, mildest and most inoffensive of people, might just have been, well . . .

Pushed?

CHAPTER TWO

Kyle would have been the first to concede that his mind was still only turning slow ahead through a fog of disbelief at that stage. There could be no question of challenging the initial presumption of death by misadventure – he couldn't even begin to propose an alternative – while some vaguely expressed conviction that the police were wrong would hardly merit serious consideration when unsupported either by evidence or even logic.

On the other hand, he held one dubious advantage. He'd spoken to the victim himself only hours before his passing, and something David had said – no, not even as tangible as that, more something David had *implied* during that now all-too-brief telephone conversation – kept returning to niggle at Kyle. Nothing specific: merely a fleeting impression McDonald had given, and one which had held little significance at the time.

Or not until now, perhaps. Not until considered in the light of its appalling sequel.

* * *

Kyle's ship had berthed at the Tilbury container terminal early that morning. Having completed a nine-month contract as chief officer, he'd planned to head for Bayswater and home as soon as he could turn over to his relief and grab a taxi – until David called out of the blue within minutes of the shore telephone line to the accommodation lobby being connected.

It had been a fragmented conversation from the start, the kind that only adults who've been inseparable as children can conduct. Kyle, long familiar with his friend's often irritating capacity for displaying bland imperturbability while he, Kyle, panicked as a matter of course, soon detected that McDonald was marginally excited.

'How long before you can get away, Mike?' David had pressed after they'd chatted briefly about Kyle's voyage past.

'Steady as you go, sport: we've only just docked. My relief hasn't even turned up yet, never mind had time to start our hand-over. Late afternoon at the earliest is my guess.'

'Late after*noon*?'

'*If* the Old Man's in a good mood. Which he won't be 'cause he's still got to take her on to Rotterdam for final discharge before he goes home.'

'Oh,' David had muttered, a bit disappointed.

Kyle remembered why it was still dark on deck then, and frowned into the phone. 'You do realize it's only half-past-six in the morning? Is my flat on fire or something?'

'*Our* flat,' McDonald reminded him primly.

'Our flat,' Kyle conceded. 'I pay the mortgage; you live in it free because, being an academic, you don't have any need for money.'

'That's all about to change,' David had retorted. 'For both of us. Although it means I'm going to need your help.'

'Help?' Kyle, already savouring the prospect of several weeks of leave packed with sloth-like unaccountability, interrupted cautiously. 'Did you say *my* help?'

'Only for a month or so. Maybe even less.'

'A *month* or so?'

'Not right away – not starting tomorrow or anything,' David assured him hurriedly. 'She's in Norway – Narvik – at the moment: won't even be here for another ten days . . .' He'd hesitated then, betrayed a tinge of anxiety. 'You're not going to be difficult, are you? I mean, well, I had to assume your agreement so's I could set things up in advance. Wouldn't have had enough time to organize otherwise.'

'Stop engines, Mister: full astern both,' Kyle urged. 'Set what up? Just what, exactly, have you assumed I've already agreed to help you with?'

'Help *us*, Mike. There'll be more than enough in it for both of us, trust me.'

'Watch my lips, sport,' Kyle advised the telephone handset somewhat illogically. 'Just what . . . precisely . . . have . . .'

'My Stollenberg research.' There was no mistaking the exhilaration by then. 'I'm pretty sure I've cracked it, Mike – come up with something exciting. Something bloody exciting, in fact, which, apart from anything else, will have every Egyptologist from Canberra to Cairo hugging themselves in delight.'

'Your Stollenberg research,' Kyle had echoed uneasily, suddenly placed on the defensive. He knew from past experience that, despite having just spent nine months in limbo aboard a seventy-thousand-ton ocean-going container truck, he was still expected to command instant recall of every tortuous thrust of David's labyrinthine military paper chases. Come to that, what had got McDonald so interested in Egypto-whatevers anyway? Wasn't he a recent history man? Since when had he become a pyramids buff?

'Manfred Stollenberg – Standartenführer Stollenberg? I'd begun to get interested in him during your last leave. You must remember my telling you about the colonel, Mike? Second Regiment, SS-Polizei-Panzer-Grenadier-Division?'

'Ohhh, *that* Stollenberg,' Kyle floundered, lost completely. 'The *German* Stollenberg.'

'You winding me up?' David demanded suspiciously.

'Christ, no. No, I wouldn't. Not about Stollenberg.'

'Well, listen. I finally managed to track down this chap I've spent months trying to trace. Thought he'd died – most of the others who were involved have. Obviously Williamson's getting on a bit himself now, but the point is that, when I went to see him, he . . .' David had paused dramatically then. 'Mike, you probably didn't think it possible, but – I've finally identified her as a Russian.'

'A *Russian*?'

'A Russian, Mike. She's actually a Russian!'

'Grief,' Kyle said, stalling desperately. He had a lot on his mind and didn't really want to get into David's obsessions right then – or spend time trying to wriggle out of whatever commitment David had apparently made on his behalf. Not when they'd be meeting up shortly anyway. Once ship's business was laid to rest he would be more than content to relax with a bottle or two between them and be bored out of his mind with the minutiae of what yet another SS man did in World War II.

'Well?'

'Well, what?'

There came a tinge of frustration. 'Well, aren't you going to react? Say something?'

'What about the Egyptian?' Kyle obliged weakly.

'You *are* winding me up, dammit.' McDonald's tone had changed then, become tight. 'This is deadly serious, Mike – and highly sensitive. Maybe even a bit dangerous in the wrong hands. The Stollenberg convoy was dynamite. God knows what some people might do if they discover I've actually managed to pinpoint . . .'

In retrospect it was all there at that moment – not only the answer but also that undercurrent of tension; almost of apprehension, only Kyle didn't want to dwell on it. He was on a high of euphoria. It gets you like that. The sailor home from the sea – voyage end – *Finished with Engines!* If only he'd been a little more aware; hadn't interrupted at that crucial point, but he did: not only compounding his idiocy but even attempting to justify it.

'You brought up Egypt,' he defended stoutly. 'I hadn't even thought about Egypt till you said Egypt.'

'Egypt*ologists* . . .' David had lightened up then: probably smiled into the phone. 'Look, you've got things to do, and I've got to rush. Want to nip over to Battersea to call on Williamson again. If his memory still holds it could just provide the last piece of the Stollenberg jigsaw.'

That was the point where the second officer had stepped across the lobby coaming. 'Relief mate's aboard and gone straight to the ship's office, Mike. Says he's ready to start the hand-over as soon as you are.'

'Two minutes,' Kyle nodded, then uncovered the mouthpiece again. 'Look, I've got to go. Not that I'm not desperately keen to hear about your Stiltonberg thing, mind you.'

'*Stollen*berg!' David corrected, but with the impish humour back in his voice. 'That's the German Stollenberg, of course – eh, sport?'

Kyle grinned back down a fibre optic cable. 'You've rumbled me.'

'You don't have a clue what I'm talking about, do you?'

'No.'

'Tonight you will have. Tonight I'm going to blow your mind. Until then you'll find a bottle of something special in the fridge if you arrive at the flat before I get back – and . . . Mike?'

'David?'

'Glad you're home.'

Kyle had smiled, feeling all happy and warm inside. 'See you later.'

But he never did. Not alive, anyway.

He'd gone for a stroll along the wharf around midday. Just for a break, to feel land beneath his feet again and gain a brief respite from the tedious slog of official paperwork demanded from those who go down to the sea in today's stopwatch-oriented merchant ships.

'Nowadays,' he reflected plaintively and not a little wistfully as he strolled in the loom of stork-fragile container lifts, 'nowadays the marline spike and rope's end have been replaced by Inward Customs formalities and Clearing Bills and Certificates of Tonnage an' bloody computers . . .'

He didn't notice the police car until it drew alongside him.

'Cap'n Kyle?'

He stopped and turned to face them. Two officers stared up at him expressionlessly from the vehicle.

'Mister Kyle,' he said, nodding upriver towards the ship. 'I'm only her Mate: just a mister – but the captain's still on board if you want –'

'He told us we'd find you here.'

They both got out and donned their uniform caps. The gesture made it all seem terribly formal. The driver came round the front of the white car with the red longitudinal stripe. Kyle remembered vaguely that they called them jam sandwiches – the police cars that was, not their crews. He thought the same source of irrelevant information had told him coppers in the Met refer to *them* collectively as Black Rats, though the etymology of such an alias was rather less apparent.

'*Mister* Kyle then, sir? You are Mister Michael Kyle?'

'Yes.' Kyle frowned, aware of a sudden flush of guilt though he couldn't think why. He hadn't even been around to break any UK laws for nearly a year and tried not to even when at home. All the same, the policemen looked too sombre merely to be pursuing an impersonal enquiry in connection with, say, ship's business.

'Mister Michael Kyle who resides at Ringtree Gardens, Bayswater, London?'

'Number Twenty One; Flat Three – between voyages, anyway. Look, what *is* this about?'

'About a Mister McDonald, sir. A Mister David Wallace McDonald. Of the same address.'

'Doctor McDonald.' From the start it had promised to be a confusing day for titles. 'Academic, not medical. Why – what's David done?'

'Got himself . . .' They glanced almost appealingly at each other. Kyle formed the distinct impression that each was hoping the other would run with it, then the driver said, 'I'm sorry, sir: there's no way to make it easy.'

He knew David was dead even before the driver had completed what must be the absolute worst aspect of a policeman's lot. Ironically Kyle found himself commiserating with the constable in return. Few officers can fail to appreciate that seldom does a sudden death destroy only one life. To be prevailed upon to break such news, albeit in the course of duty, must feel a bit like being tasked to execute the victim's loved ones as well.

Growing ever more dazed, and with the sympathetic dispensation of his captain, Kyle next found himself sharing a jam sandwich with two black rats who turned out to be anything but rattish: demonstrating only gruff understanding of the devastating blight which the London Underground Central Line had cast over his homecoming. It seemed the police, unable to trace any relative to make formal identification, had turned to a scribbled note of Kyle's ship's telephone number found in David's wallet. That, supported by municipal records showing Kyle to be co-owner of the Ringtree Gardens flat, had prompted their recruiting him to perform the necessary rite.

At Paddington police station he was given a mug of tea and a summary of events surrounding the fatality by a grey-haired duty officer. No one had come forward who'd witnessed the actual fall, which wasn't particularly surprising. When a train blasts out of its tunnel pushing a bow wave of compressed air most commuters concentrate, not on their adjacent fellow travellers but on predicting the nearest point at which a door will come to rest. All that had registered with the few on that section of platform who even conceded they *might* have spared a glance for the victim immediately prior to the horror was that David had formed part of a group of at least three – some said four . . . or maybe five? – would-be passengers. All male, most had claimed. 'No, one was a woman,' one had sworn, fiddling with his spectacles. 'Definitely a woman. Or a bloke with long hair.'

'Unfortunately station improvements meant the platform surveillance cameras were temporarily out of service, Captain.'

'Mister, Superintendent,' Kyle had demurred, trying to be a bit more specific than the witnesses. 'I'm only a mister.'

'Inspector, Mister Kyle,' the inspector had countered with matching humility. 'I'm only an inspector. Anyway, like I said, the video was down so we can't refer to that. Of course, the Underground Transport Police are still writing up their FATAC report and there'll have to be a formal inquest but, so far, the circumstances surrounding Mister McDonald's death –'

'*Doctor* McDonald's,' Kyle amended wearily, locked into auto-pilot title-wise by then while reflecting that today would most certainly have been made easier had David never gone to bloody university. 'He was a doctor. Academic, not medical.'

'. . . surrounding *Doctor* McDonald's death, sir, bear all the indications of his having overbalanced and fallen on the line before the driver could do anything.'

The inspector's fist had clenched then while his eyes grew momentarily disturbed. 'Could happen to any of us, you know. Could've been *my* best mate. Could have been the wife, even one of the kids.'

'I know,' Kyle said, liking him more for having revealed such human weakness. 'Thankfully the odds are against it.'

'You sometimes wonder about the odds in this job.' The inspector stirred: retreated behind the uniform again. 'Obviously we're continuing to interview the station staff and those witnesses who came forward, but . . .' It was then he'd given a barely perceptible shrug and eyed all the other routine reports of mayhem, citizen abuse and lost dogs on his desk.

It was that unconscious gesture which brought home to Kyle that what had happened to David was not exceptional to those who dealt with such tragedies on a daily basis. The random slaughter of yet another creature in the ants' nest that was London invoked their concern and demanded judicial resolution, but hardly justified mobilization of a Scotland Yard murder squad – or not unless they were given at least some cause to consider it a suspicious death. But *was* it? At that stage, although he found David's cryptic remarks deeply disturbing in retrospect, Kyle had neither opportunity nor, for that matter, the spirit to confront their deeper implications.

If, indeed, there were any.

That moment of his greatest uncertainty also marked the point when the inspector himself chose to raise an unexpectedly perceptive eyebrow. 'You said you'd talked to the doctor just beforehand. I don't suppose anything came out of the conversation that struck you as pertinent?'

Kyle hesitated, still unable to focus on much beyond his impending visit to the mortuary yet aware that, if he did seriously suspect an alternative scenario based on malevolence rather than misfortune, now had to be the time to make his reservations known. But what reservations? Just what, precisely, *could* he tell the inspector?

Some vaguely formed sailor's paranoia? he reflected dubiously. About the perceived anxieties of an inoffensive historian who'd awakened uncharacteristically early to greet the morning of his own death? The possible involvement in that death of a formerly nameless Russian currently located in Narvik – maybe female, maybe not – who'd finally been given a name but one which Kyle didn't actually know? The further assumption that a second person might also be connected who did, at least, have a name – Williams or Williamson, he thought David had said – but about whom he knew nothing else other than that he lived in Battersea, and that David had reckoned the chap – Williams or Williamson or whoever – must be getting on a bit by now and might reasonably have been expected to be dead already?

Kyle frowned uncertainly at the stack of daily reports on the inspector's desk. Could he really invite the harassed officer to open yet another file of suspicions as vague as those he harboured? Then suggest he complicate it a little by throwing in David's enigmatic comment that Egyptologists would somehow be duly impressed and – just to emphasize he wasn't proposing ordinary, run-of-the-mill, crack-it-overnight detection here – go on to explain that finding the keys to *those* riddles might only mark the opening phase of his investigation even then, that their resolution appeared to be entirely dependent on the Metropolitan Police first unravelling a fifty-odd-year-old World War II mystery surrounding some Waffen-SS Colonel called Stollenberg?

Not that he knew what the actual nature of the mystery was, he would be obliged to concede. Nor anything at all about Stollenberg himself. Other than that he'd definitely been a German Stollenberg.

Kyle framed his denial carefully. 'I can't think of anything David might have said which would be helpful as things stand, Inspector.'

'His ticket was for a return journey to East Putney, which meant changing to the District Line at Notting Hill Gate. Any idea of who he might have been going to see over there – in Putney, I mean? Anywhere in the Wandsworth, Battersea area come to that?'

'Nobody I know,' Kyle said with absolute truth.

The inspector toyed awkwardly with a pencil on the desk. 'I have to ask, sir. Did the doctor leave you with any impression that he might have been, well, depressed or anything?'

'He didn't jump, if that's what you're implying,' Kyle protested.

'People do. Quite often it's the most unlikely candidates who go and top themselves. And where there are no witnesses – or not ones worth a tuppenny damn, like in this case – then I can only come to an educated conclusion, submit it to the coroner, and hope it doesn't distress anybody.'

'David McDonald did *not* commit suicide.' Kyle thought a moment longer, remembering David's careful attitude to money.

17

'And anyway, how many prospective suicides buy a return ticket for what they intend to be a one-way voyage?'

'A logical argument – presupposing suicides could be held to have acted logically in the first place. Still, I'm sure the coroner will give your view due weight, particularly as there's no present reason to dispute it.' The inspector glanced discreetly at his watch. 'Nothing further then, Mister Kyle? Nothing more you'd like to add before my constable takes you round to the mortuary?'

It was then that Kyle realized there was only one way open to him to go about seeking justice for David. And that way didn't – couldn't possibly – involve policemen. Not unless he was prepared to risk being detained in a rather special cell and examined by lots of men in white coats while the Stollenberg trail, if indeed one existed, grew cold.

'Only to thank you for the tea, Inspector.' Kyle found himself rising: steeling his nerves for the ordeal to come. 'It was nice tea. Very welcome indeed.'

One hour later Kyle had said his last farewell to David and wished the young constable all success in his career. At least he was able to feel he'd had some small part in moulding it. It seemed unlikely the boy would ever forget to close a curtain in a mortuary again.

'I'm sorry, sir,' the lad had volunteered awkwardly before he left Kyle amidst the crowds of office workers beginning to make their way homewards. 'About Mister McDonald and everything.'

'DOCTOR McDonald!' Kyle had tried to call after him only to find he couldn't because of the loneliness constricting his throat. '*Academic*. Not medical.'

Kyle watched him go, a brand-new helmet taller than everyone else. Suddenly he wasn't so sure about having helped shape his career after all – but then he wasn't entirely convinced that he was quite cut out to become a Hammer of Justice himself.

18

Recognizing clues and following leads and everything?

He felt more confident about handling the judicial end-of-voyage routine, certainly. About ringing down *Finished with Engines* on whoever may have been responsible, should idiot's luck succeed in establishing that David's death *had* resulted from a push rather than a fall. Possessing a seaman's ability for improvisation, Kyle knew he'd find a way to perform that most useful function.

Executing a murderer.

CHAPTER THREE

The flat seemed very quiet when Kyle let himself in.

Deathly quiet.

It was strange how the traffic noises he'd remembered from the nearby Bayswater Road sounded respectfully muted. Or maybe such an apparent phenomenon wasn't exceptional at all, and had nothing to do with David's passing. By four bells in the middle watch – two a.m. in shoreside terms, as he'd have to get used to thinking in again – there was little traffic around, even in central London.

It felt uncharacteristically warm, too. A cloying, greenhouse-tainted sort of warmth which enveloped him before he'd withdrawn his key from the lock. But then Kyle had found himself sweating profusely in the taxi that brought him from the dockside, and that hadn't been anything to do with temperature: more a physical manifestation of the dread he felt at confronting this moment of truth. Maybe he should have grasped the nettle right away, taken the more courageous course and come straight to the flat as soon as he'd left the young policeman, rather than return to the ship to complete his hand-over as he'd so dispiritedly elected to do.

It meant that now, in the middle of the night when human resilience is already at its lowest ebb, he was about to embark upon what would surely prove the most harrowing exploration of his life.

Kyle hefted his sea gear into the narrow hallway, closed the door uneasily behind him, then hesitated yet again in a stark-shadowed overspill of orange street light filtering through the open sitting room door.

Now the whisper of traffic had been replaced by the erratic tick of the grandmother clock at the end of the hallway. The one David had bought in the King's Road years ago on the spur of the moment and pushed halfway across London strapped to the crossbar of a bicycle because he'd always wanted a grandmother clock. Kyle had never quite understood why David had wanted a grandmother clock in particular. To Kyle grandfather clocks were more imposing; much more, well . . . *grand* than grandmother clocks – especially a grandmother clock that lost at least two minutes a day during its more accurate phases despite being rebalanced precariously on little piles of cork and cardboard every Sunday morning then regulated yet again in what would become, for David, a stubborn ritual of tongue-protruding concentration.

'Get a GRIP, Mister!' he determined bleakly. 'Recognize these nostalgic deliberations for what they are – diversions avidly seized upon to further delay what has to be done. Focus on the task for which only you, in all conscience, are properly fitted because it won't – it *can't* – be avoided. Everywhere you venture in this formerly so-precious refuge you will be confronted by evidence of a moment frozen in time. That instant when David departed this place for eternity yet left everything on hold in anticipation of a happy return. It will reflect his life as he was living it, not in termination but in domestic suspension, and that poignant incompleteness is going to hurt grievously, perhaps even unbearably, yet still you will have to bear with –'

That vaguely familiar odour permeating the hallway – it wasn't so much greenhouse on reflection as . . . ? Kyle frowned, eased a finger inside his collar. Lord, but it really *was* warm in the flat, diversion or not. Which was doubly odd because normally David, never affluent, did tend to be careful beyond the point of miserliness when it came to flashing up the central heating. The barely tolerable temperatures at which he appeared content to maintain the bloody place had provided several bones of contention between them during previous winter leaves when Kyle, cosseted by the air-conditioned and comfort-controlled environment of shipboard accommodation, would complain petulantly and to no avail before ostentatiously shrugging into a fisherman's oiled-wool sweater so thick and chunky it was otherwise only deployed when they went on occasional hill walking sorties up in Scotland.

More vacuous nostalgia on his part? Avoiding the unavoidable again?

A red Cyclopean eye blinked at Kyle from the telephone answering machine by the door – three blinks, then a pause. Three messages awaiting a response from David; but not, presumably, in the middle of the night.

Automatically he reached to straighten the framed dragon print he'd once brought back from Hong Kong. It had probably hung crooked since the last time he'd squared it away nine months ago. To be fair to McDonald, one of the reasons why his grandmother clock couldn't tell the time and kept developing yet another list, whereupon its pendulum began to swing in increasingly eccentric arcs, was because the whole bloody flat tended to be lopsided; a bit like one of those crazy houses that seemed to exist at the end of every seaside pier when he and David had been kids. The buildings in Ringtree Gardens were mostly old and Dickensian and prone to subsidence. Even the simple process of selecting a door or window to open without the aid of a crowbar usually ended up as a benign version of Russian roulette. Pencils had a disconcerting habit of rolling off tables in the middle of the night: *dwelling house of character* invariably appeared somewhere in any advertisement marketing properties in the area.

Kyle frowned; listened intently. A further and indisputably alien sound had begun to register. Continuous. Persistent. Distinct from the intermittent whisper of distant traffic – a steady *hiss* . . . ?

And this time he wasn't imagining it. No way!

An unreasoning apprehension gripped him: a conviction that something was terribly wrong. Without even delaying to trigger the hall light Kyle took a concerned pace towards the open door on his right – only to halt yet again and stare incredulously within.

Their sitting-room – or the furnished cupboard euphemistically described as such by the agent who'd sold them the flat – had boasted a very large and overly efficient gas fire when they'd taken possession. It must have been in place a hundred years and they'd never had the heart to replace it. Victorian, the fire was: all floral tiles and cast iron surround with huge latticed fireclay elements which wouldn't have seemed out of place inside a brick kiln. They'd only lit it once, and since that eventful experiment had never risked commissioning it again, not even on the coldest of nights and long after their eyebrows had grown back. Put simply, to venture within arm's length of the infernal machine was to invite two-fold assault from incipient heat exhaustion aggravated by scorched trousers.

Yet now, despite the relative mildness of the night, it glowed and hissed full-throttle in the orange-tinted shadows, spitting turbo-heat which flared against Kyle's cheeks like a tropical sun.

Somebody had lit it, and judging by the stifling temperature emanating from the room, quite a few hours ago. But who? Not David, surely? Not simply lit it then blithely forgotten about it and just gone off to Battersea while their usually somnolent gas meter whirled itself to a Dervish-like frenzy and the flat gratefully absorbed more thermal units in the intervening hours than had probably been afforded it during the past several years.

So who had? Even more significantly perhaps – *why* had they? And how, for that matter, had 'they' gained access to the flat in the first place?

Kyle drew a mystified breath, choked convulsively, began to cough – and *that* marked the moment when his unreasoning anxiety converted to meticulously reasoned panic!

Having made several voyages in tankers Kyle had become acutely aware of the alchemy of potential disaster. In particular he'd learned to be alert to the invisible dangers inherent in the transport of volatile cargoes.

On the other hand, he'd come to accept with a tankerman's equanimity that, although lethal within certain parameters, the actual flammable range of petrochemical vapours when released into atmosphere is relatively narrow. Under normal operating conditions a ratio of between two and eight per cent hydrocarbon gas must be present in air before explosion occurs, and only then assuming a source of ignition is introduced. What he wasn't so sure about was what ratio of domestic gas to London air encompassed the scientific criteria for *Bang!*

He didn't think he had overmuch time left to mull on that essentially technical issue, either. Not by then. Not having finally registered that the greenhouse smell apparent on entry had nothing whatsoever to do with pot plants and everything to do with metropolitan service mains – that an atmosphere which had to be fast approaching holocaust quality had long been accumulating within the confined space in which he, insensitized by his own prevarication, had squandered far too much staying-alive time already.

Not that Kyle's fraught situation was entirely devoid of advantage. At least he wouldn't need to waste further reaction time in speculating on *how* ignition – due at any microsecond now – would occur once the build-up of gas did reach a mix volatile enough to cremate not only his apartment but also the rest of

Number 21 Ringtree Gardens and probably most of Numbers 19 and 23 on either side.

Not staring vacantly, as he found himself, at the naked flame inexplicably issuing from every orifice of that hyper-active Victorian heating contrivance less than a panic-stricken lunge away.

Apart from a facile inclination to tense every sinew in anticipation of dismemberment, Kyle's initial reaction to concluding he could well be dead by the next eccentric tick of a grandmother clock was to experience a perverse satisfaction at discovering his blackest misgivings justified. A mysterious gas leak? A fire, never normally lit in the first place, left burning while David went off to have a fatal accident?

Logic argued that domestic catastrophe simply didn't happen on cue. Not to ordinary people – to uncomplicated chaps like them. No more than did having their lives abruptly foreshortened by tripping in front of the 7.53 London Underground morning service as it entered Lancaster Gate station!

'Awwww Jesus!' the logic in Kyle bawled as frozen comprehension finally took second place to practical terror. Launching across the room he scrabbled frantically for the antiquated gas tap hidden in deep shadow – brass; slippery, stiff with lack of use; too small and too bloody hard to fin . . . *found* it! Wrenched it through ninety degrees to *Off*. Forced himself to wait while white-hot elements dulled to a reluctant red and began to die – and only then started running again towards the most likely alternative source of that lethal miasma.

He was right again! The instant he shouldered the kitchen door a pent-up volume of gas-saturated vapour collapsed across the threshold, leaving him breathless and faint in its frustrated wake: despatching potentially high-explosive tendrils racing and tumbling and seeking detonation into every corner of the hallway and through the already gaping sitting-room doorway.

Listening in semi-darkness, acutely aware that even to trigger a light switch invited an electrical arc initiating explosion and fire, Kyle could nevertheless detect the open-throated sibilance of wide open but unlit burners. It sounded as if every single cooker ring was spewing invisible filth at full bore. The entire kitchen had inexplicably – *no, negative 'inexplicable', Mister!* Maybe the motive was still inexplicable, but the actuality, the physical evidence of what was happening, was all too bloody explicable. David McDonald's kitchen space – an already-dead man's kitchen space – had deliberately been converted to a time bomb in countdown.

Even as he stumbled, retching, to grasp a kitchen chair and hurl it carelessly through the window glass before whirling to kill the flow of gas, Kyle's panic turned to dull rage. The uncertainty of the previous nightmare day – the sick-in-the-gut uncertainty that had made his grief doubly harrowing – became replaced by a bleak conviction that this was no coincidental misadventure. That he could only be experiencing a further chilling insight into the ruthless determination driving whoever had contrived the death of his dearest friend.

Even more chilling in concept, Kyle reflected savagely, than the brutality of David's own elimination: a comparison he would formerly have rejected as obscene but now horribly valid in view of the indiscriminate carnage promised by this most recent atrocity. While some link, however tenuous, must have existed between David and his killer – or killers, for that matter – which ultimately led them to engineer his death, those targeted tonight could only be considered innocents. Ten, perhaps twenty families lived in close enough proximity to ensure that many would have died or been hideously mutilated hours ago had it not been for a door having emulated the intransigent behaviour of clocks, pencils and other rightfully inanimate objects in that suddenly accursed place and – further aided by the brisk wind breaching the kitchen through a multitude of draught-inducing gaps – closed of its own volition to temporarily contain the cooker's lethal emission.

Shaken as he was, at least the incident catapulted Kyle from his earlier, self-indulgent apathy. By the time his pulse had slowed to only twice its normal rate he'd even begun to think positively.

The perpetrator or perpetrators hadn't stayed lucky second time around. It afforded him some small comfort to realize that he . . . she . . . *they* weren't invincible, weren't guaranteed to prove any more fireproof than he.

Apparently nobody in the adjacent properties had heard the sound of smashing glass. Or the handkerchief-muffled imprecations as Kyle struggled to lever open the flat's other windows more discreetly than by heaving the rest of its bloody furniture straight through and into the backyard. Either that or they'd prudently decided not to get involved.

Somewhat embittered at not having been hailed as a saviour, he concluded darkly that even if the bloody place had blown up, the residents of Ringtree Gardens would have doggedly persisted in their nocturnal slumbers.

They'd have just slept rather longer than they'd planned to. That's all!

He'd slumped outside on the stone-flagged and reassuringly chill first floor landing for a long time after that, knees drawn up and back against the wall waiting wearily for the gas to clear. And, to cap nervous frustration, found himself wrestling, not with conundrums already posed, but with yet one further riddle.

'Why, for Heaven's sake?' he kept brooding. 'What possible reason can anybody have to blow up a man's apartment *after* they've killed him?'

The only conclusion he could reach was that, somewhere inside the apartment itself, something must still remain that compromised David's killer. Something not instantly apparent, or presumably it could have been removed rather than destroyed. Some artefact, some jotting, some evidence that somebody had intended to incinerate in tandem with David's neighbours.

The premise did hold water. To anyone more concerned with destroying evidence contained within a building than the lives of its residents, then not only would purging it with a fireball afford a highly efficient solution, but also a bonus in that it might well be presumed an accident. An unexceptional domestic tragedy caused by the absent-minded negligence of some historian who'd occupied Flat Three on the first floor – an occasional failing of David's which, had Kyle not been given prior cause for doubt, even he might have felt obliged to concede.

Better still, the accused could hardly be called to defend himself against such a charge, having died himself a mere few hours before. Accidentally.

But who, precisely, had arranged these 'accidents', and why?

Considering he wouldn't recognize a clue if he collided with one in mid-ocean, Kyle had little option but to assume that David himself had provided the only lead so far. *Highly sensitive; maybe even a bit dangerous in the wrong hands* was the caution he'd expressed only an hour or so before he died.

A *bit* dangerous, for cryin' out loud?

Or had that low-key expression of concern merely been the ultimate mark of McDonald's penchant for understatement? Had David, while Kyle had been prattling so idiotically on the telephone, been standing in actual fear for his life? Surely not. Not even he was as laid-back as that. More likely he really hadn't anticipated such barbarous extremism. No more, God forbid, than he'd suspected he was voicing what was, so soon thereafter, to prove an all-too-accurate prophecy.

So, perceptive though David had previously been at feeling his way through the fogs of history, Kyle's working hypothesis had to be that yesterday's ghastly outcome had indeed resulted from his friend's failure to appreciate the power of evil which, despite the passing of over half a century, still protected the core subject of his investigation.

Kyle's problem was that, well . . . didn't that assumption suggest, in turn, that not mere danger but Death itself must stand equally ready to stalk anyone else reckless enough to embark upon the fifty-year-cold trail of a former Nazi called Manfred Stollenberg?

The 'anyone else' being him – Kyle – in this instance?

CHAPTER FOUR

There was no sign of forced entry from the landing so far as Kyle could tell. It didn't necessarily mean whoever had rigged the Ringtree Gardens DIY cremation kit actually possessed a key – for instance, they could have done something clever to open the arguably inadequate front door with a credit card or whatever, as Kyle had seen them do on TV. He resolved to have the lock changed as soon as the shops opened in the morning.

By the time he considered it prudent to re-enter, the grandmother clock was hazarding a rough guess it was five to four in the morning. His Taiwan counterfeit Rolex reckoned nearer to twenty past. Both were equally accurate. Either way, the occasional whisper of distant traffic had increased to an intermittent rumble as the city utilities geared themselves for another routine day while Kyle, in contrast, felt physically and emotionally exhausted. There was nothing routine about murder and attempted mass extermination.

He should have slept then, or at least tried to, but the moment he stretched out on the too-short settee in the lounge he found himself restored to a Judas wakefulness; simply staring up at the street-lamp-patterned ceiling in adrenaline-driven uncertainty and trying to imagine what a proper detective would do next.

His most prudent move would, of course, be to find out. To go straight round to the local police station and make his suspicions known despite his earlier reticence with the Paddington inspector. But what corroboration could he offer even now? Precisely what hard evidence could he lay before the Metropolitan Police that would persuade them to launch a murder enquiry?

A front door that showed no sign of having been forced? A cooker turned on that hadn't been lit? A fire left on that *had*?

If he drifted off at all it was only to wake, shivering, a few minutes later. It was getting cold with the windows having been left open. Any residual heat had long escaped from the room along with all traces of gas. Eventually Kyle hauled himself gloomily erect again and headed across the still darkened hallway to the kitchen where he plumbed his absolute nadir of misery on encountering two champagne glasses neatly placed side by side on a tray, ready for the bottle of Bollinger '86 in the fridge. He hadn't noticed them earlier, having been too preoccupied with throwing chairs through windows.

Blinking fiercely, he made a coffee strong enough to stand the spoon in, too depressed even to care about the stray shards of glass crunching under his feet, then wandered, cradling the mug pensively, through the darkened flat in search of Holmesian inspiration.

Not that he expected to come across a file marked *Stollenberg* or something equally obvious that might resolve all his uncertainties in one straight read. He knew McDonald didn't work like that. With the flat being too cramped to store much in the way of hard copy, David tended to do his research in the Imperial War Museum archives and the British Library – another probable reason being that they were a bloody sight warmer – then enter key references into a portable computer. A fairly old Toshiba so far as Kyle could recall.

So, while he did make a cursory search of the lounge for what could have proved the all-critical laptop, it was more with a sense of resignation than anticipation. He was pretty sure McDonald hadn't taken it with him to Battersea or it would have been found among his personal effects recovered from the accident scene. The chances were that David had left it lying around in the flat during what he would have expected to be a brief absence. Simply begging, as things had turned out, to be lifted by the same intruder who'd then, presumably, rigged the place to self-destruct in order to erase any further, less apparent loose ends of evidence.

Wary of possible pockets of gas that might still be hanging in the flat, he decided not to switch any more lights on than he needed. Apart from the prudence of such reticence, he didn't yet feel emotionally prepared enough to enter David's bedroom – not to pry into that most intimate personal fiefdom of any individual which is normally only surrendered to the eyes of others following the act of dying – and it wasn't as if the Toshiba's discovery would have helped immediately anyway. Any sensitive information it held would almost certainly be password-protected, even allowing for David's frustrating, per-haps ultimately lethal, naiveté, while Kyle's limited experience with shipboard software didn't extend to computer hacking. Even had he succeeded in finding it he would have to rely on outside help to retrieve any information it contained.

So far, he reflected morosely, the list of expert backup he was beginning to need included a computer nerd, an Egyptologist, a World War II pundit fluent in German and Russian, a glazier, a locksmith to improve the flat's security and, most particularly, the director general of Interpol.

Returning to the lounge, Kyle switched the light on for the first time and began to rummage desultorily through a mess of books and papers on the desk. Whether anyone had raked through it before him he couldn't tell: whether, come to that, it had been turned over with a pitchfork would have been impossible to establish. David may have ridden the information superhighway professionally but he'd never been the most disciplined of domestic administrators.

Ironically, one of the topmost items littering the desk was a letter threatening firmly that, if Doctor McDonald didn't settle the enclosed account within the next seven days, his supply would be terminated. The ultimatum was from British Gas, and dated sixteen days previously.

If they'd had the courtesy to cut off people's gas when they bloody promised to, Kyle reflected darkly, then it would've prevented one helluva strain on *his* nervous system for a start!

One publication buried at the back of the desk did strike a hopeful chord – a slender, cheaply bound volume entitled *Waffen-SS: Death of a Folk Myth*. Extracting it from beneath the debris of correspondence, he thumbed through it expectantly, but the contents consisted largely of black and white photographs with only cursory explanatory text. More a war photographer's archive than a treatise in depth. The plates had obviously been selected to illustrate the book's title, emphasizing the demise of that darkest of Hitlerian military machines whose men and women had worn the Nordic runes – the feared double lightning flash in silver on black – to such terrible effect in World War II.

Certainly one page *had* been marked with a scrap of paper, but turning to it Kyle couldn't imagine why. Like most of the others it was simply another battlefield shot – this one taken amid the ruins of some former industrial complex and posed for largely by contorted dead men. The part of principal corpse in the foreground was played by a camouflage-smocked SS soldier staring sightlessly skyward from under the steel rim of his coal scuttle helmet, disillusioned at last with the promises of the Third Reich. The cause of such ultimate disappointment probably had a lot to do with the bullet hole impacted just above the rim of that same helmet.

For a moment Kyle wondered if he could have been Stollenberg

– if that was a link – but even though his knowledge of SS rank markings was non-existent, he didn't think the corpse looked old enough to have been a colonel. More a class prefect at school, he reflected bleakly. The trappings of an iron warrior: the slack-smooth features of a child spawned to die in blind allegiance to a monstrous ideology.

Four British soldiers stood over him, staring indifferently into camera, fatigue etched into each dirty face. One – a sergeant with a Sten gun balanced gamekeeper-casual in the crook of his arm – had a cigarette dangling from his mouth in post-battle relaxation. It struck Kyle how reminiscent the tableau was of those sepia-toned big-game hunting records prized by a somewhat earlier if no more compassionate age, though admittedly the trophies in such Victoriana hadn't carried stick grenades and Schmeisser sub-machine guns.

The caption read: *Twilight of a God. Bremerhaven: May 1945.*

Closing the book, Kyle turned to a stack of magazines – mostly old ordnance brochures and military publications – balanced precariously between the desk and the corner of the room. Sifting through them, he noted that one had been folded back as if to mark the page, though once again he couldn't imagine why. It featured an aerial photograph of a ship, whereas David's professional interest in naval matters had been peripheral at most. Even more uncharacteristically it was of a merchant freighter: not even a man-of-war. Referring curiously to the magazine's cover, he found it to be a NATO-inspired recognition journal dated *November 1976* and comprising photographs, silhouettes and line drawings accompanied by technical details – a catalogue of killing machines ranging from former Warsaw Pact armoured vehicles, naval units and aircraft to the then-latest weapons technologies deployed by the Western Powers.

She didn't appear to be an exceptional ship. Kyle had seen clones of her in virtually every seaport – an old Soviet three-island general cargo vessel identified by the hammer and sickle funnel markings and taken, in this case, by a Nimrod surveillance aircraft overflying the Western Approaches. The caption even confirmed her as being: 'A typical Warsaw Pact intelligence-gathering freighter – the *Yuryi Rogov*. Note the ultra-sophisticated electronic interception array abaft the bridge: very much at odds with the purported trading status of such vessels.'

In commercial terms she'd been clapped out even by the Seventies when the photograph was taken, he reflected absently. With limited cargo-handling capabilities and high manning requirements she couldn't have competed with Western freight rates: not without the massive subsidies the Soviet military afforded its merchant fleet in those Cold War days in order to allow them to roam the world at will to fulfil their hidden eavesdropping agenda.

Still, David must have had *some* interest in her?

Kyle shivered, resolved to rig something to insulate the broken window before he froze to death, then forced himself to take a spell before attempting further to pursue the ghost of SS-Standartenführer Manfred Stollenberg.

His nervous system reasserted its fragility when, while completing a tongue-protruding damage-control exercise with plastic bin-liners in the kitchen, he was startled by an abrupt clatter from the front door. Poised to retaliate with a drawing pin, he shakily realized it was only David's morning newspaper being propelled through the letter box to crash-land on the mat . . . Lord, was it *that* time already? Yawning promisingly, he walked through the hallway to retrieve the folded broadsheet.

The blinking red telltale on the telephone answering machine caused him to hesitate in passing. He'd forgotten about the waiting messages, what with having nearly been blown up and everything. Carefully he put down the cup and pressed *play*. The machine whirred into scratchy rewind, then spoke.

A young girl's voice. 'The Hoover you left for repair is ready for collection, Mister McDonald.' Kyle frowned. The kid didn't say collect from where, so he philosophically added one vacuum cleaner to David's *items missing* list. Then he realized he could always try letting his fingers do the walking through the Yellow Pages looking for local Hoover service centres, and felt inordinately pleased. Trouble was, even mustering that degree of investigative resourcefulness had more or less exhausted the level of sleuthing he felt qualified to undertake.

Hackman came next. Kyle didn't know who Hackman was. Nor who Lightwood – the apparent reason for Hackman's call – might be either . . . or might have been, considering it suggested he was dead too.

'Hackman here,' the gravel voice carrying a vaguely northern inflection announced. 'You were right about Lightwood, Doctor. The bloke never did make it home. KIA a few hours after the event. A casualty of what we call friendly fire nowadays, the word was: but seemingly it *was* him who blew the whistle to the Provos – not that they would've done bugger-all in the circumstances, what with him bein' a goner by that stage and unable to give formal evidence.' The disembodied Hackman paused. 'Probably hadn't felt all that inclined to, for that matter. Summary justice you might say, eh? Look, there's more. Some of it pretty interesting stuff. Gimme a bell when you get home an' we'll meet over a glass of ale. Bye!'

Kyle replayed that one, frowning just as blankly at the conclusion of Hackman's electronic encore. There was nothing that specifically tied it to David's Stollenberg research, although KIA – killed in action? – undoubtedly implied a war-related incident, but *which* war, dammit? And 'friendly fire'? The reference to the Provos confused him in that respect. So far as he was aware, the IRA hadn't been overtly active during World War II, yet, on the other hand, if David's trawl through history had steered him into more recent terrorist waters . . . ?

But, peace accords apart, didn't today's men of violence, with their sophisticated weaponry, incline more towards the use of Semtex rather than Victorian gas fires when attempting to blow up people's houses?

Apart from which, while Hackman's reference to summary justice sounded plausible, was it likely that such paramilitaries required someone to give formal evidence before they meted it out?

Kyle decided he definitely needed to talk to Hackman, but didn't think *Hackmans* would feature generically as a trade classification in the Yellow Pages. He resolved to make a careful transcript of that particular message before he finally wiped the tape, then triggered call number three.

It was from Jagjivan Singh. As soon as he recognized the precisely modulated accent Kyle decided that his coffee getting cold demanded a higher priority than anything Mister Singh might have to say, and stopped the tape. Singh was a ship broker and crewing agent with an office near Covent Garden. Formerly a postgrad student at Kings with David until he'd abandoned academia for the pursuit of making money, good old 'Jaggers' Singh invited only dislike from Kyle, invariably representing, as he did, foreign flag coffin ships. Particularly the kind whose owners had a greater vested interest in collecting the insurance pay-outs generated by their vessels sinking en voyage than the profits accrued from their arriving safely at their destinations.

Presuming on his friendship with McDonald, Singh had once persuaded Kyle to help him out by temporarily filling a berth on a clapped-out Monrovia-registered freighter to enable her to sail on schedule. Her original Turkish first officer had been hospitalized – or so Jaggers had sworn. Turned out the mate had actually jumped ship in Singapore, an' no bloody wonder! Kyle had spent most of his watches below on that particular voyage lying fully clothed in his bunk with his lifejacket a regularly practised grab away, his cabin door hooked back so's it wouldn't jam should she capsize without warning, and ears straining to catch the first rumble of sea water free-surfacing on the wrong side of her rust-eroded hull plates.

Not that such meticulously rehearsed paranoia would have helped. Her lifeboats had been anything but. Kyle had been horrified to find them even more structurally hazardous than the ship, suspended as they were from falls so corroded that the parting wire strands bestowed upon them more the appearance of a terrified cat's tail.

Still, Singh *had* been a friend of David's. He'd call him later. Let him know before he heard from someone else about what had happened.

Kyle found himself blinking again, and felt the sterile emptiness of the flat closing around him. Sniffing, he rummaged in the telephone-table drawer, found a spare recording tape, ejected the original which held Hackman's message and shoved it back in the drawer, then continued down the hall to scoop up the newspaper. Carrying it back into the kitchen he resolved to finish sweeping up the broken glass while he finished his coffee, then try once more to get his head down.

All in all he felt a little better. He'd passed, and overcome, the psychological low brought about by encountering David's celebratory champagne earlier – or at least, he thought he had.

In actual fact he was scheduled to become a lot more miserable in the next few minutes. Not that 'misery' – or not 'misery' *per se* – quite embraced the gamut of emotions Kyle was destined to experience on making his next discovery in the apartment that he'd formerly assumed he shared only with a gentle, albeit pretty damned untidy historian.

His finding the corpse, that was.

Of the naked girl?

In the hall cupboard?

CHAPTER FIVE

That particular body had been compressed into the cramped utility space with considerable force. It had also been despatched with extreme violence.

'Bloody *hell*,' the older of the two policemen who'd first responded to Kyle's garbled emergency call muttered, appalled.

Then they'd turned to appraise his six-foot-two frame pointedly. Or the one who'd passed the comment did, anyway. The other, much younger, had hurried back down to the street by then looking pale.

'I was only trying to find a brush,' Kyle explained defensively. 'To sweep up the glass from the broken window in the kitchen.'

'Why was it broken?' the remaining bobby asked, still shaky.

'Because I threw a chair through it.'

'Ah,' the policeman nodded understandingly. 'A domestic, then.'

'A domestic what?'

'Argument. Went too far after the two of you'd had a right old set-to, did you?'

Kyle frowned. He hadn't thought of that. Of their assuming *he'd* done it.

'*I* didn't kill her,' he assured his interrogator carefully. 'She was there when I opened the cupboard door.'

'Like you said – while you were trying to find a brush. At . . .' the officer squinted ostentatiously at his watch, 'ten after seven in the morning? Usually do your housework at seven in the morning, do you, sir?'

'That depends on which clock you go by,' Kyle qualified.

The second policeman came back through the front door trying not to look in the cupboard. 'Called it in from the car, Bill. Confirmed it as a murder shout. Don't touch anything, they said: CID'll be along in a minute.'

It was bizarre. Shock, Kyle supposed. All three of them just talking in conversational undertones there in the hallway in company with a dead woman who, this time, was unlikely to have been a random victim considering she had been skewered forcefully and vertically through the underside of the chin by what looked like a butcher's boning knife.

Precisely where David and he used to hold buttercups to little girls' throats, Kyle remembered uneasily. To discover if they liked butter, wasn't it?

Or had it been to find out if they loved them?

Had she loved him, Kyle wondered. That once-pretty girl with the raven-black hair and the olive skin now beginning to discolour in death? Had he, David, loved *her* at one time, come to that? He'd never referred to any current romantic involvement in his sporadic letters, but then maybe there was a lot about McDonald that Kyle didn't know. Might David have concealed darker, more sinister appetites from Kyle for all these years? Could, for that matter, his brother in all but blood really have committed such an appalling act then meticulously placed champagne on ice and telephoned to welcome him home before departing the flat to invite his own Nemesis under the wheels of a train?

Kyle didn't think so. David couldn't – wouldn't! – have done *that*. Not slaughtered the girl in the knowledge that Kyle would almost certainly have been the one to find her – apart from which there still remained the question of who'd rigged the flat to blow. Most certainly McDonald wasn't the kind of monster prepared to incinerate the innocent.

Was he?

'Presumably you do know who she was, though, Mister McDonald?'

The query rekindled a dispiriting sense of déjà vu. 'Doctor McDonald. Academic, not med – No: I don't know who she was. Not this time.'

'*This* time?' The older policeman frowned. 'Let me get this right. You saying you're not a medical doctor, yet you've been involved with other corpses recently?'

''Course I bloody haven't!' Kyle flared somewhat ill-advisedly in the circumstances. 'Well, only marginally. Only one other corpse – yesterday, was it? And I'm not any kind of doctor, actually. My name's Kyle, Michael Kyle. Just plain mister.'

The copper muttered, 'Stick close to this one, Tom,' then walked down the hall to stare intently at David's little brass nameplate on the front door. A professional nomad, Kyle had never considered it worthwhile to include his own tally.

When the constable came back he was already fumbling for his handcuffs.

'How'd you force the doctor's door so neat, Kyle?' he demanded tersely, obviously relieved to identify some offence he could even begin to cope with. 'Use a credit card, did you? Like you seen 'em do on TV?'

He was hardly more coherent during his questioning by CID; particularly when accounting for his movements during the preceding twenty-four hours. Life after David's death had regressed by then into an absolute of disbelief rather than a time and motion record of a nightmare. To make matters worse his earlier illusion of normalcy, bizarre enough in itself, had long given way

41

to a surreal detachment from any emotion at all.

He didn't think he'd made a very good impression because they eventually isolated him in the sitting-room under tight-lipped scrutiny by his uniformed apprehenders, feeling not so much like a prospective Hammer of Justice as having been hammered by Justice. It probably didn't help his case when, with little to do other than attempt vainly to interpret the sounds of increasing activity in the hallway, Kyle eventually succumbed to sheer fatigue and slipped into a fitful doze. By that point he'd long given up caring about any impression of grisly insouciance such a laid-back attitude by a suspected serial killer may have afforded the Metropolitan Police.

Even so, as he'd drifted in his twilight world Kyle could sense things weren't going smoothly with the constabulary – that there was some kind of hold-up. Every so often he surfaced to observe the door opening, whereupon a new face would poke through to frown, a little disconcerted he thought, at his slumbering form, then the door would close again to be followed by low muttering on its lee side. He did his best to ignore the interruptions; to build some reserve for the pressures he knew were still to come.

A bit longer, more footsteps arrived, and the muttering from the hall became quite truculent. Heated, in fact.

Eventually Kyle was roughly shaken into startled wakefulness as most of the Metropolitan policemen went away, his uniformed escorts reluctantly taking their empty handcuffs with them, having surrendered Kyle – and the investigation, apparently – to yet more policemen who said they were from . . . well, from *Special* Branch?

'I thought you people only got involved where spies were concerned,' Kyle remarked nervously to the first of the New Wave: a morose-looking man in a slightly shabby tweed suit who'd introduced himself as Chief Inspector Cox from SO13, whatever that was. Kyle kept his voice as level as he could

42

because he figured that if CID had understandably judged him insane, then it was vitally important for his new interrogators to see him as calm and well balanced.

'You're thinking of Five, sir,' Cox muttered absently, frowning into the cupboard. He appeared every bit as disquieted as Kyle by what had been stored in there, which struck him – Kyle – as being rather odd considering their respective roles. 'Bit of a grey area nowadays, but basically MI5 do the spies; we do subversives and civil disorder. Even used to call us the Political Branch once.'

Three of the new arrivals had climbed into white overalls and snapped on rubber gloves. Now they were opening brief-cases packed with scientific-looking kit, while a leather-jacketed photographer loaded film into a Pentax.

Chief Inspector Cox spared Kyle a moment of grudging concern. 'All right out here in the hall, are you? We can go back and chat in the lounge. Keep out of the way of my sergeant and the scenes of crime boys if you're feeling squeamish.'

'I'm not squeamish. I'm long *past* being squeamish,' Kyle protested stiffly. 'Nor am I political – and I don't think I qualify as a subversive.' He thought about that for a moment. 'Not unless you count being a member of NUMAST, the Merchant Navy officers' union. So why can't I stay arrested by proper policemen?'

The Branch man had the grace to appear disconcerted. 'CID didn't think to tell you? Sorry about that, sir, but you're not under arrest any longer.' He stopped looking apologetic and qualified, 'Well – not for the moment, at least.'

'I'm not?' Kyle echoed weakly, slightly deflated even.

'Seems your ship confirmed you didn't sign off until after midnight, and I don't need a pathologist to tell me this happened some hours before then. Rigor's well established in the arms and trunk which suggests she was killed anything from twelve to twenty-odd hours ago. Lividity's marked and, apart from anything else,' he indicated the carpet before the open cupboard door, '*that's* had time to congeal.'

The stain; the one Kyle had never noticed before because he hadn't risked switching on more lights than he needed to, looked so obvious now: all glinting and spiky. Further smears of dried blood marked where something had been dragged from the front bedroom – David's bedroom – but Kyle hadn't hoarded enough reserves to feel able to dwell in detail on how or why they'd got there. Or on who might have provided the traction.

'CID are also satisfied that the interval which elapsed between your leaving the mortuary and returning aboard in late afternoon didn't allow you enough time to nip over here and,' the chief inspector deployed his index finger again, 'do that.'

Kyle felt a surge of relief: not so much at learning the threat of a murder charge had been lifted as for his not having been able to summon the emotional courage to enter David's bedroom earlier, in the course of his brief search for the missing laptop. Had he done so he might have stumbled upon sights even transcending, by their gory implication, the compressed horror of what had ultimately proved his lot to discover.

'Your friend Doctor McDonald, on the other hand,' Cox continued, patently awaiting a reaction. 'Now the doctor's a different kettle of fish altogether, wouldn't you say?'

Kyle's relief evaporated to be replaced by what had already become a familiar conflict between loyalty and, on the face of it, logic. Either he had to concede the possibility that David *had* killed that still-anonymous girl – had become crazed enough and bestial enough to lift a knife clear through her throat with such maniacal energy that it had almost certainly skewered her brain – or remain firm in the conviction that David McDonald had been set up for rather more than his own murder.

Loyalty still won by a short head. Loyalty, reinforced by a telephone conversation involving Waffen-SS colonels, convoys that were apparently dynamite in World War Two, Russians, Egyptians . . . no – Egypt*tologists*!

'David didn't do it either,' he declared firmly.

'Somebody did,' Chief Inspector Cox observed mildly. 'And if you're arguing coincidence, then I have to say the notion of the doctor's accidentally falling under a tube train only hours before a young woman's corpse is discovered in his flat would tax the credulity of most people to the limit.'

'You believe David killed her then committed suicide?'

'With respect, you've introduced the possibility of suicide. I'm still open-minded.'

'Why?'

'Christ, wouldn't you expect me to be?' Cox retorted, a bit perplexed.

'I meant why would he kill her? What possible motive could he have had?' The bloodstained inference leading from the bedroom suddenly made Kyle appreciate the vacuity of the question and he changed tack quickly. 'Look, I'm probably missing something but, if it's that straightforward, why are *you* here? Special Branch?'

'Because some bright DC thought to check the registration numbers of cars parked out in the street. The computer came up flagged "notify SO13" when he called for a PNC on a particular Ford Mondeo.'

'David didn't have a Ford Mondeo,' Kyle protested blankly. 'Didn't have any kind of car, as far as I know.'

'I don't recall claiming he did,' Cox endorsed blandly.

Kyle felt his eyebrows meet. It was hard to understand why David's *not* having purchased a particular make and model of motor car should automatically trigger a computer-initiated investigation by Special Branch. Not unless the Ford Motor Company possessed considerably more clout with the law than he imagined possible.

'So?'

'So standing orders task CID to call for Branch advice regarding vehicles registered to persons suspected of terr sympathies.'

'Terr?'

'Terrorist.'

'Doctor McDonald wasn't a terrorist,' Kyle protested as a matter of course. Making disclaimers on David's behalf was becoming routine by then, what with his having already denied

McDonald's being a sexual deviant, a murderer, a bomber, a suicide and a Ford Mondeo owner.

'At the risk of repetition, sir, I never said –'

Kyle's thought processes caught up with his mouth then.

'You mean it was her car – she's the reason you're here? That she's . . .' He found himself staring incredulously at the waxwork girl in the cupboard. Undoubtedly she'd been beautiful once upon a recent time. Very beautiful. Far too beautiful to imagine her as being '. . . a *terrorist*?'

CHAPTER SIX

'Does the name Abdeljalil mean anything to you, Mister Kyle? Did Doctor McDonald ever mention it, for instance?'

The chief inspector's voice, framing the unaccustomed syllables with care, interrupted a daze which encompassed corpses on sterile display, corpses in cupboards, corpses in photographs, Waffen-SS men, Russians, thought-to-be-dead Williams – or maybe Williamsons – and now, introducing perhaps the most paradoxical element of all into the increasingly lethal equation bequeathed to Kyle by David McDonald, the terrorist factor.

Or *was* it the first suspicion of McDonald's involvement with terrorists? The mysterious Hackman's message had already hinted at a former Irish Provo connection, although Abdeljalil hardly sprang first to mind as a name associated with Guinness and the Blarney Stone.

'No,' he forced himself to respond. 'Is . . . was that her name?'

'Cover name,' Cox qualified. 'Moroccan passport. 'Course, that was a shoe – a fake? – as well. Been resident in Chelsea for about eighteen months, Munich and Frankfurt before that. Called herself Loukach there according to German Bfv.' He chewed his bottom lip and looked strangely uneasy again. 'Worked up the Fulham Road. They reckoned she was a good hairdresser thereabouts.'

'David loathed terrorism,' Kyle assured him defiantly. 'He also happened to be Queen and Country to his bootstraps. Would've turned anyone in he'd suspected of acting against British interests.'

'I'm sure he would, sir,' Cox agreed enigmatically. 'But then, the doctor might not necessarily have been aware of the young lady's subversive affiliations. Terrorists don't wear badges. His relationship with her could have stemmed from a perfectly innocent meeting – as could her murder. In other words, she could have been killed because she was a woman, not because she was a terrorist.'

'Doesn't that presuppose she and David *had* a relationship in the first place?' Kyle found himself giving way to a degree of truculence.

'Disregarding probability, I'd have to concede that her dead body turning up in the doctor's residence doesn't actually prove they'd ever met at all.'

While Kyle congratulated himself on having scored a point in David's favour the Branch man supplemented slyly, 'All the same, when you identified the doctor in the mortuary, you didn't happen to notice –'

'What, Chief Inspector? Apart from noticing the fact that my closest friend had just been run over by a fucking railway train – notice *what*?'

'If he'd, well . . . had his hair cut recently?'

'Am I allowed to ask who she really was?' Kyle ventured when he'd calmed down; acutely aware that the more he learned from Cox, the closer he'd get to whoever had left a dual-titled corpse in his temporary stewardship.

'Why not? It'll be all over the bloody papers within the next couple of days anyway.' Cox succumbed to momentary frustration at the diligence of the British press, then shrugged. 'We'd tentatively identified her as having been born Inadi. Syrian national; thirty-two years old or thereabouts.'

Three patronymic options now.

'Didn't she have a Chris—' Kyle was going to say *Christian* but recognized the improbability just in time. 'A first name?'

'Steady on, I had enough trouble saying Abdeljalil,' the chief inspector muttered. 'She was known as Wanda to the locals, as far as I know.'

''Scuse me, gentlemen, but can I get started in there?' the scenes-of-crime photographer interrupted anxiously. 'I still got a rape to do before end of shift.'

'Don't you touch nothing before the pathologist gets here, Harry,' Cox cautioned. 'We're in the shit enough as it is without handing CID grounds for complaint.'

Kyle simply had to ask. 'Why, exactly, are you in the shit, Chief Inspector?'

'She's dead, sir: that's why.' Cox managed to inject a plaintive note. 'She's not supposed to *be* dead. Embarrassing for the security services. Next thing the press'll be hinting we did it on purpose. Got the SAS or whoever to take her out and save the taxpayer the cost of surveillance.'

Kyle reflected on David's credentials again, his close connections with matters military, but decided he could never have been an SAS man; not even secretly. He'd hated rough games too much. And no bird as intelligent as he would foul its own nest.

'If you were watching her, then why's she in my cupboard?' he pursued with what he felt was inescapable logic.

'I meant metaphorically speaking we were watching her. We couldn't physically watch her all the time. It's all down to resources. The public gets the safety umbrella they're prepared to pay for. Double the establishment of the Met, allocate most of 'em to Special Branch, and we might just keep our finger on a quarter of the potential bombers, stringers, moles, ravens, swallows and other assorted anarchists currently working to undermine the State in Greater London tonight.' The anti-terrorist officer thought about that claim for a moment, then qualified, 'Well, till roughly three o'clock in the bloody morning anyway.'

'It's gone three o'clock in the morning,' Kyle reminded him.

'There you are, then. Proves my point exactly.' Cox spread his hands triumphantly if somewhat obscurely. 'Trouble in her case,' he jerked his head again to encompass the frozen enigma before them, 'practical economics demanded we classified her as low priority, a sleeper: an inert subversive. One potential threat among hundreds. Poncing old ladies' hair in Chelsea like any alien legal till she's activated – if she ever is.'

'I suppose so,' Kyle conceded dubiously. It wasn't Cox's cupboard she'd ended up in.

'I mean, it's not like we're the old Soviet Union or what-ever. KGB and Cheka an' Mafia informers eavesdropping every-bloody-where.'

'Nobody would want that. Not here in the UK.'

'We do try, you know,' the Branch man persisted, experi-menting with pathos.

'I'm sure you do.'

'Even with long-term threats like Wanda Whatsit there. Had some of Five's best flaps and seals men monitor her mail down Central Sorting Office from time to time. Intercepted a few interesting items over the months along with the electric bills and irresistible direct mail offers. Routined them through to Interpol – not the free offers; just the intelligence take. Helped our Collator and Wiesbaden Database keep tabs on the rest of her cell.'

'Wiesbaden?'

Kyle couldn't help it. It was the second reference the chief inspector had made to Germany, and Stollenberg had been a German. Definitely a German. Though how the connection could be anything but tenuous he couldn't imagine, what with her being an Arab and everything. Come to that, she hadn't even been born until a quarter of a century after the Waffen-SS ceased to exist.

Cox eyed him perceptively. 'Strike a chord, does it. Wiesbaden?'

'Seemed strange, that's all,' Kyle parried weakly. 'A Syrian involved with a German terror group.'

'Mostly German certainly. Chips off the old Red Army Faction block. Call themselves *Entsagung* now – Renunciation. Mostly old-fashioned anarchists nostalgic for the Baader-Meinhof happy times of the Seventies, and ambitious to make a comeback by recruiting new talent before they start drawing their pensions. According to her file at CRO we'd linked Wanda to them even before she fell out with her former paymasters.'

'Who were?'

Cox threw him an interrogative look. 'Why would you want to know, sir?'

It was Kyle's turn to wave at the cupboard. 'Hard not to take a proprietary interest under the circumstances.'

The Branch man scrutinized him a moment longer, then shrugged. 'The Frankfurt cell of the PLO originally. Like I said, it's not exactly classified stuff. Any good newsroom will have most of what I've told you on file in case the day ever dawned when Wanda lit the fuse that could've made her famous.'

The chief inspector hesitated, frowning at the dead girl. Kyle could see something was niggling him. 'She won't be needing her matches now,' Cox added vaguely.

'Didn't that demand a pretty fundamental change of allegiance? From PLO militant to Meinhof?'

'Why? Most German and Arab terror groups share a historic hatred of Jewry. Going way back, sir, the Entebbe airport fiasco and the Lufthansa Mogadishu hijack were both joint operations. While that one's activities suggest she continued to do her bit for Izzal-Din al-Quassam, the armed wing of Hamas – providing intelligence on the leading lights of Chelsea's Jewish community for them, among other things – the official view is that she direc-ted most of her energy into supporting Entsagung after Arafat's Gaza peace initiative made blowing up Israeli citizens politically incorrect. A cynic would argue Wanda still wanted to. Wasn't too fussy about siding with any group prepared to provide the Semtex.'

'But you're not a cynic?'

'I suspect it went deeper than that with her. Word was she'd got herself romantically involved with one of the new-breed Meinhof Appreciation Society. Decided to stay with them despite what happened to her lover.'

He afforded a thin smile when he saw Kyle's expression. 'Terrs can experience love too, you know. They've got emotions like everyone else. They just don't give a damn about everyone else's.'

'It was more your previous comment that intrigued me.' Kyle kept it as casual as he could. 'What did happen to her lover?'

Cox smiled again but without any humour at all. 'Half a magazine from a machine pistol, compliments – or so speculation had it – of GsG9.' He anticipated Kyle's inevitable supplementary. 'Grenzschutzgruppe Neun, sir – the German counter-revolutionary warfare team? His killing caused a stir of press debate at the time. Alleged some of GsG9's hard men might have taken the lad out a bit unsportingly while he tried to place a bomb under a Bundesbank official's car. Seems some of the shots left close-range powder burns to the back of his head. Of course they denied it – the Germans – but who believes anything Special Forces say?'

Kyle felt a stir of excitement. 'Remember his name?'

Cox screwed his eyes tight for a moment, then shook his head. 'Damned if I do. Does it matter?'

There was a slim chance it mattered a lot but Kyle could tell the Branch officer was uncomfortable with what he'd given him already, and didn't dare push his luck.

He'd also had a sudden thought. 'You referred to Wanda there lighting the fuse that could have made her famous.' Kyle nodded through the lounge door towards the now safely inert fire. 'I can't imagine why, but might she have been trying to last night?'

'The build-up of gas you referred to in your statement?' Chief

Inspector Cox afforded Kyle's criminological thesis grave consideration before asking solemnly, 'Would that have been before or *after* she stabbed herself in the throat then hid her own corpse in your cupboard, sir?'

Cox might as well have told him bluntly to stick to navigation: leave the detective work to the professionals, but Kyle wasn't in any mood to be patronized.

'What I *really* don't understand,' he complained, still smarting a few minutes later, 'is why, if Special Branch knew she was a potential threat, you didn't have the Home Office sling her out as undesirable.'

The chief inspector shrugged. 'I told you we were monitoring Wanda's mail. Sometimes it contained references to her Entsagung cell's cross-border movements, vehicle numbers, UK associates, safe houses; you don't kill a goose that lays even the odd golden egg.'

'Somebody did.' Kyle gained a certain childish satisfaction from turning Cox's earlier phrase back on him.

'You not finished your snaps yet, Harry?' Cox diverted down the hall, conveniently irritable. 'They're not bein' featured in bloody *Vogue*, you know.'

'If a job's worth doing, Skipper . . .'

'All bloody artistes now,' the chief inspector grumbled. 'All his so-called new breed of copper – you sure you're still feeling all right, sir? Don't want us to book you into a hotel or something till we're through here?'

'No, thank you. I'm fine.'

Absently Kyle produced a cigarette and fumbled for his Zippo, wondering why Cox was allowing him to stay. It never occurred to him it was his house anyway. He didn't mind. Not so long as he didn't look too keenly into the cupboard.

'Grateful if you wouldn't, sir,' Cox murmured. 'I'm not worried about your contaminating the crime scene so long as you stay with me, especially seeing you've been trampling around destroying evidence for half the night already, but ciggies can mask intangible clues – perfume smells, aftershave, body sweat, drugs? We can't preserve them in an exhibit bag but even the hint of, say, a smoker's recent presence might just turn out to be significant.'

He sniffed loudly, expertly: an olfactory connoisseur of murder. 'Apart from residual traces of town gas, I haven't identified anything else untoward so far. Otherwise I'd have got Snappy there to witness it.'

Kyle glanced at his watch and then at the grandmother clock. A quick interpolation between the two suggested it was nearly ten a.m. Or, he reflected yearningly, four bells in the morning watch had he still been aboard ship. Preferably somewhere in the Pacific.

Cox misread his gesture as veiled criticism.

'Sorry for holding you up, but both the Poet and the Home Office pathologist will want to view the body in situ before we move it. They've been called to a suspected terr shooting in St James's. Fingerprints and forensic will keep working through the rest of the flat till then.' The chief inspector eyed the cupboard gloomily. 'She's goin' to be a bugger to get out of there by the time they've finished, I can tell you. All wedged in like that.'

Kyle couldn't help wondering aloud what a poet had to do with murder. Cox smiled sardonically.

'Byron. Detective Chief Superintendent Byron, my ultimate guv'nor. Appointed SIO – Senior Investigating Officer – on this one. Heard of him?'

'No.'

'You won't warm to him: he can be a bit of a terror himself. Mostly involved with the Mid-Eastern Fundamentalists over here; not an IRA-inclined man at all, stand-down or not. Always deplored the Fenians.'

Kyle thought about Hackman and his implied Irish connection again, but decided not to push it. Cox was too sharp at picking up on obscure points. 'He doesn't deplore Islamic extremists?'

'He understands their point of view. What drives them,' the chief inspector conceded cautiously. 'It makes him more dangerous to them.'

'*Nos amis, les ennemis*, eh?'

'Our friends, the enemy?' the Branch man mused. 'That's good, that is. And very apt. You can't afford to hate too much in my trade: it can cloud your judgement.'

''Scuse me again, gents,' the photographer broke in tersely. They moved down the narrow hall keeping clear of the bloodstains while a further barrage of flashes and motorized whirrs from the Metropolitan Police Pentax created a mini-Alamein behind them.

'Mind you, I attended the Horse Guards bomb when I was a young constable just transferred into the Branch,' Cox reflected expressionlessly. 'That made me hate, all right. All those poor dumb animals? Brushed shiny with pride by one man, yet their bellies deliberately ripped open by another.'

Involuntarily, Kyle glanced back at the cupboard. The girl's raven hair was still shiny too, like those mutilated horses must have been. Liquid black cascading over bowed and naked shoulders and briefly highlighted under the staccato interrogation of the lensman's flash. Doubled up like that they wouldn't know about her . . . well, about the rest of her until they'd eased her from her grotesque repository.

A utility cupboard. Specifically a convenience for the disposal of temporarily expedient objects? Kyle frowned uncertainly. Might that imply some macabre satire? Some unconscious or even, for that matter, intentional message from whoever had killed her?

David had enjoyed obscure little jokes. On the other hand he'd never inclined towards being any more meticulous when it came to tidying things away into cupboards than in tackling his domestic paperwork.

'It's a point, sir,' the policeman who apparently felt more deeply for horses than for people agreed politely. 'Psychological, of course, but nevertheless worth a thought. Mind you, one would have to discount the fact that the perpetrators of most impulse sex crimes tend to act in much the same way – except they're usually trying their damnedest *not* to send a message. They panic. Tend to act irrationally, hide their victims in the oddest places.'

Kyle glowered. 'Like in cupboards, you mean?'

Cox softened slightly. 'Look, Mister Kyle, I appreciate your concern for Doctor McDonald's possible involvement in this bloody awful mess. For what it's worth, I agree with you on one point. I don't believe he would have had any truck with Abdel-whatever had he been aware of her subversive background, while, as far as I know, we've nothing on Branch files to question that assumption.'

'But?' Kyle invited resentfully, knowing there was one to come.

'But I still say show me a nude female corpse between nine and ninety years old, and like as not I'll show you the victim of a sex crime. Unless forensic turn up something that contradicts present indications, then I'm bound to reiterate my gut feeling that we're not dealing so much with a terrorist-related killing as with the illogical, the irrational and the plain bloody sick. Now, whether that puts the doctor in the frame or not isn't a function of SO13 to decide. CID can have the case file back with Special Branch compliments. There's crazies in that particular can o' worms just crying out to be apprehended – the sex offender files, I mean: not in CID.'

Kyle resolved not to make any further inane observations. Like on the exquisite irony that he read into the dead girl's posture. Her left arm, still rigidly crooked despite having been released from the constriction of the cupboard door, remained stubbornly raised in the clenched fist salute of the internationally oppressed. He didn't dare suggest such a phenomenon implied any swan-song of defiance in Miss Wanda tentatively-born-Inadi's case, though.

It was a pretty safe bet that Cox would have dismissed it simply as the result of her having been forced carelessly into

56

a confined space, allied with natural depletion of the nucleotide
– er, adenosine triphosphate was it? – in her body tissue.

And that encapsulated what was becoming an all-too-familiar
quandary. Every policeman he'd met so far seemed to evaluate
things in absolute terms, whereas there was nothing absolute
about the Stollenberg riddle. Dammit, by Kyle's own reckoning
there was little enough to qualify even as being *vague* about
the Stollenberg riddle, the supposed Stollenberg riddle! David
hadn't actually pointed him towards one single piece of verifiable
evidence he could present to Cox – or none other than a passing reference to some still-apparently-surviving enigma called
Williams or Williamson who purportedly lived in Battersea: the
area which David had declared an intention to head for on his
last morning alive.

Even for Kyle to repeat David's warning that his research was
sensitive, maybe dangerous in the wrong hands, risked courting
constabulary derision. Madmen *do* fantasize, don't they? Become
paranoid? Imagine themselves the focus of bizarre conspiracy?
All said and done, doesn't falling prey to such delusion mark
the point at which a man *is* considered mad?

So what was he, Kyle, to do in the face of such likely disbelief? Even confident, by virtue of his privileged knowledge, that
the forensic process would ultimately point to the murderous
involvement of a still-unsuspected third party, how long would
that scientific support take to come forward? Certainly longer than
Kyle could afford to delay before the Stollenberg trail grew cold.
In the meantime Cox obviously didn't intend to launch into hot
pursuit of the terrorist issue – not so long as he inclined to the
theory that Wanda's death had been determined more by her
having possessed lustrous black hair and silk-bronze skin than by
any subversive affiliations she'd formed with Germany.

Kyle, on the other hand, knew the route to proving David's
innocence had to start from the hidden agenda of their telephone conversation. Which meant, in turn, he had to convince

the Chief Inspector that he, Cox, should disregard a lifetime's experience of being a policeman and accept, without a vestige of proof, an itinerant sailor's assurance that the girl in the cupboard was actually the second victim in the past twenty-four hours of a Waffen-SS field officer still capable, apparently, of inspiring murder more than fifty years after his regiment had ceased to exist – no, it wasn't *that* straightforward, dammit – after the colonel himself had, by any stretch of statistical probability, ceased to exist as well!

Kyle decided his safest course had to lie in continuing to be as economical with the truth to Special Branch as he'd been with the inspector at Paddington – which meant he couldn't dare risk giving the chief inspector cause to search his seabags which he'd previously moved from the hall into the lounge, where he'd taken care to stack them inconspicuously clear of the tramp of policemen's boots.

Cox might have wondered why Kyle, acting more on impulse than logic during the brief interval between his bemused telephone call announcing Wanda's discovery and the initial police response, had hastened to conceal certain items in that battered, globe-trotting luggage which even the most naive of witnesses should have recognized as being material evidence under the circumstances.

The two publications Kyle would probably have got away with – one picturing a time-worn Soviet merchantman, the other an even older battle between men in khaki and men wearing Nordic runes. Innocuous in themselves, Cox probably wouldn't even have made the connection with David in the first place. Not even Kyle himself knew quite why he'd hidden them.

But the tape he'd removed from David's telephone answering machine? The one recording his friend's incoming messages on the day he died? The chief inspector would most certainly have taken exception to Kyle's withholding that from his enquiry. Particularly as it identified a man called Hackman as one of the few people so far known to be connected with at least one aspect of McDonald's research.

Effectively it meant that Kyle had distanced himself from any official back-up or protection. He would be on his own now, looking to confront an apparently psychopathic spectre wearing the uniform of the Waffen-SS.

By the next morning – no, it must have been by the morning *after* the next morning – two whole days following the start of the nightmare and nearly twenty-four hours mercifully devoid of any association with corpses, policemen and nearly getting himself blown up by gas that hadn't even been paid for – Kyle had achieved little other than snatch a few further hours of sleep, order a new lock in tandem with the services of a glazier, and otherwise restore the flat to a habitable state following the eventual departure of the by-then discreetly coffined Wanda aboard a collapsible chrome undertakers' trolley.

The police and the coroner's officers had made tidying up a lot easier, having taken many of the furnishings from the flat for more detailed forensic examination. They included particularly the bloodstained carpet and mattress from David's former bedroom, all of his clothes, the contents of the kitchen utensils drawer and, mercifully, the hall carpet itself.

They also took with them the papers from McDonald's desk. Or most of them. They left the gas bill along with a sheaf of other accounts that David had omitted to pay.

They hadn't come across David's computer during their search, despite Kyle's having explained to Cox, after he'd commented on the lack of hard copy references, that all research records would most likely exist only in electronic form. The confirmation of its disappearance dashed any hope Kyle had previously cherished of finding the Stollenberg answers committed to hi-tech memory.

The laptop's not being there didn't prove anyone else had taken it: only that it had gone. Worse, its disappearance could just as easily be construed as further evidence of David's guilt. Until persuaded of a third party's involvement, the police were justified in assuming that not only had David disposed of his records himself, but he had further intended to incinerate the place where he had lived. After all, if a man in torment can be moved enough to bring about the violent destruction of his present life, then why should he not wish to obliterate all traces of his past as well?

Kyle got fed up with glooming over old ground and cast hopefully about to find distraction in irrelevancies. A quick time check indicated it was either five past or half past six, too early for the morning paper delivery. Remembering the broadsheet dropped through the box just before he'd met Wanda, Kyle found it still lying where he'd left it in the kitchen and spread it before him on the table.

Despite the newspaper's being two days old, he still hadn't enjoyed such prompt access to the British press in the nine months he'd been away. One glance reassured him that not only had his deprivation been bravely borne but that he wouldn't need to rush avidly for the current edition when it did finally reach the doormat. Apart from the journalistic staples of Royal voyeurism, financial gloom and political speculation, the news headings appeared generated largely by people's private unhappiness. *Elderly couple assaulted; Actor's top billing in court; Welsh factory blaze; Kent floods; British tourist –*

London Underground horror!

It caught him entirely unawares – just a few lines buried in the latter pages, fighting for column space between *TV Tonight* and sport. The bald reporting of David's dying: 'Morning commuters watched helplessly as a man sustained fatal injuries when struck by a train entering Lancaster Gate Underground Station shortly before 8 a.m. yesterday . . .'

Reality returned: a rush of ice through Kyle's veins. He hadn't thought – hadn't expected it, somehow. Not to be there; not confirmed in black and white for casual consumption with everybody's breakfast cereal. A reflex aversion to reading further compelled his eyes to scan in search of less traumatic diversion.

Hit and run . . .

Battersea . . .
WILLIAMSON . . . ?
Jesus!

KILLER VEHICLE FAILED TO STOP

Battersea resident Mr Ted Williamson, 83, is believed to have been the victim of a hit-and-run driver near his home on the Fairchild Towers Estate yesterday afternoon. Mr Williamson, who died shortly after admission to hospital, leaves a wife, Margaret.

According to one witness, no apparent attempt was made to apply the vehicle's brakes when it was seen to veer erratically, mount the pavement and strike Mr Williamson before continuing at speed in the direction of Wandsworth. A Metropolitan Police spokesman said later that the possible involvement of so-called joyriders cannot be ruled out.

It is understood that a black BMW 5-series saloon, reported stolen only minutes before the tragedy and later found abandoned and burning on waste ground nearby, is being examined by forensic officers in connection with the incident.

The dead man, a retired Post Office worker, was well known to Battersea residents as an active campaigner for local charities. A former Commando, Mr Williamson was awarded the Military Medal in 1945 having served in North Africa, France and Germany . . .

CHAPTER SEVEN

Fairchild Towers Estate turned out to be a failed example of late-Fifties town planning. Made even more desolate by rain, it was easy to imagine such a dispiriting conglomeration of concrete egg crates providing a spawning ground for joyriders – kids charged either on drugs or perverted ego competing for local notoriety on a full-throttle high.

Except that joyriders hadn't been responsible for the death of a seemingly indefatigable old gentleman called Ted Williamson. Kyle knew it, and whoever had stolen that black BMW knew it. Perhaps the police would recognize the possibility of malice aforethought once their enquiries were completed, but that would take time. It also seemed highly unlikely. Crimes involving vehicles undoubtedly formed a considerable part of the local constabulary workload. As far as Kyle understood, the majority of offenders were never apprehended.

He had to ask several people for the whereabouts of the Williamson flat before a harassed girl pushing a pram and trailed by two complaining children directed him to the third floor. With growing trepidation he climbed echoing, concrete stairs past murals of graffiti, asking himself what the hell he was *doing* there. How was he going to broach a topic about which he knew almost nothing?

One thing was for sure. He could hardly knock on a newly widowed woman's door and baldly inform her that her husband hadn't been killed by accident, whatever the police had told her, but had almost certainly been murdered.

Red-rimmed though her eyes were, she nevertheless presented a dignity of composure when she answered Kyle's hesitant knock. He felt for her. Not only had he so recently been called upon to marshal much the same empty pretence of normality himself, he was also acutely conscious that his sense of loss could only be but a pale counterfeit of the emptiness she must have been enduring.

'Mrs Williamson?'

'I'm sorry. If it's my husband you came to see, he's . . .'

She died a little herself, then. Couldn't quite find the courage to complete the sentence. Her hand, work-worn yet delicate with the translucence of age, tightened frail white on the door handle.

'I know about Mister Williamson,' Kyle said. 'I really am very sorry.'

'John's just gone down to the registrar's for me, then he was going to take Mary and the children to the park for half an hour. She wanted to stay but I told her not to fuss.'

'John?'

'He drove over from Wimbledon the same night, as soon as they told him. He was a Royal Marine until recently, you know. A colour sergeant.' Irrelevant though the fact was, the pride was evident, almost defiant, in her voice.

'Well, at least you've got someone to turn to. Someone qualified to take charge,' Kyle responded weakly, taken aback by her apparent willingness to talk.

'Mary came too. To make sure I managed all right.' The sudden animation in her eyes faded as she hit the reality barrier again. 'Are you from the police?' she diverted uncertainly.

'Sorry, no. My name's Kyle, actually. Not that it matters. I really came to ask if you feel able to help me, Mrs Williamson.'

'Help *you*?'

'Please, it's quite important or I wouldn't intrude at this time – but I believe your husband might have received a visit recently from a friend of mine. From a Mister McDonald?'

Kyle held his breath. Was he about to take his first faltering step closer to Stollenberg?

'Don't you mean *Doctor* McDonald?' she said, gently admonishing him for having disregarded David's years of study by not affording him his titular due.

She'd been visibly upset when Kyle explained as gently as he could that Doctor McDonald, too, had died. He didn't want to lie so he avoided elaborating further, other than to say that his friend had been engaged in a research project of considerable importance which he, Kyle, had vowed to do his best to complete as a sort of tribute.

'Such a nice gentleman.' Mrs Williamson ushered him into a neat sitting-room while giving the impression that she was commiserating more with Kyle than he with her. 'And so clever. Young, too. Compared to Ted anyway, who was, well, getting on, I suppose. Some might say he'd lived the best years of his life a long time ago. Unlike many, Ted enjoyed his war – the proper war, I mean. Hitler's war. Or most of it.'

'I suspect that was why David came to see him. About his experiences in the army?'

'Tea first,' Mrs Williamson prescribed firmly. 'We've both had a difficult time of it. A nice cup of tea should buck us up no end.'

She fussed about, plumping up cushions and urging him to be seated. Kyle hadn't intended to impose but, if nothing else, it seemed his presence was helping to counter the loneliness a little. Take her mind off things.

'You mentioned John, Mrs Williamson?' he called through to the little kitchen, trying to make conversation. 'He's your son, presumably?'

'Not really. But every bit as good as.' She reappeared with a tray. Kyle took it from her and laid it on the table. 'Ted and I weren't blessed with family, you see. Arthur and Elsie Lewis – John's parents – were our next-door neighbours. And our best friends. When he was little, John spent as much time playing here as he did at home. Even now, despite his real mum and dad both having passed away, he still looks after me and –'

Mrs Williamson remembered again, then gathered herself. 'Well, just me now, I suppose. He and Mary have been a big help already: seeing to the forms and things and sorting out my pension. But you'll know all about that too, unfortunately.'

'I'm all right on the pension.' Kyle smiled. 'It's David's research I'm a bit stuck on.'

'Oh, dear, I don't know how I can help you there,' she said as she poured tea. 'Ted and the doctor talked for a long time, I remember. He never said much about it after, not to me anyway, but I know he really enjoyed your friend's visit. Seemed to cheer him up quite a lot, in fact – put a spring in his step he hadn't had for years, he said later.'

Mumbling awkward appreciation Kyle took the proffered cup.

'But you don't know exactly what?' he ventured. 'What part of the war they discussed?'

'They were only talking generally. About the D-Day fifti-eth anniversary ceremonies when I took the biscuits in,' Mrs Williamson offered apologetically. 'Ted was there as one of the veterans – we both were. In France. Went over with the British Legion. They organized special trips. Ted marched past Her Majesty the Queen at Arromanches. Seven thousand of them did, you know – seven thousand old soldiers, sailors and airmen? He said it was the second proudest day of his life.' She smiled wistfully. 'He was always considerate. Careful to insist that marrying me had been his proudest day of all. September the tenth, nineteen forty-two.'

'He wasn't just being considerate. I'd bet serious money he was telling the truth,' Kyle assured her while covering his own disappointment.

She sniffed, looked a bit pleased, then rose and walked over to the mantelpiece. When she turned she held a photograph in a silver frame.

'That's my Ted. Early nineteen forty-four. I insisted he had it taken when he came back from Africa after he'd been wounded. You can see from the stripes he was a corporal then. *And* a very difficult patient. He was ever so relieved when they got him fit enough to return to his unit in time for D-Day.'

Kyle said, 'May I?', then took the photograph, more because he felt he should for Mrs Williamson's sake than with serious interest. Originally monochrome, it had been hand-tinted in the fashion of the day so that the khaki uniform had reverted to a muddy brown with the flesh colours garish and unreal. It seemed highly unlikely, Kyle reflected, that such a hard-looking soldier wearing *Commando* shoulder flashes would have been wearing lipstick, as the finished print suggested.

It was then that he frowned.

'You said Mr Williamson was a corporal when this was taken. Does that mean he got promoted later?'

'To sergeant, then company sergeant major. But his CSM's rank only came after VJ Day, when the war was over. Ted always joked they never gave him time to get used to being called "sir" before he was back to being plain "mister" when he was demobbed.'

Kyle was still staring hard at the picture when the front door banged and two children came rushing into the room without ceremony. The little boy was shouting 'Daddy bought me a Happyburger an' Coke, Nan,' while his older sister, blonde and more susceptible to the presence of a stranger, just eyed Kyle shyly then walked to hug her surrogate grandmother's knees with a compassion far beyond her years.

'William and Nancy,' Mrs Williamson said, blinking suspiciously moist eyes. 'Say hello to Doctor Kyle, both of you.'

'Just mister,' Kyle demurred. 'I wasn't as clever as David.'

It wasn't hard to imagine that the man who followed had been a Royal Marines senior NCO. Just something about him – the hard edge to strong features, a military self-assurance which belied the casual dress. Even the way he appraised Kyle was interrogative without implying arrogance.

'My baby,' Mrs Williamson said without the slightest sense of ridicule.

Kyle grinned sympathetically, understandingly at John Lewis.

'Mister Kyle came to ask about Ted's war experiences,' Mrs Williamson supplemented.

Lewis didn't smile back.

He didn't see much of either John or what turned out to be a rather pretty dark-haired Mary after that. 'Clean up before lunch, you two. Leave Nanny to talk to the gentleman in peace,' Mary commanded as soon as she'd said 'hello' to Kyle, then the Lewises had withdrawn from the sitting-room *en famille*, leaving only echoes of childlike protest.

'I really must go. Thank you very much for the tea, Mrs Williamson,' Kyle ventured shortly thereafter, aware of how anxious the old lady must have been to make the most of her adoptive family. He'd begun to move towards the door when a thought struck him.

'You mentioned that David's visit cheered your husband up – put a spring in his step he hadn't felt for years. You can't think of any particular reason why, can you?'

'Just Ted being silly. He was always a bit of a dreamer, especially after he came home from the war. Used to joke about how he'd fixed things in the army so's he'd be able to keep me in a manner I wasn't accustomed to. It was only later, once he'd been with the post office a while and come back to earth, he gradually stopped pretending – until the other day. He started on about it again the other day. The first time in years – how we could soon be well off after all. Be able to afford a proper house beside the sea.'

'He said that *after* he'd spoken to Doctor McDonald?'

She nodded. 'Even asked me whether I fancied living somewhere exotic, like maybe Blackpool or Brighton, the daft ha'porth. "Oh yes, Ted Williamson," I said right back to him, "and I suppose you're going to tell me next just who's going to *pay* for all that, are you?"'

Kyle smiled at an old lady's vision of exotica. 'And what did Ted say?'

'I told you he could be a daft ha'porth.' Mrs Williamson smiled too, but in a tolerant, wistfully reminiscent sort of way. 'He said Hitler was going to pay for it. That's who Ted joked was going to make us rich, Mister Kyle – Adolf Hitler, of all unlikely people.'

As soon as Kyle returned to the flat in Ringtree Gardens he went straight through to his seabag and rummaged for the book he'd concealed before the murder squad had arrived. *Waffen-SS: Death of a Folk Myth*.

The British sergeant with the cigarette in his mouth and the sub-machinegun cradled sportingly in the crook of his arm? Even without the aid of a magnifier Kyle felt a surge of cautious elation. There was no question that the Second World War soldier posing with post-battle-relaxed comrades over the corpse of a dead SS trooper could well have been the subject of the hand-tinted photograph he'd just been shown of Corporal – later promoted to Sergeant – Edward Williamson. Who'd most certainly fought in Germany during the closing months of that conflict.

And who, immediately prior to his dying as the consequence of a violent, albeit apparently random event, had seemingly felt encouraged enough, following contact by David – the coincidental victim of yet another recent and allegedly indiscriminate

68

killing – to reiterate for the first time in years the belief that he, Williamson, was destined to become wealthy after all. A conviction initially evinced on the former soldier's return from active service over half a century before.

But that was where Kyle's satisfaction petered out: where reason gave way before the ludicrous. Because, according to ex-Commando Sergeant Williamson, deceased – or, if Kyle was brutally realistic, according to eighty-three years *old* ex-Sergeant Williamson, deceased – the source of funding for the veteran's regenerated optimism represented about the most improbable benefactor anyone but a lunatic could devise, other than, say, an elderly soul suffering the onset of dementia.

Kyle lit a cigarette and leaned back pensively in David's chair. *Why Hitler? Why not Napoleon, eh Ted? Or Julius Caesar, for that matter?*

Unless, of course, Williamson had been speaking metaphorically. Had lumped them all together – all Hitler's children of the Schutzstaffeln. Maybe even gained the battlefield edge that had enabled him to survive from visualizing the face of recent history's most reviled dictator in every death's head badge that came under his gun sight.

Including, perhaps, the insignia of a field officer called Stollenberg?

He closed the book and drummed his fingers uncertainly on its soft cover, lost for inspiration. *Waffen-SS: Death of a Folk Myth.* The title was printed in red – the red of blood spreading sluggishly across a snow-chilled battlefield. It hadn't struck Kyle before, but the illustration the jacket designer had chosen for the cover was a many-times-enlarged segment of the photograph in which Williamson himself appeared. But Williamson hadn't been afforded the ultimate accolade of making it to the cover. All the blow-up showed was the helmeted head, the arched neck, the slack-spread shoulders, the disillusioned, upturned eyes of a near-child German super-soldier observing, but not comprehending, his own personal *Götterdämmerung* in the smoke-obscene sky above his defeated Fatherland.

Kyle braced as a thought struck him. Didn't most military uniforms display regimental or divisional insignia or whatever? Which, if identifiable from the photograph, should at least settle one fundamental uncertainty – whether or not Williamson's and Stollenberg's units had even *met* in battle in the first place!

He examined the book jacket again, minutely. Damn! The part he wanted, the hinted-at collar patch under the waxen chin, had been overprinted with the author's name. The upper serif of the 'L' in Lightwood just cut into the picture enough to blank out . . .?

*Light*wood?

'Photographs by *Tom Lightwood*?'

The anonymous Hackman's Lightwood? The Lightwood apparently reported KIA 'a few days after the event'? Who never made it back 'to give formal evidence to the Prov—'? Kyle's deliberations, previously sluggish, slammed into turbo. '. . . to the *Provos*!' A term which didn't necessarily *have* to refer to any former Irish Republican kill-and-fade-away terror faction, as he'd initially assumed. Not when taking into account the possibility of a silent 't' in its pronunciation.

'ProvosT' . . . 'Prov-*O*'?

Delivered that way, Hackman's reference left itself wide open to interpretation. Might it not equally have applied to a rather more benign version of rule by terror?

Being one of the British soldier's more charitable euphemisms for his own Corps of Military Police.

CHAPTER EIGHT

'Blown up you say, sir?' the photographer frowned.

'Fortunately no,' Kyle retorted thankfully. 'Managed to turn the gas off before –'

He registered the photographer's bemused expression. 'Sorry, thinking of something else. Yes – two, please. One enlargement of the whole page if you can manage it. Big as possible. And another one concentrating on the area of the soldier's head and shoulders. Magnify them even more.'

'Which soldier?'

'The German.'

'He'd be the dead one?'

'Looks like it,' Kyle agreed.

The photographer peered at the open Lightwood book and sucked a critical tooth. 'They'll be no less grainy than the repro on the jacket. Pixels like pebbles. Poor quality. I don't like to do poor quality work, sir. Can't afford to. Not with Boots and Pronto-bloody-Print just round the corner with their fancy press-a-button-an'-turn-'em-out-like-sausages machines.'

'I don't mind. I'm not planning to hang them on the wall.'

'Apart from which I got the Rotary presentation pics and the Sloanes' wedding album for Friday. Be Monday before I can get round to it.'

'I was thinking of a hundred quid,' Kyle suggested. 'Cash?'

'Can you come back in an hour?' the photographer said.

He hunted through the military history section of the nearest book store until he found a thin publication covering Waffen-SS uniform and insignia, then went back to the print shop and collected the still-damp enlargements. Kyle felt quite pleased with himself as he set a return course for Bayswater Gardens. A brief scrutiny while the blow-ups were being wrapped had satisfied him that the badges on the dead German's camouflage uniform were now perfectly legible.

'It's not so hard,' he thought. 'Being a detective.'

Mind you, he was still prepared to allow that such new-found self-assurance might be a little premature. He hadn't tracked down Hackman yet, whoever Hackman might turn out to be. Not even traced the repairer who was holding David's Hoover to ransom, come to that.

By late evening, having studied the book from cover to cover and made endless frowning comparisons between printed lists of diagrams and the insignia sewn to the battlefield corpse's 'tiger jacket' smock, Kyle had reverted to conceding he'd no aptitude for sleuthing whatsoever. Another day gone and all he'd been able to prove was that the boy soldier who'd died fifty years before *had* been a member of Hitler's Waffen-Schutzstaffeln – a breakthrough which, considering the title of Lightwood's book, didn't exactly invite his yelling 'Eureka!'

An Unterscharführer, or senior corporal, according to the silver piping on the black shoulder strap supported by evidence of a single collar pip. There was a hint of another silver-grey-on-black sleeve patch in the form of an eagle, but it was lost in a fold of material and Kyle couldn't make out whether it was the standard issue eagle or the special SS-Polizei emblem. No unit badges. No indication at all as to which regiment, or even division, the cadaver had belonged.

'Well there's one thing for sure. He isn't – wasn't – Stollenberg,' Kyle gloomed, staring pensively at the cards propped against the wall. 'David undoubtedly referred to him as Standartenführer – even called him Colonel if my memory serves me – whereas that young man was simply a squaddie.'

He sat for a while, thinking how proud the kid must have been when he'd first donned the uniform. A bit like the young policeman who'd piloted him to the mortuary had been of his. The boy soldier's parents too, come to that . . . or *had* they been quite as proud of their offspring as one might imagine? Might they not have harboured an unspoken fear of what they'd helped to create? The kind of apprehension that couldn't risk expression in Hitler's Germany: not even between husband and wife. Either way they'd probably afforded pride of place to a silver-framed photograph of their son in some little house in Dortmund or Hamburg or wherever. Just as Mrs Williamson still did in her neat flat, where Commando Ted stared granite-jawed from the mantelpiece at this moment, and never grew a day older.

Come on, Ted, Kyle thought. *Who deliberately ran you down in your sunset years for something you must have done – must at least have been aware of – when you were young and fit and hard as nails, and controlling the executive end of a machinegun? Which brings us back to our mysterious Mister Hackman's comment about 'friendly fire'. Might he, for instance, have been hinting that it was a bullet from that same weapon you're holding so casually – not from any SS Schmeisser – that took the life of a battlefield photographer called Lightwood? And if so – why? What could Tom Lightwood have discovered about you, Ted, that caused him to be murdered by one of his own before he could give evidence to the Allied military police?*

But all that was a conclusion too far. David would have chided him for such a giant leap of presumption. While Inspector Cox of Special Branch? Well, he'd simply deliver some devastatingly logical put-down equal to any launched by Holmes upon the hapless Doctor Watson.

Kyle made another coffee around midnight, splashed a tot of rum in it for consolation, and returned to the lounge. On his way back through the hall a bizarre unease touched him and he couldn't resist casting a tentative glance into the cupboard. Just to satisfy his escalating paranoia. Make sure no one had left another bloody corpse in it while he'd been out detection shopping.

He sat, becoming colder and colder as the flat chilled down, thumbing aimlessly through lists of regimental names which positively thundered Aryan triumphalism. SS-Freiwilligen-Panzer-Grenadier-Division *Nordland*. SS-Gebirgs-Division *Prinz Eugen*. SS-Kavallerie-Division *Florian Geyer*, Panzer Divisions *Horst Wessel* and *Das Reich* and *Totenkopf*, *Leibstandarte Adolf Hitler* . . .

As Kyle's enthusiasm faltered for what had become a seemingly fruitless study of military trivia, his attention wandered to the background detail of the enlargements: particularly in the full-page blow-up featuring four British Commandos standing shooting-party casual over the remains of a vanquished school prefect. On first retrieving Lightwood's book from the chaos that was David's desk, he'd merely registered that what he'd already come to think of as Ted's Battle had taken place within an industrial complex. Now, aided by magnification, he found himself able to identify the site as having been part of a shipyard. The out-of-focus legend, *Bremerhavenschiffswerft*, painted across an overhead gantry, hardly needed translation.

There was even the distance-fuzzled silhouette of a nearly completed ship on the skyline, were further confirmation needed. He guessed that much because the after samson posts were still missing and no lifeboats were yet housed in her davits . . . the yard's fitting-out berth, Kyle mused, subconsciously appraising the new-build freighter's lines with a seaman's eye. Classic six-hatch general-cargo motor vessel with 20-ton heavy lift derricks at both masts, well-proportioned funnel and a graceful sheer –

typical of the days when ships looked like proper ships and not like twin-screw power stations.

For a moment his spirits revived: wondering if he might just have come up with a lead after all. Merchantmen in war made him think of convoys – and hadn't David referred to Stollenberg having been involved in a convoy? Kyle remembered considering it odd at the time – that a soldier should have had any connection with ships and shipping. Unless the Standartenführer's duties had been concerned with, say, military supplies: evacuees, troop movements? He frowned a few minutes longer at the silhouette, then gave up. But David had definitely spoken about the *Stollenberg convoy*. 'The Stollenberg convoy was dynamite,' he'd even said.

He'd also concluded with, 'God knows what some people might do if they discover I've actually managed to pinpoint –'

Pinpoint *what*, David? And who were the 'some people' you had in mind that caused even you, despite your often-delightful naiveté, to feel apprehensive?

It was odd. How, when Kyle finally drifted into a restless doze a face materialized to hang, persistent as the Cheshire Cat in Alice, before his fading subconscious. But the features weren't those of the murdered Wanda Inadi. Nor of Sergeant Ted Williamson, or of a brutalized warrior-child sprawled on a snow-speckled battlefield. Not even of David McDonald, his brother in every meaningful sense.

No!

Curiously, the image that went to sleep with Kyle was that of a man he'd only glimpsed for a moment, and had hardly spared a thought for since then.

The Williamsons' boy – former Royal Marines NCO John Lewis – no, *not* the Williamsons' son, the son of the Williamsons' best friends – Arthur and Elsie, hadn't the old lady called them? Arthur and Elsie Lewis? Who'd lived next door?

Kyle was fortunate. He hadn't realized he should have made an appointment beforehand to talk to one of the research assistants at the Imperial War Museum. But an attendant was very helpful when he arrived unheralded at the main building in Lambeth Road: directing him past displays of military hardware and under the loom of the great Polaris missile that dominated the ground floor, to the Department of Documents.

Even his decision to go there filled him with unease. Might he possibly be about to betray David's confidence by triggering unwanted interest in some wartime event which McDonald had clearly been at pains to keep secret? But Kyle had awakened to an acceptance of reality – that he couldn't hope to find David's killer without direction, and that direction in the first instance had to lie in discovering whatever he could about Stollenberg.

But discreetly. Without giving anything away. Play it as if he didn't quite know what he was doing or where he hoped to go. Which wouldn't require any acting on his part.

'Stollenberg, Mister Kyle?' the girl who responded to his tentative approach at the enquiries counter confirmed after assuring him he wasn't being any trouble at all. She had long dark hair and was unsettlingly pretty. Didn't look at all bookish, as Kyle had imagined young women with an interest in history inevitably must. But then he recalled another girl with raven tresses, and her macabre role in the scenario which had brought him to this place where the paper bones of companies, battalions, regiments, divisions, whole armies, navies and air forces of long-dead and not-so-long-dead men of battle lay interred in filing cabinet coffins or compressed on electronic disk, and shivered just a little before dismissing such inappropriate thoughts.

'He was a German. Definitely a German,' Kyle supplemented without needing to be deliberately vague. 'A colonel or half-colonel, far as I know. Served in the SS.'

'A full colonel – Standartenführer Stollenberg, ahhh . . . Manfred?' She screwed her eyes momentarily with the effort of recall. 'Third – no – *Second* Regiment, SS-Polizei-Panzer-Grenadier-Division.'

Kyle blinked, utterly disconcerted.

'Good God!' he said and, before he could stop himself, leaned over the counter to frown at her legs.

The girl stepped back in alarm. 'Mister Kyle?'

'I was trying to trace the wires,' Kyle explained, feeling idiotic. 'To the computer implant you obviously carry in your head.'

She giggled. 'It's called short-term memory. No wires needed to remember a subject I've already tasked the database with recently. Not even in here.'

Suddenly Kyle didn't feel inclined to return the smile. The Waffen-Schutzstaffeln had mustered several hundred thousand members at its peak and, for much the same reasons as Chief Inspector Cox, he too had lost all faith in coincidence. Particularly when it involved a surfeit of corpses.

'You're saying someone else has called here in the past few days to enquire about an SS colonel called Stollenberg?'

'Two, three weeks ago at most.'

But, of course . . . His frown cleared. 'David. David McDonald.'

'Do you mean Doctor McDonald?'

'You knew him?' Kyle said, studiously rising above the cut and thrust of the by-now inevitable reproach.

'He comes in often. One of our regular researchers. In fact he used to work here at IWM, I believe.'

Kyle was summoning the resolve to tell her that David wouldn't be calling again when he realized she was shaking her head. 'But no. Doctor McDonald wasn't the one who made that last enquiry. About the Standartenführer.'

A flush of excitement stirred in him. 'Can you remember who did?'

She wrinkled her eyes again in recall. 'A youngish man? We meet a lot of people.'

'But it – he – *was* a man, not a woman. Can you describe him?'

She smiled again, unaware of the importance of recollection. 'I'm good at names. I'm dreadful at faces.'

'Try the name.'

'Smith. Mister Smith.'

'Smith!' Kyle echoed hollowly. Weren't hotel registers reputed to be full of Smiths – particularly Mr and Mrs Smiths? And while many of them might even have been born 'Smith', he suspected that hadn't been the case in this instance.

'Tall or short. Thin or fat?'

'Tall . . . ish. I do remember he was very polite. But authoritative in a quiet sort of way.'

The description struck a chord. Cheshire Cats . . . and Royal Marines?

'Like someone used to giving orders? A soldier, say?'

'Possibly.' She hesitated then, and added hesitantly, 'Please don't think I'm trying to fob you off, Mister Kyle, but if the matter's important, and as you already know Doctor McDonald, might I suggest you contact him? He's a freelance researcher with considerable expertise in the history of the former SS regiments. I'm sure he'd be happy to come to an arrangement with you.'

She must have seen the sudden emptiness in Kyle's eyes then, and misinterpreted it as censure. She flushed awkwardly. 'I'm sorry. That was outside my terms of reference. It was just that Mister Smith . . . '

'What about Mister Smith?' Kyle heard himself prompt in a level voice.

'Well, I made the same suggestion to him – even put him in touch with Doctor McDonald – and as he hasn't been back I can only assume . . . '

'. . . that they met?' Kyle finished for her.

He didn't have the heart to tell her where cold gut instinct told him that meeting had taken place. Or when.

Okay, so it was still a factually unsupported assumption, dammit. But he sensed it had been at Lancaster Gate Underground station. Five days ago. At exactly 7.53 in the morning.

He didn't say it because – if he *was* right for once, and had allowed the rage of frustration which was swamping him to take charge – then, when it all came out, she might just recognize herself for having played a crucial, albeit well-intentioned role in facilitating the calculated slaughter of David McDonald.

And Kyle didn't wish to inflict a terrible burden like that on anybody.

She'd muttered an uncomfortable 'Excuse me . . . ' a moment later, and moved to speak to an elderly man at the other end of the counter. In the interim Kyle had waited, stunned and disconsolate, not quite knowing what to do or who to turn to next – whether or not to even pursue the agenda he'd set for himself that day. He'd set out that morning in a positive frame of mind, determined to find some common factor – some link between Manfred Stollenberg's life and David's death.

He'd found one, all right. One every bit as elusive as the Egyptian and the Russian. A will-o'-the-wisp called Mister Smith.

When the dark-haired research assistant returned, the man she'd engaged in conversation trailed accommodatingly in her wake. She wore a shocked expression.

'I'm so sorry,' she said. 'I wasn't aware that Doctor McDonald had –'

'Not your fault.' He forced a wan smile. 'The papers didn't say much. He wasn't even named in the early edition I saw.'

'Was he a close friend?'

Kyle nodded. 'Yes.'

The waiting man coughed discreetly and she turned.

'Mister Kyle, this is Professor Rushby.'

'Rushby,' the new face said. 'Prof sounds far too formal.'

Kyle warmed to him immediately. 'Kyle.'

'The professor and Doctor McDonald collaborated on several papers concerning the history of the SS.'

'Lisa means we argued a lot.' Rushby beamed. 'Chalk and academic cheese, we are.' His smile faded, and he gave an apologetic shrug. 'Sorry, dear boy. It's just that young McDonald used to accuse me, jokingly of course, of being a straight-down-the-middle-of-the-archives old buffer. In short, a fuddy-duddy. I shot back by claiming he was only masquerading as a history man – better fitted for a career as an investigative journalist. Tended more towards the fanciful approach. Damn good mind, though. I'll miss our little disputes.'

'Fanciful?' Kyle frowned, trying to rise above the reminder that any reference made to David must now be in the past tense.

'All right – unorthodox. But I'm of the old school that argues facts are facts. Leave no room for interpretation. McDonald, on the other hand, saw fact as merely providing a springboard for speculation.'

'I'm good at that,' Kyle muttered wryly. 'Speculation.'

'So I gather from Lisa.'

'I wasn't being serious about the computer implant,' Kyle protested.

'I think the professor means your interest in the Standartenführer, Mister Kyle,' Lisa said.

'You've told him as well, then?' Kyle muttered, glancing uneasily along the counter to ensure no one who looked like a Smith was eavesdropping. He hoped the professor wasn't planning to travel home by tube. Given the extent of the helpful Lisa's discretion, there wouldn't be a military historian left alive in London by the time the bloody trains stopped running!

'Now don't get on to Lisa. Nothing secret about Stollenberg. Or young David's special interest in the chap,' Rushby assured him, blithely protective of a woman who, in Kyle's paranoid imaginings, might just have signed the old boy's death warrant. 'Always been something of a cause célèbre among us post-war ferrets, has the colonel, even though, as you know, most of us consider McDonald was wasting his time on a wild-goose chase.'

'I didn't know,' Kyle denied weakly.

'Thought you were one of us. An historian?'

'I'm a sailor.'

'Ah, that explains it, dear boy.' Rushby nodded somewhat obscurely. 'Then you couldn't be expected to know.'

'Know what?'

'About the myth, of course,' Professor Rushby said. 'The Myth of the Stollenberg Convoy.'

CHAPTER NINE

The professor leaned back appreciatively, cradling his second brandy. It had been a good lunch. Had Kyle been hungry, he would have enjoyed it too. Either way he didn't grudge a penny of what it would cost. Not if it helped narrow the half-century-wide information gap between him and Stollenberg.

'You say you're a naval man, yet you're interested in McDonald's Stollenberg researches. Might I ask why?'

'He . . . we'd talked about them before my last voyage.' Kyle kept it casual, defensively vague. 'I've got some time on my hands. Now he's . . . gone, I wondered if I might be able to . . . '

He trailed off. It sounded a lame subterfuge. Rushby didn't press the point. 'Chase a wild goose or two?'

'So you keep saying.'

'Where would you like me to start?'

'Idiot's guide level?' Kyle suggested.

Rushby made a face. 'In 1939 Britain went to war with Germany –'

'I meant regarding Stollenberg,' Kyle interrupted hastily. 'I know there was a Second World War and everything.'

'A charismatic man. Classic background for an SS officer. Born 1915, if memory serves: third son of a Dresden police inspector. Joined the right-wing paramilitary Freikorps while still at school. Became an enthusiastic member of the National Socialist Party a year or so later and, shortly thereafter, a volunteer in the SA.'

'SA?'

'*Sturmabteilungen*. Stormtroopers or brownshirts – the then-expanding Nazi Party's private army of part-time bully boys, led by a particularly unpleasant deviant called Ernst Roehm.'

Kyle frowned. David hadn't died without leaving some legacy of knowledge. 'Thought Roehm fancied himself as more a rival to Hitler than an ally. Wasn't he eventually shot on the Führer's order?'

'On 30th June, 1934. Along with several hundred of his key henchmen during what became known as The Night of the Long Knives. A company of the deserving Damned.'

'But obviously Stollenberg escaped that purge?'

'He assisted with the executions. Was even awarded the coveted Nazi Party's *Blutorden* – the Blood Order – for services with meat hook and Luger. An excellent career move for such a young man. He would have been, what – nineteen at the time?'

Kyle reflected on the dead child-soldier in the snow. His career move hadn't proved as adroit. 'Why do you say "move"?'

'During the early twenties a select group was formed within the SA to act as Hitler's bodyguard. At first they bore the title of Stosstruppe Adolf Hitler. They later became known as Schutzstaffeln, or Protection Squads.'

'The SS?'

'Out of little acorns oak trees grow. Even in 1929, when that colourless nonentity Heinrich Himmler was appointed to command, the embryonic Schutzstaffeln could only muster some 280 men. By 1933 when Hitler seized absolute power – which, incidentally, marked the time when young Stollenberg was astute enough to read the writing on the wall and rethink his allegiance to Roehm – they'd grown to over thirty thousand. Three battalions of what had effectively become a movement within a movement: every last pure Aryan fanatically loyal to the New Order.'

'So where did our man go wrong?'

Rushby permitted a wisp of a smile. 'Perceptive of you.'

Kyle shrugged. 'Having been born with what one might call a Nazi silver spoon in his mouth, Stollenberg could at least have expected to make lieutenant-general or whatever. Yet he was still a colonel by the end of the war. That suggests he must have blotted his copybook somewhere down the line.'

'His blot was that of being too good a soldier. And as I pointed out initially, he was also charismatic. Too charismatic an up-and-coming young Turk for the High Command to overlook and, as such, a threat to his immediate superiors. At the outbreak of war Manfred Stollenberg had already become a Hauptsturmführer – a captain – in the Flak Regiment of probably the most elite formation of the Waffen-SS, Sepp Dietrich's Division-Leibstandarte Adolf Hitler.'

'Until?'

'Until, having advanced through Holland and into France – fighting by all accounts valiantly – Stollenberg's battery reached the outskirts of a small town by the name of Wormhout. They arrived there on the 27th of May, 1940, and unlimbered their guns near a group of farm buildings known locally as Le Paradis.'

Kyle began to feel even more vulnerable. Once again he was finding that the core subject of his supposedly discreet enquiry was, apparently, common currency in academia. He'd assumed from his last conversation with David that the colonel had come under scrutiny as a result of some discovery made only recently by McDonald, and kept secret at that – the implication being that, whatever bizarre mystery surrounded Manfred Stollenberg in the present, the man himself had long faded into historic obscurity. Yet here was one of David's colleagues reciting chapter and verse: places, even precise dates, virtually the martial curriculum vitae of one former middle-ranking SS officer among thousands?

His table companion misinterpreted Kylc's evident disconcertion. 'You afford me unwarranted credit, sir. To any student of recent wars, the massacre at Wormhout will endure in the annals of infamy.'

'The massacre?'

'Appreciate the times, Kyle. The Allied Expeditionary Force was retreating to Dunkirk. To gain breathing space to evacuate those falling back on the beaches, the infantry of the British 2nd Division had been ordered to defend the Béthune area to the last. One of the forces committed to that desperate endeavour was the 2nd Battalion of the Royal Norfolk Regiment. They held their positions with the utmost gallantry until, by late afternoon, they had been reduced to less than company strength. Virtually out of ammunition, and denied medical facilities to tend the wounded, they had no option but to surrender.'

'To Stollenberg's outfit?'

'No. To another German assault group: the SS 2nd Standarte of Totenkopf. Immediately following the battle, and despite being under protection of the Geneva Convention, all 98 British prisoners – wounded included – were then taken to a meadow in the proximity of Le Paradis.'

'Near where Stollenberg's battery was dug in.'

Rushby nodded: his expression sombre. 'There the Norfolks were lined up and machine-gunned. Mown down in swathes. Only two men evaded the slaughter by feigning death, eventually crawling away under cover of a rainstorm later that night to be captured and hospitalized by a unit of the Wehrmacht – the regular German army. All others who survived the initial massacre were bayoneted or pistolled.'

Kyle went cold. Such a callous multiplicity of grief. Of white-shocked parents and widows. Of weeping, fatherless children. 'On Stollenberg's order?'

'On the order of a Totenkopf company commander called Fritz Knochlein. To the best of my belief Stollenberg could

84

have had no preknowledge of what took place adjacent to his position.'

For some utterly illogical reason Kyle felt relieved. 'Then why . . . ?'

'I told you, dear boy. His immediate superiors were already seeking an excuse to discredit him. So, while the barbaric affair was effectively hushed up during the course of the war – largely because the SS refused to concede the Wehrmacht's authority to investigate an incident they considered embarrassing rather than monstrous – they still needed a scapegoat. The presence of Hauptsturmführer Stollenberg's battery at Le Paradis provided their opportunity.'

'While the real perpetrator – Knochlein – went free.'

'Eventually to become a lieutenant-colonel, having been awarded both the Iron Cross and the Knight's Cross in the process.'

'That's what I meant,' Kyle retorted bitterly. 'He got away with it!'

'Fritz Knochlein was hanged in Hamburg in 1948 for his part in the Wormhout Massacre: convicted largely on the evidence of the two Norfolks survivors. Of small comfort to his victims' relatives, Justice did in the end prevail.'

'And Stollenberg?'

'Moved sideways. Professionally buried. Posted to the Second Regiment of what had always been regarded within the Waffen-SS as an inferior division – the Polizei-Panzer-Grenadiers. Raised initially from poorly trained and ill-equipped Ordnungspolizei – civilian police – they never distinguished themselves, although, having spent the early part of the war on occupation and security duties in Russia, I have to concede they did fight well on the Wolchow River. Stollenberg earned himself an Iron Cross there. Even climbed back on the promotion ladder by being gazetted Sturmbannführer.'

'Just shows you can't keep a good man down,' Kyle muttered dryly, for want of something to say, then thought how appropriate that inane comment had actually been, considering the

85

man in question was, apparently, still killing people over half a century after the Allies had either shot him, blown him to pieces or at least taken his bloody gun away!

What he actually followed with was: 'Why did you say "myth" earlier, Rushby? The Myth of the Stollenberg Convoy?'

The Prof smiled again, but kindly. 'McDonald's wild goose?'

Kyle risked revealing a hint of proprietary interest. 'Mine too, now – if I knew what I was looking for.'

'Be prepared only to find disappointment, Kyle. And, with respect, the frustration suffered by many rather more qualified researchers who've gone before you. I speak as an old Stollenberg trail campaigner myself.'

'I'm already becoming familiar with the feeling. Where did he go after Russia?'

'To Bohemia-Moravia on further security duties with his regiment, then on to Poland, followed by anti-partisan stints in Yugoslavia, Slovakia and, in early '44, Greece. The Polizei-Panzer-Division was certainly guilty of committing atrocities there, particularly in the Larissa area.'

'Was Stollenberg directly involved?'

Professor Rushby shrugged. 'Frankly, I don't know. Although Wormhout had been duplicated a thousand-fold by the SS during the intervening years, by the time he arrived in Greece the spectre of approaching defeat was beginning to evince itself to those as perceptive as Stollenberg. Officers such as he had learned to withhold self-incriminating entries from their combat reports.'

The frustration Rushby promised hadn't waited long to rear its head. 'What I still don't see,' Kyle appealed plaintively, 'is how all this leads us to our man's involvement with the navy.'

It was his mentor's turn to look confused. 'What navy, Kyle?'

'*I* dunno. The German Navy, presumably. The, ah . . . Kriegs-marine?'

'Why do you assume – ?'

'The convoy. You've even referred to it yourself, Rushby. The Stollenberg *convoy*.'

The Prof smiled a smile of sudden understanding then, and minutely inspected his empty brandy glass.

'Bring the bottle, please,' Kyle suggested to a passing waiter. The way the five-star lunch meter was ticking, he could only hope the goose David was chasing would turn out to be more golden than wild.

'Obvious now that you're a seafarer, dear boy,' Rushby chuckled. 'Automatic association of ideas and all that?'

'All that what?' Kyle growled, irritated by his seemingly routine predilection for constantly falling into traps laid by his own naiveté.

'The Stollenberg convoy was a *land* convoy – a column of military vehicles. Trucks, Kyle, not ships!'

'In January of the final year of the war the SS-Polizei-Panzer-Grenadier-Division was recalled to the Fatherland. They were immediately sent to defend the Polish border and, within hours, committed to heavy combat in the Stettin area. By the time they'd been driven back to Danzig, Stollenberg's regiment had been decimated.'

The professor stole an appreciative sip. 'Our man had gained his Standartenführer's collar laurels by then: an achievement somewhat lacking in lustre, one might suppose, considering defeat had become a certainty. The Third Reich was crumbling: the Allies were approaching the gates of the capital. Hitler was rapidly disintegrating into a hysterical, shambling, sunken-eyed lunatic clinging to an impossible dream. Panic was setting in. It was time to begin hiding the last of the loot.'

'Loot, eh?' Kyle echoed, and cheered considerably. 'The notorious Nazi Gold David talks . . . talked about.'

'Far more than precious metal. And far more than the Nazis' own federal reserves. The treasures looted from the former Occupied Territories, Kyle. Exquisite works of art: gems, securities, narcotics, forged and genuine dollar and sterling notes, Swiss francs, collections of stamps, coins and porcelain which alone were worth billions at today's values. During four years of war they had been accumulating in the Berlin vaults of the central Reichsbank and the Foreign Office until – in August of 1944 – a top-secret meeting took place at the Hotel Maison Rouge in Strasbourg. The attendees consisted of leading Nazi financiers, industrialists and Party glitterati under the chairmanship of Economics Minister and Reichsbank President, Doctor Walther Funk.'

'Less than two months after D-Day.' Kyle guessed what was coming. It seemed Stollenberg hadn't been the only one with a crystal ball.

'As a result of that meeting, although none dared openly concede the possibility of defeat, a decision was taken to "reposition" the assets held in the capital. A precautionary measure, naturally. Only in order, should the unspoken occur, to facilitate the rebirth of an even more monstrous Fourth Reich, or . . . ' Rushby afforded a dry smile then, 'at worst, to maintain certain high-ranking Nazi officials in a style to which they had become accustomed.'

'So the rats began to make plans to leave the sinking ship.'

'At first high-value convertible assets were smuggled to neutral countries in Europe: Spain, Portugal, Turkey – not forgetting Switzerland, of course. At the same time hastily redeployed U-boats headed for the non-belligerent shores of South America carrying bullion cargoes worth billions. It still wasn't enough – the invasion clock was ticking too fast. As the Allied net began to close, the pressure stepped up. To gain breathing space, two priority-routed armoured trains codenamed *Dohle*, meaning Jackdaw, and *Adler* – Eagle – transported ton after ton of treasure trove to hiding places within Germany itself: to what were, even then, fondly believed to be the impregnable fortress areas of the Bavarian Alps and the Austrian Tyrol – the so-called National Redoubt. There the loot was salted away at the bottom of lakes and under the floors of barns, down mine shafts, concealed in the attic spaces of municipal buildings.'

'Stollenberg,' Kyle steered the Professor gently back on course. 'Where did Stollenberg come into all this?'

'Splendid brandy, dear boy,' Rushby observed pointedly. 'Absolutely splendid.'

'Care for a top-up?' Kyle tempted, reaching for the bottle.

'By the last week of April '44, the Polizei-Panzers had been reduced to a limping shell-shocked remnant of a division retreating westwards from Danzig. It was then that Standartenführer Stollenberg was called to regimental headquarters and given secret instructions. He was given one hour to select fifty battle-seasoned men – the hardest, most fanatical Polizei Schutzstaffeln who had so far survived. From there he and his troopers were flown to Berlin. One can only guess at the mixture of emotions they must have experienced as their Dorniers, groundhopping to avoid Allied air patrols, approached the burning capital.'

'I'm experiencing a few myself,' Kyle pointed out with fast-waning restraint. The brandy was obviously inspiring time-consuming lyricism from the academic who'd previously proclaimed himself a dates-and-places-only man. 'Please, Rushby: can we fast-forward to the convoy bit, now?'

'From Tempelhof he was taken by staff car directly to the Führerbunker – by then a subterranean hellhole inhabited by gaunt, hopeless Troglodytes. Imagine the scene, Kyle – mildewed concrete walls shuddering continuously from the detonations of the Allied barrage: even the emergency lighting flickering and shorting out. A rancid nether-world stinking of urine, antiseptic, boiled cabbage, body sweat, the vomit-reek of fear.'

'No need to imagine. I've been there,' Kyle said, thinking inconsequentially of the Monrovia-flagged coffin ship David had persuaded him to sail in as a favour to good old Jaggers. He *must* remember to phone Jagjivan Singh when he got back to the flat. Posthumously return the shipping agent's call to David as a matter of reluctant courtesy.

'There Stollenberg was marched under close escort to a vault in the deepest recess of the bunker. Two men awaited his arrival. The first was the Nazi official placed in charge of the final evacuation of reserves – Economics Minister Funk's closest aide, Reichsbank Director Hans Alfred von Rosenberg-Lipinski. The other was Reichsleiter Martin Bormann.'

'Hitler's personal secretary?'

Rushby nodded. 'The meeting was brief. But then, neither Bormann nor Rosenberg-Lipinski cherished long-term plans to stay. Neither man was found in the Führerbunker when – one day later, on the second of May 1945 – Berlin fell.'

It was Kyle's turn for cynicism. 'But at least Stollenberg achieved his ambition. He'd caught the eyes of those highest in command.'

'Not only the eyes of his masters.'

'Someone else was in that strong-room?'

'Some*thing* else, Kyle. Something without life, yet possessing the most compelling gaze. An artefact, a work of perfection. Probably the most exquisite man-made object Standartenführer Manfred Stollenberg had ever seen.'

By the time Kyle returned to the flat that evening he'd learned all about the Stollenberg convoy. All about the legend attached to it – or rather, as much as any man was ever likely to know according to Rushby, who Kyle had eventually poured into a taxi to go home rather than risk the old boy's meeting Mister Smith while he waited, already teetering and off-balance, for the next tube train to come blasting towards his platform.

Yet, perversely, Kyle didn't feel euphoric as one might have expected. Not considering the measure of success he'd achieved in one day, bolstered by the quantity of brandy he'd consumed.

But that was because David was dead, and nothing could change that. And so was ex-Commando Sergeant Ted Williamson. And a once-beautiful young woman with lustrous black hair and a history of hate who'd inexplicably met her Nemesis in his cupboard. And perhaps even a combat photographer called Lightwood, who might or might not have been murdered by his own side in that terrible war of sixty years before, and whose only valediction now stood propped against the kitchen wall exuding grainy challenge.

But above all, Kyle didn't feel euphoric because . . . well, because he was still no closer to solving the mystery – apart from understanding the Egyptian connection. He knew now about the Egyptian part. But, other than that, he'd learned nothing about Manfred Stollenberg that hadn't, apparently, lain in the public domain for many years. He still didn't know who Hackman was – or the Russian. He couldn't begin to imagine how some woman in Norway fitted into the bizarre scheme of things. He couldn't even hazard a guess at why David had felt compelled to set up whatever it was he'd set up in anticipation of his – Kyle's – return from voyaging . . . and to top it all, he'd still lost David's Hoover!

Something else that bothered him was the way he kept thinking of Cheshire Cats – no, *not* Cheshire bloody Cats! – that was just the brandy playing tricks . . . of former Royal Marine Lewis: the Williamsons' neighbours' boy. Yet why should a chap he'd only glimpsed briefly assume such a high profile in his subconscious? Was it the manner by which Lewis had made evident his displeasure at Kyle's visiting old Ted's widow, that had triggered his dozing thoughts of the previous night? And why, for that matter, had the vague description of Mister Smith offered by the War Museum's dangerously obliging Lisa immediately conjured a further association with Lewis?

A warning bell began to penetrate Kyle's alcohol-slurred reflection. Association – 'Automatic association of ideas and all that,' the Professor had derided, astutely labelling him as having a penchant for jumping to ill-founded conclusions. A convoy, but a convoy of military vehicles, not ships. Yet despite that flaw in his reasoning, surely there was – there *had* to be – some merit in considering the succeeding generation, those who followed Stollenberg and Williamson *et al*, as being in the frame detective-language-wise?

All right, Mister. So let's lay aside the admittedly tenuous connection with John Lewis for the moment. What about the most obvious candidate: Stollenberg himself? The Standartenführer was still the key – it was *his* bloody myth that had triggered a chain of killings of otherwise seemingly unconnected victims. Had he left a family . . . children? Might *he* have passed down the secret behind his own legend as some form of legacy? The Stollenberg Legacy?

Assumptions again, always making bloody assumptions.

Kyle gave up as brandy-fuelled conjecture retreated before increasingly black depression. Tomorrow David's funeral would take place. He would cry then, he knew that. He didn't want to cry. He was frightened of being seen to cry.

On his way through to the lounge cradling a double-strength black coffee he noticed the red eye of the telephone answering machine blinking. It made him think wistfully of a port hand buoy in a navigation channel somewhere: anywhere – ideally a whole ocean away. Red flash, pause, red flash, pause. Damn, he'd forgotten to phone Jagjivan Singh *again*. It was too late now, but tomorrow evening for definite . . . unless, of course, good old Jaggers attended the funeral and rendered the call superfluous. Not that Kyle thought he would. There was little profit in funerals, other than those of seamen who'd sailed in overinsured coffin ships managed by people like Singh.

The message was from Cox. Detective Inspector Cox of Special Branch.

'Kyle? To satisfy your understandable curiosity regarding Inadi's background. Her lover – the Entsagung terrorist who got himself taken out by GsG9 a few years ago? I looked up the file. The young man's name was . . . '

Kyle replayed the tape three times at that bit. Just to make sure he hadn't misheard the Christian name.

'Stollenberg,' Cox's professionally jaded voice assured him. '*Gunther* Stollenberg!'

CHAPTER TEN

The sky helped Kyle. It wept on his behalf to save him embarrassment. A multitude of proxy tears falling from an overcast as sombre as a field-grey Schutzstaffeln service tunic.

He didn't cry because he'd determined not to. David's life had been a joy to him, and they'd celebrate it together – he and the ghost of the boy who'd been his brother: the bespectacled academic who'd later grown as close as any father.

Not that his evidencing grief so openly would have mattered as things turned out. There was a handful of mourners at the chapel, and only two of them familiar to Kyle. Old Prof Rushby was there, more to offer his respect as a former professional colleague of McDonald's than as a social acquaintance. He stood in a group which obviously represented those fellow researchers David had worked amongst. The professor looked a bit under the weather, considerably less ebullient than on the previous day, and risked only a bow of condolence to Kyle before gingerly taking his leave. Just as well, perhaps. Had Rushby waited, Kyle would have felt compelled to have asked him there and then if he knew whether Stollenberg *had* fathered a son called Gunther, and that would have been a foolish impulse. He would have long regretted permitting a terrorist's death to impose on David's very special moment.

Inspector Cox was there, too. But very much in the background, accompanied by another who was also evidently a plain-clothes policeman, if such an observation couldn't be considered a non-sequitur. They had clearly come to see if Mister Smith turned up. No, that couldn't be right! They didn't *know* about Mister Smith, or even that David had been murdered as opposed to having committed suicide. And the police knew nothing whatsoever about Stollenberg. The truth was that, because of his – Kyle's – withholding possibly crucial evidence, Cox was lagging half a century behind. Still pursuing the Case of the Corpse in the Cupboard, not the one on the electrified underground line, and his presence at David's funeral simply suggested the Special Branch officer hadn't moved far from his initial theory regarding who killed Wanda-whatever.

Jagjivan Singh didn't attend, much as expected. Kyle felt a bit guilty at that, despite his brandy-hazed bitterness of the previous evening. To be fair to the little creep he may not even have heard of David's going, thanks to Kyle's own tardiness – no, outright bloody-minded disinclination! – to contact him. He really *would* have to.

There were a few who Kyle didn't recognize. Four or five men wearing token black ties and hovering outside the clutch of historians, who might either have been social acquaintances or, for all Kyle knew, purveyors of domestic services paying their last respects to a sadly missed customer. Remembering the unpaid bill, Kyle didn't think any of them was likely to be representing British Gas, although one of them might still be holding on to McDonald's Hoover?

There were also three not-unattractive young women standing self-consciously apart from each other, who David may well have known at a more romantic level. While all were dewy-eyed, none of them was actually sobbing so Kyle assumed – no, Kyle *surmised,* because he'd given up making assumptions – that none of the romances had held promise of permanency. As none of them looked Russian, Kyle didn't approach them. He didn't want to approach any of the mourners right then. This was a private time. A time between him and David.

Only it wasn't. It wasn't permitted to be so.

Because even while he prayed for David's soul, and tried desperately to see the end of the virtual sibling-hood that had sustained him since he'd been a seven-year-old orphan as reason, not for grief but for thanksgiving, Kyle still couldn't prevent the spectre of Manfred Stollenberg from imposing on his sad reflections.

'Some*thing* else, Kyle,' Professor Rushby had said of the object that preoccupied those three desperate men in the mildewed vault of the Führerbunker. 'Something without life, yet possessing the most compelling gaze. An artefact, a work of perfection. Probably the most exquisite man-made object Standartenführer Manfred Stollenberg had ever seen.'

'This artefact,' Kyle heard himself mutter with almost childlike fascination. But then, he'd thought he was about to learn why David McDonald had died. 'What was it, Rushby?'

But Rushby had refused to be drawn. Apart from being enthused by his subject, there was still a good third of the bottle left. 'To understand the myth, Kyle, first you must appreciate the history that generated it. You have to appreciate the significance of the Kaiseroda incident.'

'Oh, for *fu* —! No – no, I *do* apologize! Sorry, Rushby: just tell me about the Kaiseroda incident,' Kyle had surrendered resignedly. 'Not forgetting the dates an' stuff, of course.'

The heavy irony was lost on his companion. Or was it? Kyle couldn't quite be certain, but wasn't that a blearily mischievous twinkle in the professor's eye?

'On the morning of April 6th, 1945,' Rushby emphasized with unabashed precision, 'two US military policemen, Privates First

Class Anthony Kline and Clyde Harmon, were patrolling the already occupied German village of Merkers, some thirty miles south of Mulhausen in Thuringia. As their jeep reached the limit of the patrol they came upon two young women resting by the roadside, one of whom was clearly pregnant.'

Ohhhh shit, this story's going to take longer than the bloody war did, Kyle thought and reached determinedly for the bottle.

'The young women turned out to be displaced persons – French forced labourers – so the MPs gave them a lift into the village. On the way they passed the entrance to an old potassium mine – the Kaiseroda mine.'

Rushby paused a moment then for dramatic effect. And refill.

'As a result of a casual remark made by one of the women, by late that afternoon seven hundred troops of the United States 357th Infantry Regiment, supported by armour from the 712th Tank Battalion, had sealed off all five entrances to the workings. On the following day the Kaiseroda mine was entered by senior officers from 90 Division Headquarters. They were preceded by an army engineer company sweeping for booby-traps, and German mining officials.'

'Look, I really am sorry, Rushby,' Kyle felt bound to interrupt, 'but according to you, our man Stollenberg was still fighting Russians in northern Poland at that point in the war. He hadn't even been flown to the Führerbunker then. So what possible – ?'

'In good time, dear boy. You'll understand in good time. Eventually the Americans were taken by a somewhat dubious lift to a point nearly half a mile underground. When the lift door opened they found themselves confronted by a short run of tunnel. Sacks of high-denomination paper currency, later recorded as nearly a billion Reichsmarks'-worth, lay stacked in untidy piles along its length. The end of the tunnel was blocked by a steel door set into a one metre thick brick wall. The engineers dynamited the wall.'

The professor's persistence had paid off. For that moment at least, Kyle was hooked.

'They had gained access to over thirty miles of further tunnelling linking great vaulted galleries hewn from the salt rock. In those chambers were stored many of the treasures looted from the occupied world – and stored in great haste. Paintings by Rembrandt, Van Dyck, Titian, Renoir, propped several layers deep against white-glistening walls as carelessly as if they'd been sheets of corrugated iron. Thousands of priceless antiquarian books including the Goethe Collection from Weimar, all piled in bins like cat food in a hyper-market. Mountains of golden coin in sacks. Pyramids of bullion. Bales – not simply boxes, Kyle – of dollar bills and sterling notes, rail-truck loads of Nazi High Command records overspilling into suitcases crammed with spectacles, watches, jewellery, gold fillings prised from the teeth of concentration camp victims.'

'The point,' Kyle urged, abruptly recalling why they still conversed in that now otherwise-silent dining room. 'We have to move forward to the point where Stollenberg became involved, Professor.'

'The point, dear boy, is that out of all the billions'-worth of booty recovered by the Allies from the Kaiseroda potassium mine, one prize stood above the rest.'

Rushby sat back then, and watched for Kyle's reaction as he sprang his trap. 'It was a single artefact, Kyle; a work of perfection. Probably the most exquisite man-made object those high-ranking American officers had ever seen.'

Kyle had stared at the professor for a long time then, before finding his voice. 'But you – you've already *used* that expression. A few minutes ago. Only I'd thought you were referring to Stollenberg's visit to the Führerbunker.'

'I was.'

Then what subtlety had he missed? Kyle frowned hard at the label on the now almost empty brandy bottle. It had been an excellent vintage. Potent. But not that potent. He was still capable of comprehending the anomaly so evidently intended in the professor's tale.

'Can we go full astern for a moment?' Kyle proposed carefully. 'You chose your words deliberately, didn't you, Rushby? Used exactly the same phrase to describe both an event which occurred on April 7th '45 in some Thuringian backwater called Merkers and a virtually identical – no, the very *same* event, if I'm to take your implication at face value – which didn't take place until the following month. In Berlin!'

Rushby chuckled, but not unkindly. 'You asked for the background to the myth, Kyle. The riddle most war historians have long given up on, but that our mutual friend McDonald was still bent on solving. I say again: the myth, Kyle. Always remember that caveat – the Stollenberg *Myth*!'

'I think,' Kyle muttered, 'you should elaborate a little more. What was this exquisite man-made object?'

'A statuette. A three-thousand-year-old statuette, Kyle. Some twelve inches high and crafted from pure Egyptian gold.'

Kyle did feel a surge of excitement then, despite his growing confusion. Egypt? Egypt*ologists*! One piece – the very first piece – of the jigsaw?

'What form did the statuette take?'

'The likeness of Nefertiti, Queen to Akhenaton who ruled the Land of the Pharaohs fourteen centuries before Christ was born.'

Kyle mulled dubiously over that. An antiquity of merit undoubtedly, but of great enough value to justify David's risking his life for? If, indeed, that was what McDonald had been trying to trace. Rushby read his uncertainty.

'Before the Second World War the Nefertiti was Germany's most important national treasure, Kyle – the single most precious artefact ever to be acquired by the Berlin Reichsmuseum. Beyond price. Absolutely beyond price.'

'There you bloody go *again*, Rushby!' Kyle yelled before he could stop himself, much to the disconcertion of the last courtesy waiter slumped at the far end of the room. 'You said it again – *the single most precious item*, you said! Yet a moment ago you quite clearly implied there were *two*. One in

Thuringy-wherever an' . . . an' another a month later. In the Reichsmuseum!'

'Führerbunker.'

'The Führerbunker then!'

'Precisely.'

'I *knew* you'd say that, too,' Kyle surrendered.

Professor Rushby cocked an amiable eye at the bottle. There was a good inch left at the bottom.

Kyle squeezed the neck very tightly as he poured.

'Let us suppose, Kyle, that not one, but *two* Nefertiti statuettes had been discovered by German archaeologists in the tomb of Akhenaton some two decades prior to the Second World War,' Rushby propounded.

'And were there?'

'So rumour had it among Egyptologists of the Twenties. The rumour persisted, even gained currency until August 1939 when Hitler's invasion of Poland ignited the most terrible war the world has known, whereupon a dispute which had previously threatened to assume the proportions of an international archaeological incident became increasingly irrelevant.'

'You keep saying rumour.'

'Remember the key word, Kyle – myth. An allegory: a parable; a fine line between fact and fiction so blurred it becomes impossible, even for the most learned historian, to identify where the actuality ceased and the embroidery of time began.'

'But what *I* don't understand, Rushby,' Kyle protested plaintively, 'is why uncertainty needed to have arisen in the first place. If two Nefertitis had been recovered in Egypt, then why didn't they put them both on display in Berlin or wherever and scotch the myth before it began? If one was priceless, then presumably a pair would have been . . . ' Kyle got a bit stuck then. 'Well, twice as priceless, I suppose,' he trailed off vaguely.

'They couldn't risk doing so. According to those who still believe in the existence of a second golden statuette, although the first Nefertiti was purchased legitimately for the German nation, its twin had been taken from Akhenaton's tomb illegally. Smuggled out of Alexandria aboard a Hamburg-bound tramp steamer.'

'Why smuggled?' Kyle shrugged. 'Why not ship it back to the homeland on a Kriegsmarine gun-boat with an oompah band playing Bavarian bravura for the world's press corps? The Germans were hardly shrinking violets when it came to using *force majeure* against weaker nations, even in the Twenties.'

'Because that decade also marked a period when restriction on the international movement of important *objets d'art* was gaining momentum. Egypt's King Ahmed Fuad, justifiably resentful of the rape of his royal ancestors' graves during the previous century, had begun to flex the economic muscle afforded him by the building of the Suez Canal: even threatening to ignore its treaty status and deny passage through it to vessels of any flag which persisted in such vandalism. The then-German Republic's Weimar government had little choice but to place an embargo on displaying the second Nefertiti publicly for fear of triggering such a crippling trade sanction.'

'While subsequently, when Hitler came to power, it wasn't in his interest to upset the economic apple cart either,' Kyle mused. 'He would have considered it prudent to allow the second Nefertiti –'

'The *alleged* second Nefertiti.'

'. . . to hover between fact and fiction for a few more years until his blue water navy was complete, his Blitzkrieg ready to roll. He knew he wouldn't have to wait long. He was planning to launch a war intended to allow the Third Reich first pick of the riches of the world anyway.'

'Well reasoned, dear boy. So if indeed the statuette's twin did exist, it was probably kept hidden in a top-secret vault below the Reichsmuseum until the Allied air offensive against Berlin gathered pace, at which time it would have been secretly transferred to the even more bomb-proof sanctuary of the Führerbunker.'

'Where Stollenberg came to learn of it.'

Rushby shrugged. 'If speculation is correct – yes. But I emphasize once again that it is speculation, Kyle. No surviving inventories of the German national art collection shed light on the second Nefertiti's veracity or otherwise. No documents have since been found that refer to it. Of those few privileged Nazi officials who might have set eyes on the twin artefact, none admitted to having done so. Not even during the war crimes tribunals, when deals to sidestep the shadow of the hangman's rope must have loomed large in their thoughts.'

But some of them *had* seen it. Hitler's secretary, Martin Bormann, for one. A Reichsbank Director called Hans Alfred von Rosenberg-Lipinski; and an SS colonel called Manfred Stollenberg. Kyle sensed that now, knew that the second Nefertiti *did* exist, for all the professor's scepticism. But then, he had the advantage over Rushby, just as he had over Cox of Special Branch. Because David had sounded too excited during their last telephone call: too confident to have been harbouring any lingering doubts regarding his wild goose.

It was then he became conscious of a renewed prickle at the nape of his neck. More and more he was beginning to realize that the bizarre events of the past few days only went to prove he wasn't alone in that belief. That his – Kyle's – faith in the research skills of his closest friend were already shared by another, by the individual who had killed David and at least two other people so far to ensure, for whatever still-inconceivable motive, that the Stollenberg Myth remained just that.

The chill passed, the implied threat only fuelling Kyle's determination.

'Tell me about the Stollenberg convoy, Professor. And I don't give a damn how mythical the experts say it was or wasn't.'

Rushby smiled. 'Oh, the convoy itself exists firmly within the realm of fact, Kyle. As did Stollenberg's meeting with Bormann and Rosenberg-Lipinski two days before Berlin fell: this time corroborated, you'll be relieved to learn, by the daily diaries recovered from Hitler's last concrete bolthole, as well as by eye-witness reports on the progress of Stollenberg's column.'

'Progress where?'

'Northerly, then westwards to the North Sea coast. A circuitous route intended to keep the convoy behind the protection of the last-ditch German lines.'

'What part of the North Sea coast?'

'Bremen? No, Bremerhaven if memory serves. Does it matter?'

It mattered. Bremerhaven. As in *Bremerhavenschiffswerft* . . . ?

'Yes, the port of Bremerhaven. At the mouth of the River Weser.'

Kyle knew where Bremerhaven was. He'd discharged ship there often. Apart from which he had a big grainy picture of it. Propped up in his kitchen.

'SS-Standartenführer Stollenberg's orders from Bormann were simple, to the point – and in military terms, possessed only one drawback.'

Rushby offered a laconic shrug. But then, to the venerable historian the slaughter of battles past had become an abstract paper exercise. For him they no longer generated harrowing images of lacerated flesh, sundered limbs, of blinded, eviscerated men screaming for the cradle of their mothers' arms throughout countless wars.

'Considering the appalling conditions that reigned on the refugee routes to Northern Germany, his mission was virtually impossible to carry out.'

Rushby had begun to lose focus a bit after that, the last finger of brandy triggering his earlier preoccupation with matters more technical than relevant to Kyle's self-imposed quest. Kyle's head was beginning to spin too, while a second brigade of waiters appeared to begin resetting the tables around them for dinner. It wouldn't be long before they were invited, with five-star discretion, either to take their leave or consult the evening menu.

'We already know that Standartenführer Stollenberg had

recruited fifty of the toughest, most seasoned campaigners the Polizei-Panzer-Grenadiers were still able to muster: every man still loyal to the Schutzstaffeln blood oath to serve his Führer unto death.'

'And maybe even past it,' Kyle muttered.

'Pardon, Kyle?'

'It doesn't matter,' Kyle retreated hurriedly. 'Tell me about the convoy itself.'

'It consisted of nine vehicles in total. Seven heavy trucks escorted by two Panzerspähwagen Puma armoured reconnaissance cars.' The Professor blinked owlishly then, and brightened. 'You may wish to note, Kyle, that the eight-wheeled Puma was a most interesting variant of the Sonderkraftfahrzeug marque – particularly the two model SdKfz two-thirty-four oblique threes commanded by Stollenberg.'

'Why seven trucks?' Kyle hastily piloted the academic back on course. 'The Nefertiti was twelve inches high. Stollenberg could've carried it in a bag.'

'Because, dear boy, the gold statuette wasn't the only treasure closeted in the Führerbunker two days before Götterdämmerung. Apart from various irreplaceable *objets d'art* and antiquaria, Stollenberg's column was tasked to evacuate other items vital to Germany's eventual resurrection. Meticulously forged treasury master plates for example, which would have enabled a Fourth Reich High Command in exile to print any of the world's leading currencies at will. Negotiable Weimar and Westphalia bearer bonds to the tune of millions of dollars. Records and plans from the Reich Patent Office. Secret documents related to the development of future Nazi secret weapons, including,' Rushby changed gear into minutiae mode again, '*including*, Kyle, the final stage blueprints for the then-revolutionary Mark Three Rheintochter anti-aircraft rocket first developed by Doktor Konrad of Messerschmitts. A most exciting design concept capable of –'

'Why?' Kyle urged, desperate to clear the final hurdle.

The professor looked surprised. 'Why? Well, because even

then Hitler, drowning in his own megalomania, believed next-generation weapons such as the Rheintochter could stem the tide of war.'

'I meant why Bremerhaven? Why was Stollenberg ordered to make a run for there when you yourself argue he'd been given a mission impossible?'

'Because it was a last desperate gamble. And because of the U-boat.'

'What U-boat?'

'U-536. A Type-VIIC Atlantic-class submarine commanded by Otto Erhard. She had been recalled from sea to rendezvous with Stollenberg and, thereafter, to sail for the Argentine as soon as his column's cargo could be trans-shipped.'

'But that didn't happen. You can be certain of that?'

'Kapitan-Leutnant Erhard's boat never even returned to Germany. She was depth-charged and sunk with all hands off the Frisian Islands by a Catalina of 341 Maritime Squadron.'

Rushby broke off impatiently at that point, made one last attempt to pursue his ingrained preference for the lecturer's agenda. 'Look, Kyle, you're jumping too far ahead. No serious student can afford to overlook the slightest detail, no matter how irrelevant it may appear at first sight. It's vitally important that you should understand everything about the cargo carried by that column. The mystery surrounding the consignment of Stoff 381 may, in particular, prove to be of great relevance.'

'Stoff 381?' Kyle echoed uneasily. He had quite enough mysteries to be going on with. 'And what in heaven's name was Stoff 381?'

'Ah, now *that* is the mystery, dear boy!' Rushby said, looking pleased with himself. 'Other than its obviously being a coded reference, none of my colleagues are quite sure. We can only surmise that Stoff 381 was either a derivative of, or an improvement on, the Stoff 146 already being produced in massive quantities by the Nazis' Dyhernfurth chemical facility.'

'Then what, Professor,' Kyle grated with barely contained self-control, 'was Stoff One-Four-*Six*?'

'Originally? Oh, a simple domestic washing powder, Kyle. Perfectly innocuous. In fact, before the war Stoff 146 was a leading household brand. Advertised as the most popular detergent on the German home market.'

The maître d' had begun to stare in their direction, alternating disapproval with pointed glances at his watch. And anyway, Kyle's capacity to absorb what he considered academic trivia had begun to reach overload. He chose his words carefully. Very carefully indeed.

'Are you seriously claiming, Rushby, that in the very week when the Third Reich was entering its death-throes, an SS colonel was flown to Hitler's headquarters and ordered to take command of a convoy of trucks, supported by armour which must have been desperately needed for the final defence of the Führerbunker itself, then make for a destination virtually impossible to reach, in the hope of making a rendezvous with a U-boat that might well have been sunk before it even made port – merely to deliver, to some god-forsaken South American backwater, a load of . . . of *soap* powder that washed whiter-than-white?'

'Something of an exaggeration, Kyle,' Rushby chastised with alcoholic good humour. 'Reputedly there was only one small flask of the material placed in Stollenberg's care. And I did say Stoff 381 was undoubtedly a code name for –'

'I don't care *what* you bloody said!' Kyle inhaled deeply, got a grip. 'I don't care what Stoff 146, or even Stoff 38-whatever was. I don't care how much of it there was. I don't care about any of the other kit aboard that convoy, Professor Rushby. I am only – I say again, *only*! – interested in pursuing David McDonald's research into the whereabouts of the second Nefertiti!'

'But unless you realize what the Nazi plant at Dyhernfurth was –'

'The bill, please!' Kyle requested firmly.

He didn't know it then. He wouldn't realize it for some time. But by assuming it to be irrelevant – by closing his ears to the mystery surrounding Stoff 381 – Kyle had just made the biggest mistake of what would become his increasingly more tenuous life.

There weren't many tributes at the graveside: David had never been a particularly gregarious chap. A few bouquets of flowers, rain glistening like teardrops among the petals; a large wreath from Kyle, and two smaller wreaths. Long after everybody had left, he still remained with head bowed and . . . well, if his shoulders did betray an occasional tremor, it was only a private concession. A secret between himself and David.

Eventually he made to turn away, even more reluctant than he'd been in the mortuary chapel to sever that unutterably desolate communion with his friend, then hesitated. It seemed uncharitable that no one, not even he, should care enough for other people's expressions of sympathy to afford even cursory acknowledgement of their final salutes.

By blinking fiercely, he could read the card on the first wreath without further effort. *From your friends and colleagues who retraced, with you, the paths of the Warriors.*

Water had seeped into the plastic envelope of the second. Kyle had to stoop to prise it open. The ink was already blurred.

Doctor David. The sequel of today unsolders all whereof this world holds record. Yours very respectfully . . .

'Bit naff, I suppose, sir. Got it from a book. A corruption of Tennyson,' the still-disembodied man standing over him commented a bit sheepishly. 'Don't really know what it means, but it seemed to fit the bill.'

Kyle hadn't realized that any of the other mourners had delayed their departure. He *had* heard that voice before, though, and didn't need to read the signature on the card.

'Hackman?' he said.

CHAPTER ELEVEN

It was late afternoon by the time Kyle returned dispiritedly to Ringtree Gardens. When he turned his key in the newly fitted five-lever lock, allowing the door to observe the laws of crooked walls and swing open of its own accord, the flat seemed lonelier than ever. Even David's grandmother clock had stopped ticking for want of tender loving care and a piece of cardboard.

He'd already decided to sell it. The flat, that was – not David's clock. He wouldn't need a permanent anchorage ashore for some years yet and anyway, it had ceased to be a home any more. Home should be a place of happy return, whereas the fond associations once evoked by these now-silent rooms had been clouded by violent death.

After taking his now-habitual precaution of checking that the telephone tape had no surprises on it and that the hall cupboard had no surprises in it, Kyle made coffee and sat thinking about Hackman – or rather about his coming meeting with Hackman, arranged for eight o'clock that evening in the Four Feathers pub near Covent Garden. Eliciting Hackman's view of the Second

World War while standing over David's freshly commissioned grave had hardly seemed appropriate, not even to explore the bond that evidently linked all three of them.

Trouble was, thinking about Hackman made Kyle increasingly dissatisfied with the way events had progressed in general. As with his chance introduction to Professor Rushby, he felt no sense of personal achievement at having finally encountered David's mystery caller. Both Hackman and Rushby had crossed his path, not as a result of any initiative of his, but apparently by coincidence; in fact, everything he'd learned so far about McDonald's quest had come *to* him. He was continually being placed in the position of having to be reactive, not proactive. It almost seemed he wasn't so much pursuing the myth as being pursued by it.

Oh, there was no question that his 40%-proof educational lunch with Professor Rushby hadn't resulted from pure chance. Or that the old boy himself wasn't genuine; his academic credentials had been vouched for by the well-intentioned Lisa at the War Museum. The same went for Cox of Special Branch, which had led to Kyle's one small triumph of subterfuge in learning of the existence of a second Stollenberg – no, that wasn't quite accurate – of the once-upon-a-time existence of a second Stollenberg. A Stollenberg called Gunther, who'd been shot to death several years ago by yet another crowd with impeccable credentials underwritten, on that occasion, by the Federal Republic of West Germany, and who, Kyle felt it safe to assume despite his resolve not to fall into the trap of jumping to false conclusions yet again, must have had *some* family connection with the previous generation Konvoi-Meister Stollenberg.

As well as a romantic one with the now-also-dead Wanda Inadi. Which, while forging a whole new chain of riddles, did establish a positive link between at least one Stollenberg and McDonald's cupboard.

Even ex-marine John Lewis alias Mister Smi— '*No!*' Kyle told himself firmly – now that *was* a presumption too far. And anyway, the point at issue was that even Lewis had crossed

Kyle's bows by chance, hadn't he? There was no way his, Kyle's, spontaneous visit to Ted Williamson's widow could have been anticipated by Lewis because it *had* been . . . well – spontaneous?

Which only left Hackman as an unresolved quantity. Had Hackman's approaching him at the funeral been as fortuitous as it appeared – or was the gravel-throated mystery man with an affinity for Tennyson pursuing a carefully planned agenda which must, in that case, place Hackman at the top of Kyle's ever-expanding list of suspects?

Or was he, Kyle, being totally paranoid now, and making a complete ass of himself? Ohhhh, bugger being a detective. Or a war historian. Especially being a war historian. Despite his conviction that David must have made some crucial breakthrough in his quest for the Nefertiti, how could he, an untutored lay researcher, possibly hope to penetrate the web of intrigue surrounding Stollenberg when even a professor had conceded defeat?

'It disappeared, of course, dear boy,' Rushby had slurred as Kyle helped ease him into his taxi. 'The Standartenführer's column? Took a route northwards, up through Neustrelitz and Neubrandenburg, then vanished at some point after the convoy started to turn west. Simply vanished without trace after they'd been observed traversing a lake called the Müritz See, heading for Hamburg.'

'Good night, Rushby. And thank you again for your help,' Kyle had urged as he felt his own head swimming.

But the Prof had struggled to open the window even after Kyle had slammed the door. 'Couldn't get a damn thing out of the chap, you know. Tight-lipped as a Junker he was, when I interviewed him.'

'Who was?' Kyle surrendered wearily while the cab driver activated his fare meter.

'Stollenberg.'

Kyle had blinked then. 'You spoke to Stollenberg?'

'A charismatic man. Did I tell you he was a charismatic – ?'

'You *spoke* to Stollenberg, Rushby? Meaning he actually survived the war?'

'Had a place up in Schleswig-Holstein when I met him.' Rushby smiled happily. 'A modest cottage near Lübeck. Perfectly happy to chat about the Schutzstaffeln in general, which is more than most former SS officers are, but he wouldn't talk about the Nefertiti. Wouldn't let me even broach the subject of what happened to his column.'

Kyle's excitement had returned with a rush then. 'Do you think he'd let *me* talk to him, Rushby?'

The professor had considered that possibility owlishly and at length before nodding. 'I'm sure he wouldn't object, dear boy. I can even help you find him if you really want to. He's still there, in a little town called Bad Oldesloe.'

Kyle had been halfway through punching the air in triumph as the driver pulled away. He didn't bother to finish the gesture. Rushby's inevitable caveat still hung in the air as his cab became swallowed by the Mayfair traffic.

'. . . but I don't think going to visit will help you greatly, Kyle. Standartenführer Manfred Stollenberg died in 1984.'

By six o'clock or thereabouts according to his Taiwan Rolex, time had begun to hang heavily for Kyle. He was becoming impatient to meet Hackman and wished now that he'd proposed an earlier rendezvous. It would have taken his mind off things: helped diffuse the same-day pain of David's funeral.

'Not that it'll be much of a wake even then, dear friend, to celebrate your crossing the bar on your greatest-ever voyage,' Kyle reflected morosely. 'Two blokes who don't know each other from Adam, meeting under what must almost certainly prove a cloud of mutual suspicion, to dissect your last testament over a pint of beer in a London pub.'

Kyle spent a few desultory minutes killing time by emptying crumbs from the toaster, then crawling on hands and knees to sweep under the kitchen table using the brush and dustpan from the cupboard. He could have vacuumed the flat throughout if David's bloody Hoover hadn't been . . . He found a new yellow duster under the sink and moved out to the hall to stir the layers that had accumulated since he'd become sole mortgagee of Ringtree Gardens.

When he conscientiously pulled the telephone table drawer open to dust its leading edge, he noticed David's original answerphone cassette lying among the jumble of maybe-come-in-handy lengths of string, perished rubber bands and expired ballpoint pens. It was the tape that had recorded Hackman's message about the Provos: the one Kyle had ejected and removed to the CID-proof secrecy of his seabag before the first two policemen had arrived to look knowingly at Wanda, then later, while unpacking, had shoved back in the drawer for want of somewhere else to lose it.

The tape also held his only verbal proof that David had ever owned a vacuum cleaner. As well as that message he'd ignored from . . .

Jagjivan *Singh*, for cryin' out loud! He still hadn't thought to return the call. And now he'd lost the initiative, and would no doubt be made to feel guilty that he hadn't prompted Jaggers to attend the funeral, irrespective of whether the smarmy little turd had known about it in advance anyway. Seizing the bull by the horns he looked up Singh's home number there and then, and dialled.

'Thank you for your call, which is very greatly appreciated,' Singh's answering machine patronized him. 'Unfortunately Mister Singh is unable to . . .'

Kyle hung up and dialled the shipping agency. The phone continued to ring unanswered, which seemed a bit odd. If Jaggers and his staff – his 'staff' being one part-time girl who chewed gum while pretending to work at the heart of a vast global maritime communications network where all extensions led to Jagjivan Singh's desk – if they'd both left the office, then why wasn't *their* global bloody answering machine on?

Come to that, why had Jaggers called McDonald on the very

day he died? A mix of aimless boredom and curiosity got the better of Kyle so he slipped the original tape into his device and triggered replay.

'Jaggers here, David old boy. Re Michael's trip . . . '

Michael's trip? Kyle's eyebrows met in the middle. Might *he* be the Michael that Singh was referring to? So far as he was aware David didn't know any other Michaels.

'There's been a change of plan. Do please apologize to Kyle for me . . . '

Damn – it was him in the frame!

'The *Centaur* won't be coming to London now. He'll have to join her in Rotterdam . . . '

The Centaur? What Centaur? What *was* the Centaur?

Kyle's mind slammed into conclusion mode. That was trade language Singh was talking. Meaning the *Centaur* had to be a ship, dammit! While sensible landbound people join things like the Foreign Legion or the Women's Institute or their local railway modelling society, seamen join ships. To sail in them! So was that what David had meant when he'd talked about the female who'd been in . . . in Narvik, was it, according to his cryptic remark of nearly a week ago? Yeah, in Narvik at that time, and who wouldn't arrive in London for another ten days, which would end Thursday – no – that left three more days, which meant the *Centaur*, whatever type of vessel she was, would be here Friday! Only now, it seemed, she wasn't – *is*n't – bound for London after all, but for Rotterdam. Where he, Kyle, had apparently been volunteered by McDonald to join her?

And all this time he had assumed the 'she' David had referred to had been the Russian he'd also claimed to have identified. But instead, 'she' had meant a bloody ship. Even worse – one of Jagjivan Singh's ships. Nothing whatsoever to do with Stollenberg after all.

'Tell Michael I have his appointment documents here in the office. We'll tie up later. Oh, and . . . ' Kyle sensed a Jaggers lie coming. Jaggers' lies were always concealed in the Trojan Horse of an afterthought. 'Tell him if he doesn't mind paying his own flight out, I'll make sure he's recompensed as soon as he gets back.'

That'd be bloody right. Kyle had already been there. Seen it, done it, got the T-shirt branding him as a Singh Shipping Corporation creditor. He was still waiting to be paid in full for the last trip he did as a favour to Jaggers.

. . . *including* those two days he'd spent, surrounded by Singh's brothers, in an inexorably deflating, long past its service-due-by date life-raft in the middle of the Indian Ocean waiting to be rescued.

Singh's brother sharks, that was. Of the sub-surface variety. The rather more benign kind.

'Pint of lager for you, sir, an' a bitter for me,' Hackman said, placing the glass before Kyle. He raised his own. 'To Doctor McDonald, yeah? An officer and gentleman through and through.'

Kyle endorsed the salutation, thought longingly of David even though he had placed him in the position of having to say *no way* to Singh's kind offer of a busman's holiday abroad, then sat back appraising Hackman. He saw a thick-set man in his late forties, early fifties: freshly shaved with a face marred only by a nose that had been taken to hospital more than a few times after the bout had ended. It made him feel slightly disadvantaged. He hadn't thought to wear a tie, whereas Hackman had. Dark blue regimental or club style, with diagonal red stripes.

Hackman noted his gaze. 'RMP. Royal Military Police . . . Ex.'

'Ah, the Provos.'

Hackman smiled fractionally. 'Make sure you emphasize the "T" if you hear an Irish voice in the crowd. He might be a big, ultra-sensitive bloke of the Protestant persuasion.'

Kyle had the grace to look discomfited. Particularly as it was the second time he'd fallen into that trap. 'But you were a Redcap?'

'Twenty-four years in the mob. Finished up staff sergeant in SIB.'

'I daren't even ask,' Kyle said, taking a liking to Hackman.

'Special Investigation Branch, sir. Sort of the army's CID.'

'So how did you come to know David?'

'I'm in the business of finding things out for people. Usually military things. As long as they're not still classified.'

'Then I'd be right to assume, from the message you left last week, that you were working for David McDonald?'

'Have done on and off for the last couple of years. But with respect, sir, my revealing any details of what I was doing for him depends on what your credit card says.'

Kyle scowled across the table. It seemed he'd been a bit premature in liking Hackman. 'You're proposing to charge me for this conversation?'

'No.' Hackman regarded him coolly. 'I just want to make sure you are Mister Kyle, Mister Kyle. Okay, so I know you were the doctor's friend; he'd mentioned you several times in passing, and you've obviously had access to the message I left on his machine – but he was probing a sensitive area. There's a lot of people aren't who they claim . . . a driving licence would do. Anything with your name on it.'

'D'you take American Express?' Kyle volunteered, handing it over with the warm feeling that he'd just met a really suspicious bastard who did know a bit about not jumping to hasty conclusions.

'That will do nicely,' Hackman said.

Hackman's professional caution had at least taught Kyle a lesson. Non-disclosure still had to be the name of the game: play his cards as close to his chest as possible. It may well have been, for that matter, that, despite his naiveté, David had taken the precaution of erecting Chinese walls around each facet of his investigation – compartmenting them in discrete areas of enquiry holding little significance unless one possessed knowledge of the end-game.

Hackman's message, for instance, had only made reference to the wartime death of the combat photographer, Lightwood, and that intriguing bit about blowing whistles. Hadn't even touched on the subject of SS men: in or out of convoy.

So give nothing away until he knew how much David had told the former military policeman – negative that last! – the *self-proclaimed* former military policeman, because Kyle was fast becoming street-wise too, now. Although he'd obviously worked with McDonald, Hackman hadn't volunteered any credentials other than he was wearing the right tie. Until some level of trust could be established between them he, Kyle, didn't propose to even mention Stollenberg, while no way was he going to let slip any hint of what he'd learned from Rushby regarding the legend of the second Nefertiti.

Subterfuge, Mister. Keep it casual.

'So, ah . . . how much *do* you know about Doctor McDonald's research project?' he hazarded.

Hackman drained his glass, placed it squarely before Kyle with an unspoken prompt that even Rushby could have learned from, then shrugged.

'What d'you want me to start with, Mister Kyle? The SS colonel, the Führerbunker connection – or the Egyptian Queen?'

An hour and four pints later, Standartenführer Manfred Stollenberg's convoy had once again reached the point where it had, according to commonly accepted wisdom, disappeared after having been observed by Allied agents traversing the northern shore of Lake Müritz: still heading west on its circuitous route to Bremerhaven. A column of eight or nine heavy Mercedes trucks bearing SS-Panzer-Grenadier decals with AA-mounted machineguns above each cab, escorted by either one or two Puma armoured reconnaissance cars.

'All of which ties in with my understanding of the situation.' Kyle chewed a pensive lip. 'Do we know exactly where, and on what date, that last sighting actually took place?'

'Little lakeside village called Malchow on May 2nd, '45. The day Berlin fell.'

'So Hamburg hadn't been taken then. They were still pushing on to bypass it.'

'The city itself held out for another three days, till May 5, though Stollenberg probably didn't know one way or the other.' Hackman shrugged. 'German communications had fallen apart. Regimental frequencies were often incompatible – certainly between SS units and the regular Wehrmacht. Complete bloody snafu . . . but the colonel and his boys were battlers, you got to give 'em credit for that. They didn't give up.'

'But how do we know that?' Kyle asked, reflecting on the billions'-worth of loot the Nazis had already secreted in the National Redoubt. 'How do we know Stollenberg didn't realize the game was up and do a Kaiseroda. Dump the Nefertiti and the rest of his column's treasure five fathoms deep in the Müritz See?'

'Because Doc McDonald proved he didn't,' Hackman refuted calmly. 'That's where he gained the edge over all his history colleagues who'd tried to follow the Stollenberg trail.'

He broke off then, reading the look in Kyle's eyes, and smiled.

'If you're sitting comfortably, Mister Kyle, I'll tell you a story . . .'

'A few months ago the doctor wandered into a secondhand bookshop selling military publications – one of those little specialist places off the Charing Cross Road, yeah? While browsing, he came across a book – just a small book. Second World War photos taken by a guy called Lightwood.'

'*Death of a Folk Myth*,' Kyle said. 'It's still in the flat.'

Hackman nodded. 'Waffen-SS stuff: the doctor's field of expertise. While you an' me would be scratching our heads even trying to identify the divisional badging system used by the Schutzstaffeln . . .'

'Tell me about it,' Kyle muttered with feeling, thinking about his inconclusive blow-ups.

' . . . the Doctor could practically tell which regiment a man belonged to from the weave of his uniform cloth. As soon as he glanced through that book he knew he was on to something significant. Something that tied in with what he'd already researched over past years.'

Kyle guiltily recalled those now irretrievably precious occasions when he'd allowed David's enthusiasm to go over his head. 'The Stollenberg Myth, as I've now come to realize. He was always on about it.'

'And he didn't mind admitting it. That he'd become obsessed by a conviction that not only did the second Nefertiti exist, but that it *had* been aboard the colonel's column when he left the Führerbunker on his mission to rendezvous with Erhard's U-boat.'

'So what did David do then?'

'Took himself off to Northern Germany. Started at the last point at which the column had been sighted, then followed Stollenberg's most likely route west from there. Along the way he interviewed local burghers: the older ones who had lived in the area during the war. By a process of elimination he managed to establish that the convoy had got as far as a town called Brahlstorf, a few kilometres nor' east of Schwerin –'

'I'm sorry, Hackman,' Kyle felt bound to interrupt, 'but if the Nefertiti had been that important, then why hadn't someone, some other historian or archaeologist, done that soon after the war? Why wait fifty years till David was spurred to take the initiative?'

'Until the Berlin Wall came down, Mister Kyle, the Müritz See was on the cold side of the frontier: well inside the border of East Germany. Guys wandering round asking questions, especially about military matters, tended not to come out of there.'

'Oh!' Kyle looked suitably chastened. 'So what did he discover in Brahlstorf?'

'Enough contemporary evidence to suggest that was as far as Stollenberg's convoy managed to reach. Three separate eye-witness accounts confirmed that, around May 3, '45, an SS column approaching the outskirts was strafed by USAAF Mustangs – seven, eight trucks: two light armoured cars left shot up and burning. One resident even remembered having seen the street littered with SS troopers' corpses covered by a snowstorm of paper she swore had born the legend Reichspa— 'Hackman's brows met then, until he shrugged. 'What the hell: three tours in BAOR and my German's still lousy – the Reich Patent Office logo, anyway. The point is, they had to have been the colonel's boys.'

Kyle's eyebrows emulated Hackman's. Only in his case it wasn't so much an inability to get his tongue around unfamiliar words, as a mix of confusion and disappointment. So why had David died, if . . . ?

'You're saying that's where it ended? That there was no myth. No mystery.' Then Kyle broke off as a voice in his head over-rode his disappointment: *Wait a minute, Mister! There's more to this than* –

'There were nine trucks in the Stollenberg convoy,' he said ever so carefully. 'David's trip to Germany accounted for eight at most – so what happened to the ninth, Hackman?'

'You should've been a detective.' Hackman grinned.

'Tried it. Failed the entrance exam on grounds of incompetence. But I am a navigator: good at subtraction – the ninth truck?'

'That's what Doctor McDonald kept asking himself. Until he went into that bookshop off the Charing Cross Road.'

'And?'

'One of Lightwood's pics particularly caught his attention. A snap of a dead SS senior corporal with a squad of battle-fatigued Tommies. To the doctor's expert eye it revealed enough detail to indicate that the Nazi trooper was from the Second Regiment, SS-Polizei-Panzer-Grenadier-Division – and, considering most of the Second Regiment were getting themselves neutralized up in Poland, there was only one way the KIA could've got there.'

It all came clear then. Or some of it did. For the very first time since David's death, Kyle *did* enjoy a surge of elation.

'Aboard Stollenberg's so-far unaccounted-for ninth truck!'

The elation didn't last long. No longer than it took for the bar-maid of the Four Feathers to pull two more pints of ale, in fact.

Because by the time Hackman had negotiated a reciprocal course to their table, manoeuvring his foaming cargo expertly through the late-evening throng piling in from the nearby Opera House, it had become alarmingly apparent to Kyle that if anyone had a prime motive for killing David, then that anyone had to be, well . . .

Hackman, himself?

CHAPTER TWELVE

'Cheers,' Hackman saluted, raising his glass.

'Um,' Kyle responded, toying moodily with his.

For by then he'd come to realize that not only did Hackman know rather more about Stollenberg and the Nefertiti than he did, but that the former Redcap possessed a greater understanding of one aspect of the mystery, even, than David.

He knew more about the Lightwood factor. Of how the cameraman's death in action, presumably while still in the forward battle area around the Bremerhaven shipyard on which everything now seemed to hinge, had closely followed his 'blowing the whistle' to the military police of the day. Hackman's taped intention to report to McDonald on the details of that intriguing revelation had been forestalled by his employer's untimely demise.

Although shouldn't that, Kyle tried to reason in desperate search for reassurance, argue more in favour of Hackman's innocence than his complicity? Because why would a man intent on murder leave a message on his potential victim's answerphone while on the way to push him under a train?

Which made Kyle feel a bit easier, until his current bout of paranoia versus clinical deduction did an about-face yet again as he recalled sitting on a bitterly cold landing just over a week ago, waiting for a malevolently released explosive vapour to dissipate while debating much the same clash of logic.

Why, for Heaven's sake? he'd been brooding on that occasion. *What possible reason can anybody have to blow up a man's apartment after they'd killed him?*

But on the other hand, David's having formed a hunch from a picture in a book still didn't necessarily prove there'd been any connection between the two still apparently separate wartime dramas – Lightwood's losing his life, and the rest of the world losing track of the Stollenberg convoy. So didn't that let Hackman off the prime suspect hook again?

Unless – on yet *another* hand, if such an unlikely allusion made any sense at all – Hackman's recent enquiries into the cameraman had unearthed the missing link. Might that discovery have proved crucial enough for him to – ?

Kyle rather lost sight of just what he was trying to prove or disprove at that point, and lapsed into gloomy silence. His companion noted his reticence.

'You think I had good reason to take Doctor McDonald out myself, don't you?' Hackman challenged out of the blue.

'Christ, no!' Kyle lied. 'It never even enter—'

Then he broke off, and blinked at Hackman. 'You believe he was murdered, too?'

'I don't subscribe to the suicide theory, if that's what you mean. Apart from having known him to be a pretty well-adjusted bloke, you show me a body on a railway line that was privy to the secrets the doctor carried, and I'll show you a body that didn't fall accidentally.'

There was a bit of Inspector Cox in Hackman. In fact, there was a lot of Inspector Cox in Hackman. Kyle wasn't quite sure whether that was a good thing or a bad thing. It rather depended on whose side Hackman was on. He decided he had to make up his mind pretty quickly.

'And just what secret do you think David McDonald did carry with him to his grave?' he heard himself retort with a brutal directness he couldn't have mustered before the funeral.

'One which, according to the doctor, the current German Government should consider as being worth a few Deutschmarks for a start – give or take ten million!'

'Jesus,' Kyle muttered, taken aback. 'No wonder he wasn't worried about our mortgage.'

Hackman shrugged. 'Not if you bear in mind that the original Nefertiti – the statuette later recovered from the Kaiseroda Mine – was considered so valuable that, following D-Day, the Nazis included it among the first treasures to be evacuated from Berlin. In archaeological terms it's still recognized as being Germany's most important national artefact. Produce its twin, and the Bundesbank's your oyster.'

'And you think David was about to produce it?'

'I think Doctor McDonald saw something more than a dead teenage SS-Unterscharführer in that book of Lightwood's. Some other clue which neither you nor I know about, Mister Kyle; something which told him exactly where Stollenberg had hidden the second Nefertiti.'

Kyle made up his mind to trust Hackman. Or at least to a point. It wasn't so much that he had sound reason to trust Hackman as that he had to trust somebody with a background in investigation. So far, about the only thing he'd managed to prove was that he wasn't equipped to proceed without a pilot who knew the waters of intrigue. And anyway, where was the risk? Obviously David had thought highly enough of Hackman to take the former military policeman into his confidence.

But then again, David was dead. Possibly *because* of the fact that he'd taken someone of whom he'd thought highly into his confidence.

Dammit – cut that out, Mister!

'What was your deal with the doctor anyway, Hackman?'

'A fair one, considering he'd already done the research and I only came in as leg-man on specific enquiries like the Lightwood trace,' Hackman declared candidly. 'Out-of-pocket expenses, sir, plus ten per cent of whatever he eventually negotiated as treasure trove from the Germans.'

'Or the Egyptians. If it ever did exist it's still their statue.'

'I was going to suggest that to him,' Hackman grinned. 'But later. Money wasn't his primary aim.'

Neither was it Kyle's. Revenge promised immeasurably greater satisfaction. The major joy in that revenge would derive from ensuring that David McDonald received his academic due through the plaudits of his contemporaries. But not the only aspect. Not now. Not after Kyle's visits to a mortuary, a cupboard, and the frail widow of a war hero.

'You could've claimed twenty per cent, you know. I wouldn't have known any different.'

'But I would,' his large companion rejected flatly. 'Just don't bugger me about on my ten if you ever do catch up with the Nefertiti, Mister Kyle.'

Kyle extended his hand. 'Call it thirty and use the expression "we" from now on – if "we" ever catch up with the Nefertiti. I need help, Hackman.'

Hackman's grip was firm. 'Who d'you want me to kill?'

That wasn't funny – not funny at all! Not even knowing Hackman was only joki— well, *assuming* Hackman was only joking. Mind you, on the other hand, once they *had* positively identified David's killer . . . ?

'I'd rather you explained the Lightwood connection to me,' Kyle said hurriedly.

'Following up on the book, the doctor confirmed its author had been an accredited war photographer at the sharp end. At the beginning of May '45, Tom Lightwood was assigned to cover a British assault group fighting in the Bremerhaven sector.'

'Ted Williamson's Commando – the brown jobs in the picture?'

'Thought you needed help.'

123

'Oh, I'm going to,' Kyle said with feeling, thinking about what he hadn't so far told Hackman. About his finding a spitted enigma called Wanda in David's flat, and her past subversive connection with the also-dead Gunther Stollenberg. And about Mister Smith and his curious interest in –

And the Cheshire Cat! No – that was John Lewis, about whom he suspected a great deal but still knew nothing at all, other than that he was the son of Ted's widow's next-door neighbour.

'Believe me, I'm going to need a *lot* of help, Hackman,' he reaffirmed with gloomy certainty.

Hackman shrugged. 'Fair enough. Then by May 5 the battle situation was what official communiqués described as fluid – indicating that no one knew what the hell anyone else along the front was doing. Lightwood found himself happy-snapping in a shipyard.'

'The Bremerhavenschiffswerft.'

'A pocket of resistance, the official sit-rep called it. Which usually means you've either found yourself up against a bunch of terrified squaddies with no way out and their backs to the wall, or a team of fanatical hard men prepared to hold to the last round – an' then take you on hand-to-hand in the finale.'

'And which were these?'

'No way of telling from the Divisional battle diary. In military-speak it was a minor skirmish. Five minutes of panic, wounded screaming, every soldier for himself. Blood, guts an' fear all along the front don't find any place in routine reports of enemy contact, Mister Kyle.'

'But Lightwood himself survived that particular firefight?'

'For barely twenty-four hours. Just long enough to lodge a verbal allegation with the combat Field Provost company in the forward area.'

Blowing the whistle to the Provos! Kyle felt his pulse quicken. 'Alleging what?'

'That he'd observed eight Waffen-SS prisoners being taken in the shipyard skirmish.'

Kyle's disappointment was palpable. 'Hardly an allegation. His seeing prisoners being taken.'

'The bottom line of it was, sir,' Hackman retorted flatly, 'Lightwood claimed he'd witnessed them being executed after capture. By Williamson's Commando.'

'That's where the doctor brought me in – to help substantiate, or disprove, Lightwood's accusation. I've still got contacts in the Corps. They helped me trace a veteran Provost sergeant who'd been there during the assault. He remembered the incident. Confirmed Williamson's troop was questioned later but that no further action was taken in the absence of a prosecution witness: Lightwood himself having been KIA'd by then – allegedly shot by a rogue sniper.'

'Another allegedly?'

'My interviewee had actually recovered the dog tags from Lightwood's body. I couldn't draw him on it, but he implied that German snipers didn't usually place six rounds from a British Sten in their targets. He also admitted to having turned a blind eye on the principle that, although the expression "friendly fire" hadn't been coined at that time, every soldier accepts it can happen: particularly in a confused situation.' Hackman smiled tightly then. 'Either way, there was nothing in writing about the execution of the prisoners: no statement taken by the MPs on the battleground. You don't take out your notebook and pencil while someone's tryin' to shoot the shit out of you, Mister Kyle. You tend to forget the rules.'

'A Totenkopf company commander called Fritz Knochlein probably claimed much the same defence after Wormhout,' Kyle rejoined bitterly.

'Pardon, sir?'

'It doesn't matter,' Kyle muttered. 'Not unless you'd happened to have someone you loved on the receiving end.'

Hackman gave him a curious look before draining his glass. 'And that's about it. The only positives are negatives. I can only tell you that, if German troops *had* been captured in the shipyard, then none of them were later logged as having been received in the forward echelon POW cage.'

'Not even Stollenberg himself?'

'The colonel was a survivor. We can only presume he escaped from the shipyard – was probably the only one who'd been on that ninth truck to do so. We do know he went to ground near Lübeck after the war. The military authorities caught up with him in '46 and sent him to Nuremberg for trial. He walked on those charges, eventually died of cancer in the early Eighties, and took the secret of the second Nefertiti with him.' Hackman nibbled a philosophical lip. 'There's none of us can escape the last great adventure.'

Kyle debated on whether to broach the subject of rather more recent victims of the last great adventure, then decided to leave it until he was more certain of Hackman's loyalty. One aspect of the former Redcap's involvement worried him in particular.

'You know David went to see Sergeant Williamson recently?'

'Knew he was going to. Didn't get the chance to catch up with the doctor before he was . . .' Hackman broke off and looked uncomfortable.

'So how did he make a connection with Williamson, if you were the one checking out the shipyard reports?'

'Not only Williamson, Mister Kyle. Doc McDonald was a pro. He'd retrieved the names of all the soldiers involved in the shipyard action from IWM archives and found that twelve of them had survived the war. When he tried to contact each of the twelve he discovered that, fifty-odd years later, eleven had been less fortunate in surviving the peace. The only one the Grim Reaper hasn't so far caught up with is the troop commander, Sergeant Williamson. We agreed that while I went down to RMP headquarters to suss out the background to the Lightwood affair, he'd go interview the old boy. The doctor had struck lucky in one respect – it turns out that Williamson still resides at the same London address noted on his regimental records.'

No Ted doesn't, Kyle reflected grimly. *Not any longer!* But the way Hackman had phrased his reply – his use of the present tense – suggested he wasn't aware of everything that had happened during the past week, which, unless he possessed the verbal skills of a Machiavelli, swayed the balance of suspicion even further in his companion's favour.

'David was on his way back to Battersea to confront Williamson for a second time when he went under the train,' Kyle said levelly. 'Why d'you think he felt the need to make a return trip so soon?'

Hackman shrugged. 'Without knowing the result of his first interview, I couldn't even hazard a guess. But like I said, Mister Kyle, it suggests he'd seen something in the Lightwood pictures which gave him good reason to want to follow up on it.'

Kyle was rising from the table when a last thought struck him: inconsequential probably, considering David had already pursued it. In fact he only raised the point in deference to Rushby's caution that no serious student could afford to over-look the slightest detail, no matter how irrelevant it appeared at first sight. Kyle still felt a twinge of guilt over having been so impatient with the professor over the Stoff 381 issue – the washing powder conundrum.

'You don't happen to recall the names of any other Commandos listed in the War Museum report on the Bremerhavenschiffswerft action, do you?'

'Offhand? Only one. The other troop NCO.' Hackman screwed up his battered nose with the effort of recall.

'Lewis? Yeah – a corporal . . . Corporal Arthur Lewis.'

Kyle left Hackman outside the Four Feathers after having arranged to meet again the next day for a strategy-planning session.

Updating the former MP on the current corpse situation would be a prerequisite to that exercise. Taking his hopefully unrehearsed comment at face value, Hackman still wasn't aware of just how industrious the Grim Reaper really had been during the past few days. That their only surviving contemporary source of information had been launched into *his* last great adventure by impact with a BMW, for a start.

Equally, and Kyle could only surmise an information black-out by Special Branch, no reference to the killing of Wanda Inadi alias Loukach alias Abdeljal-whoever had appeared in any newspaper he'd scanned. So Hackman couldn't have any inkling of that particularly bizarre twist afforded to the riddle, either.

Unless, of course, Hackman himself had . . . ?

Belay that, Mister! You really must put a stopper on that recurring paranoia of yours.

He decided to walk awhile before flagging a taxi for the rest of his return voyage to Ringtree Gardens. Get his head together, as the junior officers he sailed with sometimes said, although he'd never been quite sure of what it meant.

The rain began to trickle inside Kyle's turned-up collar but only served to make him force his pace with masochistic determination. One thing for sure: no matter how far he walked, he couldn't walk away from the burden he'd undertaken on David McDonald's behalf. While Hackman had been right to state that the only positives were negatives, their meeting had at least helped to reinforce Kyle's faith in his closest friend's deductive skills. Even the rationale for the second Nefertiti's remaining undiscovered for over half a century had become more clear. That in the post-war confusion, SS-Standartenführer Stollenberg's mission, insignificant when compared with the cataclysm then overwhelming Germany, had at first been ignored and, later, denied to academic pursuit once the Iron Curtain descended to divide that battle-weary nation.

Even after the Berlin Wall *had* been toppled, it was perfectly feasible that those few historians who, unlike Rushby, had believed the Nefertiti twin to be more than a myth had long concluded it had been destroyed in company with the Colonel's column itself. That subsequently, while Egyptologists lamented and successive German Ministries of Culture became ever more myopic as to who really bore responsibility for the loss of one of their greatest national treasures, everybody assumed that the priceless artefact had, at worst, been vaporized by bomb or shell or, at best, lay concealed for eternity by the mud at the bottom of the Müritz See.

Everybody, that was, except David McDonald, who'd bought a slim volume by sheer chance in a London bookshop and seen death in many violent forms within its pages but, blinded by the hope it offered him in furthering his obsessive quest, had failed to decipher its warning concerning the most important death of all – his own.

Well, everybody except David McDonald, a certain German colonel and a handful of Allied soldiers, to be precise. All of whom had survived the war, if not the peace, and all of whom carried with them the secret of what *really* happened to that 12-inch-high statuette after British Commandos surprised the remnants of Stollenberg's SS escort in the ravaged complex of the Bremerhavenschiffswerft.

The wind had begun to increase, gusting around the corners of buildings flanking Long Acre. Rain whirled and danced under the amber glare of the street lamps, causing all but the most determined late-nighters to seek shelter. The office façades were dark and silent as midnight approached, although lights still showed from those upper residential floors where people still talked, argued, made love or prepared to sleep through a night uncomplicated by thoughts of . . . ?

Kyle halted abruptly, frowning. Some vague recollection had pricked his subconscious as he'd passed the last narrow entry. Tucking his chin into his collar, he turned head to wind and retraced his steps to the corner. The street sign glistened, raindrops vibrating and twinkling under the press of the storm, reflecting the glow from the first-floor window beside it: *Shipskull Lane WC2*.

Of course . . . Jaggers' office! The pulsating heart of the

Singh Shipping Corporation's global empire – both rooms of it. Plus postage-stamp-sized entrance hall leading to washing-up cupboard with toilet and state-of-the-art electric kettle.

And that was Singh's light still shining into the night, wasn't it? A beacon of hope to destitute mariners desperate for a berth – until they found themselves clinging to a perished life-raft having decided, too late, they hadn't been *that* bloody desperate! Yet it was midnight. Surely Jaggers didn't stand a middle watch himself to demonstrate solidarity with the needy sailors he exploited? In Kyle's jaundiced view it was unlikely that Singh had ever set foot on a gangway – and he had certainly never stepped aboard one of the superannuated hulks flagged to owners he represented.

Then he realized the business of ship management continued irrespective of international time zones. Singh probably found it necessary to work some graveyard hours as well: particularly on nights when profits were put at risk by rust. Overloaded, overstressed and undermanned freighters sank at any time of day with total disregard for the convenience of agents such as Jagjivan Singh. Crews who walked off vessels stranded in Panama or Singapore because they'd been forced to live on minimal rations for six months, and not even paid for the last three of those, also tended to be unreasoningly selfish, often failing to ensure that their last hopeless protest was made within UK office hours.

Well, this was out of office hours, Jaggers old boy, and while Kyle was neither hungry nor particularly selfish, he *was* bloody resentful at having been taken for granted by both his best friend and his least respected anathema – albeit that his disgruntlement was tempered by sad affection in McDonald's case. Dammit, he wouldn't even have minded if David's having yet again volunteered his, Kyle's, help to solve Singh's crewing problems had promised to have the slightest bearing on the Nefertiti conundrum, but Jaggers' message had proved that prospect was out of the question.

Driving some undoubtedly clapped-out freighter to God knows where on the planet, instead of enjoying the well-earned leave he'd been looking forward to before the Black Rats waylaid him in their jam sandwich and tore his world apart, certainly didn't come under the category of World War II research. Apart from anything else, he'd since learned that the Stollenberg convoy had been a land-bound mission – nothing whatsoever to do with convoys of ships as Kyle, in his initial naiveté, had at first assumed.

So forget it, Jaggers. Rotterdam has no place on Chief Officer Kyle's current sleuthing itinerary. No more Mister Nice Guy!

The door from Shipskull Lane to the common ground floor entrance hall was unlocked. Nothing sinister was implied by that: merely a lack of landlord husbandry in that peeling layers of multi-coloured paint exposing, in parts, the enduring qualities of Victorian era base-coat, had simply welded the heavy key irretrievably within its lock . . . but then maybe the owners of some properties, in common with the owners of some ships, had also found a way of taking refuge from their responsibilities by hiding behind Flags of Convenience, Kyle reflected dryly, although he did feel bound to concede that the decrepit door was at least an honest door. It projected exactly the right image of the standards by which Jagjivan Singh carried on his trade.

When the door swung open even its rusted hinges creaked on cue, inspiring Kyle to anticipate a fleeting vision of the candle-flickering interior of Castle Frankenstein. Instead he found himself faced by a long stone-flagged corridor leading to a narrow staircase at its far end and lit, if such an extravagant term could be applied to its pallid output, by a single 60-watt bulb. On either side, heavily reinforced doors, most still bearing the jemmy-marks of generations of overly optimistic burglars, proclaimed the business registrations of others who strove to earn a crust within that Dickensian hub of cosmopolitan commerce. *Wang Zhendong Oriental Imports; Uncle Hiram's Jokes and Novelties Inc; Artefactos del Repúblico del Paraguay . . . To let* – no, hadn't that been *Toilet* before editing by some vandal? *Lolita's Massage . . . ?*

As a change from brooding over Egyptian relics, Kyle spent an inconsequential moment wondering about *Lolita's Massage and Relaxation Therapy Ltd* as he mounted stone stairs rendered quaintly concave, to say nothing of bloody dangerous, from two centuries of erosion by the soles of countless boots. Had Lolita always been Lolita, for instance, or was Lolita simply a coded euphemism for some enterprising lady's alternative vocation? A bit like all the Mister Smiths who weren't really Mister Smiths . . . all of which brought him back full circle to the spectre of SS-Standartenführer Stollenberg.

The imposing brass plate on his immediate starboard hand said *Singh Shipping Corporation.* It had been polished recently: looked tiddly as a tea clipper's binnacle . . . a bit of one-upmanship, Kyle suspected, in order to reassure those clients who survived the stairs that the proprietor of Singh Shipping was of a rather superior breed to the small-time traders down the foc'sle. The door, conveniently ajar, didn't even creak when he pushed it open. Oily smooth. Like good old Jaggers himself.

Lousy security, though: not having a creak, Kyle reflected as he stepped into the claustrophobic box that doubled as Singh Shipping's grand foyer. The opaque glass door facing him was closed. Anyone could slip in without disturbing either of the Corporation's staff – steal their kettle . . . anything. Even charge through and liquidate the office's occupants before they'd time to . . .

And probably have done, going by my recent track record, Kyle thought, petulantly reverting to childish fantasy. *Probably find another bloody corpse in there or something. Probably find two this time. Seems I can't even look in a cupboard for a bloody brush without finding a bloody body!*

But the clocks had struck midnight by then and Kyle was tired and fretful, and David's funeral had upset him far more than he'd let himself admit, and the rain had seeped down to the small of his back and he wasn't in any bloody mood to think happy bloody thoughts – he just wanted to say 'No!' and go.

He knocked impatiently on the glass. 'Jaggers?'

No reply. He raised his clenched fist to knock again, then thought, *Ohhhh, bugger the niceties!* and turned the handle.

The vacant outer office – reception, waiting, filing, communications centre, discarded gum wrappers in an ashtray and a well-thumbed copy of *Young Love* lying on the desk – suggested Singh's right-hand teenager was made of sterner stuff than his Third World crews, and had refused to be exploited into the clubbing hours.

Or *had* she? All of a sudden Kyle's discontentment began to give way to growing foreboding. He shouldn't have let his all-too-often black-humoured appreciation of the fine line between normality and the ludicrous take charge. He shouldn't have allowed his imagination even to touch on the possibility of discovering more corpses.

Yet another glass-panelled door beckoned. Gold leaf letters this time. Narcissistic but nice. Very tasteful. *Jagjivan Ajit Singh. Chief Executive Officer.*

'You in there, Jaggers? It's Kyle. Mike Kyle.'

Still silence, broken only by the steady trickle of rainwater overflowing from a blocked gutter somewhere on the outer face of the building.

Kyle extended an apprehensive finger to gingerly prod that most impressive door of all, allowing it to swing open. Then stood gazing within, uncertain of whether to feel relieved or . . . ?

Well, whichever spin one put on it, it was reassuring to find he'd been overly pessimistic. Deferring yet again to his acutely honed paranoia. Quite ridiculous – imagining he might have opened that door and discovered two corpses.

There was only one. The usual number.

Of corpses, that was.

And it definitely *was* a corpse. Not simply a chief executive officer with a slashed throat who might or might not still retain a tenuous hold on life.

The volume of sluggishly evacuating blood already beginning to congeal in little dark red stalactites below the edge of Jagjivan Singh's desk told a chap with Kyle's experience there was no immediate hurry to call for an ambulance.

CHAPTER THIRTEEN

Kyle would have been first to admit, once he'd recovered from the initial shock of meeting up with Jaggers again, that his primary concern hardly reflected to his credit.

Okay, Mister, the little voice inside him was yelling with more than a touch of incipient hysteria. *So just tell me how the hell you're goin' to explain THIS to Cox of Special Branch?*

But then, giving way to bouts of selfishness where Jagjivan Singh was concerned didn't necessarily have to be a luxury confined only to the agent's disillusioned crews. For a start, Cox had made it disturbingly clear that he frowned on coincidence. So while discovering one partially decapitated cadaver might have been considered an unfortunate but random event, Kyle's stumbling across two in the space of barely a week almost certainly promised to raise a cynical eyebrow on the already world-weary countenance of the inspector.

And that was the best-case scenario for the mess he'd got himself into. The *upside* of his dilemma! The downside was that Cox, once spurred by this extravagance of dead bodies into investigating other contacts made by Kyle in the past few days, would have little difficulty in establishing that he'd also recently visited the wife of a man who'd lived in Battersea – except that Mrs Williamson wasn't Mr Williamson's wife any more, she was his widow. Because old Ted, too, had died instantly after being run down, quite possibly with malicious intent, by a stolen car driven by a person still unknown, and within hours of Kyle's return to the UK.

All of which might even cause Cox to reconsider the circumstances surrounding yet one further violent death which, by a remarkable coincidence, had occurred since Kyle first disembarked to begin his holiday.

David McDonald's.

So Kyle's anxiety was understandable. Put simply, if he'd ever had cause to panic, this was it! Cox could even construe a perfectly plausible motive for his, Kyle's, having killed David if he looked closely enough. Interviewing Rushby would reveal not only that the finder of the second Nefertiti stood to make a great deal of money, but that Kyle had shown considerable diligence in researching McDonald's progress towards that particular goal – unseemly diligence, one might argue, considering his best friend had still been awaiting burial when Kyle entertained over a five-star brandy lunch.

Ohhhh, shit! The downsides were queuing thick and fast the more he scowled, a tad resentfully, at Singh's body. Because Cox would *then* want to know why, when first questioned by various policemen about Wanda-whatever's murder, he hadn't once volunteered the crucial admission that he'd spoken to David during the hours preceding his death; even a routine check on calls made from McDonald's telephone would reveal one made to Kyle's ship after it had docked.

And that would lead to more questions. Difficult questions. Pointed questions, even. Like: 'Okay, so where *did* you dispose of the doctor's computer, Kyle, once you'd decided to kill him and go for the Nefertiti reward yourself?'

Of course he could always come clean about everything, albeit a little tardily. Explain to Cox that none of this was his doing, that it was all the fault of an SS colonel who'd been given an order in the Führerbunker by Adolf Hitler's secretary in 1945 but who had subsequently died in Bad Oldesloe without mentioning it to anybody?

No, he'd better stick to its possibly having been the fault of a chap called Mister Smith. Or a Russian. Though he didn't actually know the name.

Rotterdam suddenly began to seem very attractive to Kyle. A nice cosmopolitan warren of a city. A good springboard for disappearing without trace.

The only glimmer of hope was that the police, including Cox of Special Branch, *had* seemed satisfied that David's death was a suicide. It might help put them off his track until he could sort things out.

The counter to that brief optimism was, well . . . Kyle could only think of one factor that might help a policeman differentiate between a distraught person throwing themselves on to a railway line, and a murder victim being pushed on to a railway line.

The availability of a suspect to suggest the latter possibility.

Particularly a suspect with Kyle's qualifications.

Panicking or not, he forced himself to hold his ground on that grim Victorian stage. The steps he took now, the intelligence he might glean from observation, could well dictate whether or not he remained a hunted man for the rest of his life: whether David's killer would ever be brought to account, for that matter.

Okay, then first it seemed a reasonable deduction to assume that Jaggers Singh hadn't committed suicide – and that wasn't simply Kyle's tendency, when under pressure, to take refuge in black humour surfacing again. He'd once before – well, once before if he discounted Wanda last week – found himself in a not-dissimilar situation. As Mate of a bulk carrier berthed in Bombay on that macabre occasion when her second engineer had been discovered in his cabin with his throat cut.

To Kyle's, and his captain's, untutored eyes the evidence clearly pointed to the man's having done away with himself. A lot of blood; the knife still held loosely in the dead man's hand; a 'Dear John' letter from the engineer's fiancée breaking off their engagement; and a history of depression since the letter had arrived aboard in Aden.

'Topped himself,' the Old Man had muttered. 'Case closed, Mister Kyle!'

'Not so,' the little Indian pathologist called to the quayside had begged to differ. 'This poor man has been murdered . . . observe, good sirs – the weapon is placed in the right hand, yet the angle of cut slopes obliquely downwards from to right to left. Here, sir: you wish to try it?'

'No thank you,' Kyle had resisted politely. He'd got the drift of the argument.

'Also there is only one cut – a deep and incisive cut, you see? And it is my experience that an unhappy gentleman wishing to do away with himself will almost invariably make two, perhaps even three tentative slashes before despair gives strength to his resolve.'

'I'll go see to the paperwork. Try and dredge up another bloody Second,' the Old Man had growled, turning hurriedly away. 'You carry on here, Mister Kyle.'

'Whereas a homicide victim will display evidence of a single, most positive cut delivered with considerable force by his or her assailant – observe, Chief Officer? Look closely at the wound.'

Jaggers Singh also displayed evidence of only one cut. Delivered very forcibly indeed. Forcefully enough to have completely severed his . . .

'Also, the suicide tends to be physiologically inefficient. They have an overpowering instinct to tilt the chin back immediately prior to their last desperate incision – to arch and thus expose the neck.' The Bombay doctor had shaken his head then, disconsolate at the pathological ignorance of his average client. 'A counter-productive action, sir, which causes the main arteries

138

to retreat and seek anterior refuge behind the protection of the windpipe.'

Whoever had cut Jagjivan Singh's throat hadn't made such a fundamental error. The agent's chin must have been savagely forced down to his chest in the instant when his killer drew the knife. Kyle shuddered and finally looked away.

They never did arrest anybody for the murder of the second engineer. There had been many ragged longshoremen and ste-vedores roaming the ship that day, and every last one of them looking in need of extra income. The local police had laconically concluded homicide in the pursuance of theft. Sudden death is a fact of life in Bombay docks.

Kyle had sometimes wondered later, though. After he'd heard that the container ship's technical officer, a man who tended towards fits of aggression, had got married.

To the girl previously betrothed to the dead Second.

Kyle ran out of initiative after exhausting his throat-cutting expertise. He was also running out of time. Middle of the night or no, anyone – the proprietor of an adjacent business, an oppor-tunistic sneak thief, one of Jaggers' previous employees keen to engage him in conversation after having been left stranded penniless in Manila or Malacca or wherever – might find the courage to run the gauntlet of those bloody stone steps and chance upon his open office door.

Observe, Mister. Look for something odd, he forced himself to think. *Apart from the obvious, that is. But look for something that either shouldn't be here at all, or should be here that isn't, or . . . or is here that doesn't appear quite right.*

He didn't see anything. Including the presence of any likely murder weapon more lethal than the blunt paper knife lying on the desk. Which meant that even his cut-throat expertise had proved quite superfluous, because it was hardly likely Jaggers had committed suicide then got up and hidden –

Cox again! Recollections of Inspector Cox's dry censure came into everything. This time it was his gravely considered response to Kyle's suggestion that it may have been Wanda Inadi herself who'd opened the gas tap in the flat.

'Would that have been before or *after* she stabbed herself in the throat then hid her own corpse in your cupboard, sir?' Cox had asked.

'Ohhhh, bugg—!' Kyle began to snarl at the world in general, then broke off, frowning.

There was a clip of papers lying on the desk. Several sheets stapled together. The top sheet bore the heading *Crew List – MV Centaur*. Of considerable interest, yes – particularly to a sea-qualified man seeking to travel . . . anywhere. But it wasn't that consideration which initially drew his attention.

The papers looked out of place somehow. And then Kyle realized that, while other documents scattered across the desk top had been submerged under Singh's remorselessly spreading blood, this sheaf hadn't. Although the underlying two or three sheets had similarly absorbed the gory residue – capillary action would explain that – the top sheet hadn't. Only scallop-shaped tide marks of drying blood had soaked into the paper's edges . . . which suggested even to Kyle's lay eye that the clip of papers had been placed on Jagger's desk *after* – not before – the brutal attack on the agent had taken place.

While didn't that, in turn, imply that whoever had killed Singh had unwittingly betrayed his – or her? – interest in that particular document? Must have had cause to examine it before discarding it, probably unthinkingly, to lie in the blood on his desk – but *why*? What conceivable motive for severing a man's windpipe could be concealed within papers concerning the routine administration of one voyage among many, of a ship managed by the Singh Shipping Corporation?

Crew List – MV Centaur. Voyage 289 . . . Damn right she'd steamed more than a few sea miles in her time . . . ! So where was she bound for on this trip, which increasingly promised to hold such significance to Kyle?

Narvik, Rotterdam, Naples, to Djibouti via Suez. Djibouti

would be a bunkering stop? No, that was port of final discharge; but then she was scheduled to sail further east in ballast to . . . to final destination – *Banji Beach*?

Banji Beach? That was on the west coast of India. Kyle had heard of it although, happily, never had cause to sail to it. A great wide stretch of pure white sand south of Srivardhan where ships arrived – and never left. Banji Beach was the elephants' graveyard of the sea. Any vessel bound for Banji Beach drove straight inshore at full speed until her forefoot bit into the soft bed of sand, whereupon slowly, remorselessly she would come to rest for the very last time: stranded and prey to acetylene torch and ripping tool.

Banji Beach was the most cost-efficient of ship-breakers' yards. There, as soon as a vessel came to rest, a thousand, two thousand Indian labourers would swarm over her like a tidal wave of worker ants. For a handful of rupees they would take her apart and literally put her back in the box. Her plates would be cannibalized. Her main and auxiliary engines would be dismantled for spares. Her ancillary equipment would be removed, rebuilt and dispatched abroad: anchors, cables, shafts, propellers . . . even the brass screws and hinges of her doors would be painstakingly extracted, cleaned and repackaged.

So Kyle had been right. The Motor Vessel *Centaur* was indeed turning out to be typical of those managed by Jagjivan Singh: old and finished as a commercially viable asset even to owners who lived by running such coffin ships. More so, it now seemed, than his worst apprehensions had led him to imagine. She really had to be sick if this was scheduled to be her final voyage. FWE, indeed: *Finished With Engines, Mister*. For ever!

So who else had been signed on to sail in company with him as participants in this, the *Centaur*'s desolate funeral cortège? Her Old Man, for instance? Hardly a career move, delivering your command up to be executed.

Master – Ferreiro Cavaco Barrosa, the list said. Portuguese? Barrosa was a Portuguese surname, wasn't it? Yeah – Portuguese, according to the notation in the margin. It figured.

While directly below – Chief Officer *Michael B. Kyle*! There confirmed in black and white; bordered with scalloped red.

Thanks, David, dearest friend: thanks a bunch! Probably the sole stiff upper British lip in what was undoubtedly going to prove a crew of multinational misfits – although perhaps his fondly tempered sarcasm wasn't so justified as he'd previously imagined. Not now. Not with the imminent prospect of Jagjivan Singh's name being added to the Metropolitan Police tally of corpses he was known to associate with. He could catch the first morning Eurostar out-bound through the Channel Tunnel and be in Rotterdam by afternoon. The *Centaur* was due to berth on Friday. By then, with any luck, the constabulary would only just have started putting two and two together and coming up with four times Kyle.

Second Officer William Voorhoeve. Dutch? Belgian? No: Canadian, the margin assured him. Thank God, Kyle reflected gloomily, clutching at any positive straw. At least there'll be one guy aboard who'll understand when I say 'Good morning'. Not that I'm ever likely to be given bloody cause to.

Third Officer Saifur Kamal Chowdhury: Bangladesh . . . he should be okay with English, too. If not, 3/0 Chowdhury had better learn some, an' bloody fast. Kyle's fluency in Bengali was as scant as his tolerance was likely to be on this particular trip.

Chief Engineer Mohammad Ben Saaidi. Moroccan – *Moroccan*? Hadn't Wanda in the cupboard been a Moroccan, or worked under a Moroccan alias in one of her many guises? Kyle frowned a moment longer, then put it to the back of his already over-loaded mind. Second Engineer – Maurice Beaubrun: Haitian – *Haitian*, for crying out loud? Were there actually any Haitian ship's engineers left? Hadn't all their seagoing nationals been drowned on the Haitian ferries they'd managed to sink?

Quickly Kyle scanned down the remaining crew members listed on the top page without, unsurprisingly, recognizing any names. Or being able to pronounce most of them.

There followed a tongue-protruding exercise in trying to prise

142

the bloody-edged page two apart with a pencil, and failing. When distaste finally overcame determination and he cast around for a suitable receptacle, a discarded plastic sandwich wrapper in Jaggers' waste bin offered a utilitarian solution. Ever so carefully Kyle eased the whole document from its bed of grue and placed it, dripping, in the bag. It wasn't exactly a confession, but he didn't think it prudent to leave any evidence linking his name either to Jaggers or to the last voyage of the *Centaur*. Interpol had long arms and he didn't fancy doing several months in a Djibouti jail while diplomats argued the finer points of extradition procedure.

He gazed irresolutely about him for a moment longer before retreating to the outer office, taking great care not to step in the blood soiling Singh's chief-executive-quality carpet. Fairly confident that, apart from the document itself, he hadn't touched anything within the inner sanctum, Kyle wiped its door handle as meticulously as any first trip apprentice polishing the brass plate adorning the door of his master's cabin.

It was only after he'd afforded equal diligence to the outer office, and was casting one last glance behind him to make doubly sure he hadn't missed anything with an arrow pointing to it marked 'clue', that he hesitated again. Something *had* caught his eye this time. Something on the shelves behind the reception desk. Nothing incriminating as far as he was concerned – nothing that even looked out of place in its present environment – but something that nevertheless caused him to re-enter the room as a sudden thought struck him.

It took Kyle less than three minutes to find what he was looking for.

And another three, or even five, to . . . well, to get his head together again: digest the import of what he'd just discovered. Just wondering if such a thing was possible. Just listening to the steady overspill of rainwater cascading outside the office of his dead friend's friend, and reflecting on the macabre chain of events which had brought him to this point of discovery, and on precisely how long the spectre of Standartenführer Stollenberg would lie dormant before it stirred again and attempted to kill someone else.

Probably himself next time, if his latest conclusion was correct.

He finally left Jagjivan Singh's temporary resting-place as he found it. No fingerprints, no indications that he'd ever been there. Oh, he suspected tests existed that could prove him wrong but – particularly in view of what he'd just learned – Kyle didn't plan to hang around London while a Home Office forensic scientist picked carpet strands or other trace evidence from the soles of his shoes, although his initial panic had subsided to be replaced by a calmer reasoning. It was nearly one a.m., according to his Taiwan Rolex: give or take twenty minutes. No early morning Channel Tunnel getaway, for a start. He had things to do and, if he kept his head, time to do them in. He could probably count on a minimum of twenty-four hours grace before the police made the tenuous connection between himself and Jaggers via David, and came looking for him.

Mind you, he'd already been proved wrong once that night. Had only discovered one corpse, not two. But that was simply him taking refuge in flippancy again, to help counter his mounting foreboding. He decided to make a special point of checking the hall cupboard anyway, as soon as he got home. Just to be on the safe side.

Kyle walked for a full mile at right angles to a mental course line drawn between Jaggers' office and the flat in Ringtree Gardens before burying the plastic-shrouded crew list deep in a builders' skip, then gratefully hailing a passing taxi. Another small concession to putting the police off his scent if they started questioning cabbies regarding early morning fares from the Shipskull Lane area.

He actually gained satisfaction from such masochistic diversion. The gusting wind, the icy rain cutting across his face as it did on lousy nights at sea. It made him feel alive, somehow. And that sensation alone was becoming something of a rarity among those who'd sought the truth behind the Stollenberg Myth.

Not that Kyle needed to seek further. Not any more.

Because he knew now where the second Nefertiti was hidden.

CHAPTER FOURTEEN

'*How* many bodies?' Hackman exploded.

'Four,' Kyle counted. 'Well, only three actually. Obviously I haven't asked to see Ted Williamson's.'

Hackman's face remained a triumph of impassivity as he resumed his assault on the full English breakfast Kyle had promised if he'd meet him in a somewhat less than five-star early-morning diner near Putney Bridge. His only give-away was in stabbing his egg with a savagery enough to cause Kyle to look away. But then, Kyle was becoming ultra-sensitive about knives.

A mouthful later and the former military policeman wearily consigned his cutlery to the still-full plate and stared hard at Kyle. 'All right. So can you give me one good reason why I shouldn't turn you in here an' now, Mister Kyle?'

'No,' Kyle said.

'Then did you kill them? Any of them?'

'No,' Kyle said.

'But you do realize that either way, you're in deep shit,' Hackman growled. '*Don't* you, Mister Kyle?'

'Yes,' Kyle said.

'And you also realize that, if I don't go to the coppers and tell 'em what you just told me, then *I'm* in deep shit too?'

'Yes,' Kyle said.

'Ohhhh, for Christ's sake!'

'I'm going to find the bastard who killed David, Hackman,' Kyle advised him. 'Whether you do or you don't go to the police. Now – d'you want tea or coffee to finish?'

'Tea,' Hackman decided.

'The question is, did Wanda Whoever-you-said go to your flat just to lift the doctor's computer, or for some further reason?' Hackman frowned after Kyle had ground to an explanatory halt. 'Did her killer accompany her there – or follow her? Why, for that matter, kill her in the flat anyway . . . an' why rig the gas to blow unless, as you've suggested, it was a belt an' braces job, intended to ensure any stray jotting pointing to the Nefertiti was obliterated while helping to confuse the issue – make out the doctor was a sad bastard who'd done for his girlfriend then decided he couldn't face the music?'

'If I had the answer to even one of those questions,' Kyle muttered, 'I probably wouldn't be buying you breakfast now.'

'Yes you would, sir. Because you still wouldn't know why someone, presumably the same perpetrator, also chopped your mate Jaggy last night,' Hackman countered. 'Where does he fit in anyway?'

'Not Jaggy, Jaggers – or more properly, Jagjivan – Singh. I'll tell you about him in due course but, for now, just accept that he wasn't my friend, he was David's. Couldn't stand the little turd myself.'

'I wouldn't recommend saying that to the police.'

'I'm not planning to say anything to the police. Which is why I *am* buying you breakfast, Hackman.'

Hackman ladled three sugars into his mug of tea. 'Okay. So where are we with these killings, Mister Kyle? The onc solid fact so far established, courtesy of your inspector at SO13, is there's some link between Wanda, the Stollenberg family and this German terror group Renunciation – or was a few years back, anyway. Before young Gunther took a head-shot from Grenzschutzgruppe Neun. D'you want me to check his history out? Confirm he *was* the colonel's spawn for a start?'

'Can you?'

'I could phone Frankfurt this afternoon. I still got RMP mates serving in BAOR. If they can't call GsG9 personally to give me an intro, they'll sure as hell know a man who can.'

'Just a hunch,' Kyle said, 'but while you're tapping into your old boy net, find out as much as you can about a recently discharged Royal Marine Colour Sergeant called John Lewis.'

'Lewis?' The name was ringing a bell with Hackman even before Kyle told him about John Lewis, and Mrs Williamson's obvious closeness to her deceased neighbours' son, and the Lewis family's affection for her. By then Hackman had made the wartime connection with old Ted's fellow campaigner: Commando Corporal Lewis, Arthur.

'This is your Legacy theory. The sins of the Fathers *et cetera*?'

'Can you think of a better one right now? Okay, it still leaves a wide field of suspects. Apart from Stollenberg himself, there were – what . . . twelve Brits who survived the shipyard action, including Williamson and Arthur Lewis? Any one of them could have passed the secret of the Nefertiti down to their kids. But the next generation John is the only one we know of at this time, and . . .' Kyle hesitated then, unable to put his finger on it. 'I dunno, Hackman. I only met him briefly, but there's something about the guy keeps making me think of the Cheshire Cat.'

'The what?'

'Nothing,' Kyle dismissed hurriedly, feeling foolish.

Hackman gave him a funny look. 'I can check his service record, that's about all. But there's one thing you should ask yourself, Mister Kyle. A pound to a penny whoever killed Doc McDonald and the others also ran Ted Williamson down. Yet according to his widow, Williamson had been like a second dad to ex-Colour Lewis since he was a kid. With such a close relationship, is it likely the bloke would take out his own . . . ?'

'I found a young woman with a boning knife rammed under her chin so violently it damn near exploded through the top of her head, Hackman,' Kyle interrupted tightly. 'And Jaggers didn't just get his throat cut – he'd practically been decapitated! Anyone who can do that to another human being has to be a homicidal psychopath. The rules of the heart don't apply.'

'Then remember that. Because it underlines the fact that you can't afford to trust anyone.'

'Including you?'

'You have a choice. We say *auf Wiedersehen* and go our separate ways; or I telephone Frankfurt this afternoon and we take it from there. Either way, you still pay for my breakfast.'

'It was a damn good breakfast,' Kyle said. 'By definition a few murders wouldn't put a psychopath off a breakfast like that. You didn't eat yours.'

'With *that* kind of logic, sir,' Hackman said morosely, 'it's a wonder you've even survived this far.'

'We know Stollenberg's ninth truck didn't rendezvous with Erhard's U-boat,' Kyle recapped. 'Come to that, with the city about to fall it's unlikely they would have made it to the submarine pens down-river even had the Kapitan-Leutnant survived his last patrol.'

'Whereas I'll grant there's enough evidence shown in Lightwood's photograph to be pretty sure it did reach the shipyard.'

Kyle shrugged. 'More than that. Add Lightwood's allegation of SS POWs having been shot in the Bremerhavenschiffswerft and I'd say there's proof positive that they never got any further. You're an army man – what would they have done next?'

'If it had been me,' Hackman volunteered candidly, 'it would've been *Hande hoch* an' *Kamerad, Tommy*.'

Something told Kyle that Hackman wouldn't have. He was a hard bastard, was Hackman. Comfortingly so.

'I think they reverted to Nazi Cunning Plan B. Hid the Nefertiti to await the resurgence of the Fourth Reich. Or tried to.'

'With respect, Mister Kyle, that's not deduction: it's pure guesswork. For a start you're presuming Stollenberg still had the statuette at that point, whereas it could have been aboard any of the trucks. Could've been blitzed out of existence as far back as Brahlstorf an' Lake Müritz when the rest of his column was strafed.'

'David didn't think so. He sounded too positive, too excited when I spoke to him. He must have been given reason to believe it was still there with the colonel in that shipyard.'

'Given reason by whom?'

Kyle thought back to his visit to old Ted's widow, and of what she'd told him. About the mood of optimism the sergeant had shown when he'd first returned from the war. Of how he'd claimed to have fixed things in the army so's he'd be able to keep a then still-young Mrs Williamson in a manner she wasn't accustomed to, but how, as time passed, he'd gradually stopped dreaming – until recently. Recently, it seemed, he'd cheered up again: even developed a spring in his step he hadn't shown for years. Started talking once more about how they'd soon be rich after all, able to afford a proper house by the sea – started talking like that immediately *following* David McDonald's visit to him.

'Oh yes, Ted Williamson?' the old lady claimed to have retorted. 'And I suppose you're going to tell me next just who's going to *pay* for all that, are you?'

Kyle recalled smiling tolerantly then. 'And what did Ted say?'

'I told you he could be a daft ha'porth,' Mrs Williamson had answered sadly. 'He said Hitler was going to pay for it. That's who Ted joked was going to make us rich, Mister Kyle – Adolf Hitler, of all unlikely people.'

'Williamson,' Kyle confirmed with absolute certainty. 'I think Williamson told Doctor McDonald exactly where SS-Standartenführer Stollenberg hid the Nefertiti fifty-odd years ago.'

'Oh yes, Mister Kyle?' Hackman challenged in unconscious

parody of Ted's frail widow. 'And I suppose you're going to tell me just where that was, are you?'

'As it so happens, Hackman,' Kyle shrugged with an insouciance he could only pray was justified, 'I am. Let's suppose –'

'About par for the course, the way this bloody investigation's going,' Hackman grumbled without quite being able to conceal the intrigue in his eye.

'Let us *suppose*, Hackman,' Kyle persisted heavily, 'that Williamson's Commando did eventually trap the remnant of Stollenberg's escort in the Bremerhavenschiffswerft. That he and his Waffen-SS men couldn't hope to prevent the Nefertiti from falling into Allied hands much longer. What then?'

'Carry on supposing.'

'Stollenberg was faced with three choices. One: surrender and hand over the statuette; which meant conceding the total failure of his mission. Two: conceal it then fight to the death, with much the same end result – no point in hiding something of inestimable value to the renaissance of Nazism if there's no one left to pass on its location. Or, three –'

'Hide it – then surrender? Keep shtoom under interrogation. Go back and recover it once the POW cages are emptied and the heat's died down, to help swell the coffers of their pipe-dream Fourth Reich.'

'Exactly.'

'So what *do* you reckon? Or rather, what d'you reckon Doctor McDonald reckoned? That the colonel hid it in some building, or buried it?'

Kyle shook his head. 'No.'

'Christ, you can be frustrating, Mister Kyle. Anyone ever tell you you can be frustrating?'

'If he'd done either, it would have come to light eventually, or been bulldozed into the ground for ever, and we've been through that debate. Lightwood's book shows the yard was wrecked. The post-war authorities must have cleared that whole area before rebuilding. Probably isn't even a shipyard now. Probably blocks of bloody people-pens with balconies to the River Weser.'

'Thank you for that potted social comment,' Hackman grumbled. 'Just tell me where you think the Nefertiti is now, and we can go from there.'

'Look Hackman, you're jumping too far ahead,' Kyle demurred, virtuously imitating the asperity shown by Rushby over his own lack of interest in the peripheral details of Panzerspähwagens and anti-aircraft rockets and Stoff Three Eighty-something. 'You've overlooked a fourth option. The one Stollenberg never allowed for.'

'Which was?'

'That Williamson's troop overcame the SS escort *before* they'd finished concealing the Nefertiti. Can you imagine what went through the minds of that group of combat-hardened Tommies when suddenly confronted by the most beautiful, most precious object any of those guys had ever seen? Okay, they couldn't have begun to guess at its international significance, but it was clearly worth a fortune. An ancient Egyptian artefact made of pure gold studded with gemstones? Sure as hell they would have recognized the post-war contribution it could make to their service pensions.'

'Your next supposition being that Williamson's boys decided to keep the statuette for themselves? Shot their SS prisoners to keep their mouths shut – or all but Stollenberg anyway, who'd escaped – then for an encore, fragged Lightwood twenty-four hours later after learning he'd already reported them verbally to the MPs?'

'In a nutshell, yes.'

Hackman shook his head. 'Good theory: unlikely in practice. You made the point yourself. Williamson, Corporal Lewis *et al* – they were battle-wise troops. Mean, lean and bent on surviving the war. For all they knew they still had weeks of front-line fighting ahead of them – an' you don't run so fast or dodge so nimble with God knows how many pounds of solid gold weighing down your backpack. Especially when you know that even if you *do* make it through the rest of the campaign, make it as far as the demob centre, chances are the Redcaps'll go through your kit with a fine-tooth comb anyway before they open the door to civvy street.'

'Precisely.' Kyle nodded.

'Whaddyou mean – precisely?' Hackman exploded.

'I mean that's precisely what Doctor McDonald would have reasoned as well, Hackman. It meant he was stymied. Until he came across the Lightwood book.'

Hackman showed great restraint. He didn't physically attack Kyle. Merely caused the few early breakfast clients remaining in the diner to turn, stare uneasily, then concentrate nervously on their plates.

'Then if Williamson didn't take it either, where *is* the golden fucking queen?'

But to answer that, Kyle had to cast his mind back once again. Although only for a matter of hours on this occasion.

When he'd been spurred to re-enter Jagjivan Singh's office in the wet and windy graveyard watch of that same morning, he'd done so simply because curiosity had got the better of his natural impulse to make a prudent withdrawal from the crime scene.

Though accepting, by then, that McDonald's motive had to be linked with the Stollenberg riddle, he *still* couldn't figure why David and Singh had obviously conspired – days, or perhaps only hours prior to their deaths – to appoint him, Kyle, to some ship he'd never heard of. A ship of a type, size and history that was unknown to him – other than that she was ultimately scheduled to rendezvous under full power with her own undertakers at Banji Beach, of course; which, if nothing else, gave him a pretty good idea of the condition she was in.

It was his desire to satisfy at least the latter part of that speculation that had compelled Kyle to return to the reception desk. Or rather, to the bookshelves behind it.

Lloyd's Register of Ships comes in three heavy volumes published annually. It lists the principal details of every vessel in the world – ship type, date of building, builders, present owner, current country of registry, dimensions, tonnages gross, net and dead-weight, main and auxiliary machinery, bunker capacity. Most maritime-related businesses subscribe. The Singh Shipping Corporation was no exception.

Having fashioned his handkerchief into a makeshift mitt, Kyle had leafed awkwardly through the first volume until he came to the entry he sought.

Centaur . . . Single-screw general cargo motor vessel. Owners: *Le Blanc Ship Management Pte Ltd, Brazzaville*. Flag State: *Régie des Voies Maritimes de Congo*? Well, *that* made a refreshing change from Liberia or Monrovia! Engine by Hartmann: oil fuelled. Gross tonnage: 7,688. Year built: 19 . . . ?

That's when Kyle had stiffened – checked the date of building again, hardly able to credit what he read. Quickly he ran down the *Centaur's* previous names. As with most venerable ships she'd served many owners, sailed under many national flags – often for reasons as much to do with avoidance of safety legislation as tax efficiency – but few had been rechristened as many times as this one.

Her most recent names and years of change were listed first. Ex *Lorenz Star* – '98: ex *Malungo* – '96: ex *Doric Sea* – '93: ex *Luang Prabang* – '91: ex . . .

Kyle had disregarded the Eighties, Seventies, Sixties – and Fifties.

Had stood frowning at the final entry for all of those imprudent minutes before stirring. Just reflecting on spectres, and things.

Which helped to explain why, when he did eventually return to Ringtree Gardens, Kyle hadn't felt the slightest bit in thrall to his paranoia while confirming that nothing had been added to the contents of the utility cupboard.

'A precaution amply justified, Mister,' he'd had little difficulty in persuading himself by then. 'Considering what you've already learned – and found, in Jaggers' office tonight.'

Although yearning desperately for a mega-volatile coffee following his unscheduled London Marathon, Kyle had gone straight through to the lounge and raked through David's pile of old NATO magazines until he'd extracted the one he'd previously replaced after Cox's policemen had left. Then propped it beside the enlarged photograph taken by Lightwood in the Bremerhavenschiffswerft and, while waiting for the kettle to boil, meticulously compared the two.

A typical Warsaw Pact intelligence-gathering freighter – the Yuryi Rogov, the caption under the 1970's aerial surveillance photograph of the Soviet spy ship advised him. *. . . note the ultra-sophisticated electronic interception array abaft the bridge: very much at odds with the purported trading status of such vessels.*

Those electronic listening devices hadn't been fitted at the time when Lightwood took what must have been one of his last exposures: capturing for posterity the split second in 1945 when a Sergeant Ted Williamson, a Corporal Arthur Lewis and two other unknown British Commandos posed in post-battle reflection over the body of a Waffen-SS-Polizei-Panzer Grenadier.

But, given the lead he now had, to Kyle's sea-wise eye the silhouette of the then-new freighter on the yard's fitting-out berth – the one providing the hazy background to that picture so reminiscent of a Victorian-era shooting party – and the 1974 intelligence-gatherer shown in the NATO journal, were one and the same vessel.

Only, according to *Lloyd's Register*, she wasn't called the *Yuryi Rogov* any longer, that Russian female David had sounded so pleased at having finally identified but, by his cryptic phrasing, had utterly confused Kyle who, of all people, really should have known better.

'Stollenberg hid the Nefertiti aboard a ship,' Kyle said.

'Aboard a what?'

'A ship – or rather, *the* ship. The ship still under construction in the Bremerhavenschiffswerft in 1945. Williamson's troop simply took a leaf from the colonel's book – left the statuette where the SS had already concealed it.'

Hackman's brow furrowed. Other than that he showed no response. Kyle tried again for a reaction.

'The ship that can be seen in the background to one of Lightwood's pictures, Hackman? McDonald must have registered her significance while browsing in a secondhand bookshop: the last piece of the jigsaw he'd been trying to put together for years. Helped by that he was able to work out what probably happened, then traced Williamson through regimental records to confirm his hunch. It could well have been that on the morning he was killed, he was returning to ask old Ted to pinpoint the statuette's exact place of concealment aboard her.'

Hackman still continued to frown in silence. So much so that Kyle began to wonder if he'd even registered the implication.

'*Well*?' he prompted eventually.

'Well, what, Mister Kyle?' the former Redcap finally growled. 'Either way you've as good as said we're buggered. Any ship that old will have sunk or been broken up years ago.'

'She's still afloat and working. Just,' Kyle corrected, wishing to God she wasn't because then David would still be alive and Standartenführer Stollenberg mouldering easy in his grave.

'Still doesn't ring true.' Hackman churned the sugar with his spoon as a mark of frustration. 'Williamson's troop were hard, hard soldiers who'd already committed one major war crime, then compounded it by murdering one of their own to ensure *his* silence . . . an' for why? For the same reason Stollenberg hid it in the first place. So's they could go back after the war and recover their loot.'

'Agreed. Except they never did.'

''Course they did. They must have done. She was a freighter, wasn't she? One sailor on the gangway when in port, an' him probably down the mess? They could have waited a year – five years, if that's what it took – then boarded her in some god-forsaken backwater and had it away with the loot before the rest of her crew woke up. For Christ's sake, they'd been *commandos*, Mister Kyle!'

'If they'd been the whole NATO Fleet, they'd still have had a fight on their hands,' Kyle rejoined, rather enjoying the advantage of being one step ahead for a change.

'Now you're just being silly,' Hackman grumbled.

'According to Lloyds, her first registered name was the *Yuryi Rogov*. Probably handed over to the USSR after completion as war reparations . . . either way, she sailed under the Russian flag – meaning the first forty years of her life were spent as an intelligence-gathering para-Soviet Navy vessel protected by an Iron Curtain. Every covert spy ship the Russians deployed during the Cold War doubled as a merchantman subsidized by the Kremlin: free to carry cargoes into Western territorial waters denied to Warsaw Pact men o' war.'

Hackman thought about that for a moment.

'Okay, I grant you it *could* explain why the statuette's never turned up,' he conceding grudgingly. 'The best-laid plans of mice and men, you might say.'

'Thought you were a Tennyson man?'

'Burns had his moments. Wrote some good tunes too . . . so?'

'So when the Wall came down, old Soviet spy ships became redundant. The Russians had a number like the *Yuryi Rogov* laid up – still do – while suddenly they were dollar-hungry. Along with others she was placed on the international market. She could still float even after fifty-odd years, and that was good enough for some owners.'

'It's ironic, when you think about it,' Hackman reflected. 'It was a hot war that gave ex-Sergeant Williamson and those other squaddies their chance to get rich, and a Cold War that took it away.'

Kyle shrugged, not entirely without sympathy himself. 'Until, one day, the political map changed and old Ted's dream became attainable. Only by then it was too late. Most of his remorselessly ageing Commando, including his best mate Corporal Lewis, had died, the survivors too old to go in for hijacking.'

'You could say the same for Stollenberg. He could have gone after the statuette too, when he was still young – for

157

himself even, had he ever come to accept that Nazism was dead. Could have passed his legacy of knowledge down to Gunther, presupposing he *was* his son – only Gunther didn't get the chance to go for it either.'

Which brought them full circle back to Kyle's generation cascade theory. And the part currently played in the drama, if indeed he had any part at all, by the only other suspect they'd so far identified who fitted that role. John Lewis.

'I'll be able to fill in some of those blanks after I've called Frankfurt,' Hackman said. 'Before that you'd better tell me about your man, Singh, because I'm damned if I can figure where he fits into the equation.'

'It's not as obscure a connection as you might think. Jaggers is – was – a shipping agent. He managed and crewed the *Yuryi Rogov* on behalf of her present owners, which explains . . .' Kyle hesitated then, suddenly aware of the enormity of what he'd been let in for. 'Which explains why I can't risk being detained by the police, Hackman. Courtesy of Jagjivan Singh I'm sailing for India come Friday – in that same damn coffin ship.'

Hackman's expression betrayed a mix of astonishment and slowly dawning amusement.

'Don't, Hackman,' Kyle added warningly. 'Don't even think about quoting the irony of it. McDonald had realized that getting me aboard her represented our last chance to recover the statuette before some itinerant labourer south of Srivardhan finds himself worth more than the bloody Taj Mahal!'

Kyle brought Hackman up to speed then, on David's post-university friendship with Jaggers and their benign conspiracy to press-gang him, Kyle, into returning to a sailor's lot earlier than he'd anticipated. Even admitted, not without a twinge of guilt, to having ignored the answerphone message that ultimately led to his discovering, all too late, that bloodied crew list on the by-then dead Singh's desk.

'My appointment to her would have been simple enough for him to arrange. Probably suited him, in fact. So much so he wouldn't even have looked for a backhander,' he finished, unable to quite prevent cynicism from clouding his respect for the dead. 'Jaggers was notorious for exploiting the crews he hired. He didn't exactly have queues of certificated officers clamouring for a berth, and wouldn't have questioned why David had volunteered my services too closely.'

'You don't think he was privy to the Nefertiti being aboard?'

'I very much doubt McDonald would have let him in on the secret. He liked Singh but I don't think he trusted him particularly.'

'Either way it seems the mere fact he was connected to the ship was enough to trigger his killing.'

'Which still doesn't help us find the motive for Wanda's murder.'

'Oh, I dunno.' Hackman moodily rearranged the sugar again. 'All we got to do now is figure how a female Arab terrorist fits into a scenario involving World War II, a superannuated Soviet spy-ship an' Doctor McDonald's bloody cupboard.'

It struck Kyle inconsequentially that Hackman wasn't the only one who could latch on to the odd irony. 'They did actually have something in common, Wanda and the *Yuryi Rogov*. They'd both changed names quite a few times since they were born.'

He paused then, wondering what the hell kind of nightmare he was about to sign himself aboard from Rotterdam outward. 'She's called the *Centaur* now,' he added vaguely. 'The ship, I mean. Not the girl.'

'Enjoy your trip in her, Mister Kyle,' Hackman offered mischievously. 'They say it can be very nice in the Indian Ocean at this time of year.'

'I'm sure we will, Hackman,' Kyle agreed amiably.

Hackman smiled at the joke. 'For a moment I thought you said "we".'

'I did.'

Hackman's grin became fixed. 'No, I meant –'

'Williamson may have been persuaded to describe the Nefertiti's precise location aboard the *Centaur* to Doctor McDonald – but as he's past telling anyone, that won't help me to find it. Certainly not on my own.'

'You're not expecting *me* to go with you?'

'Affirmative.'

'Spend my time ferreting in the . . . the bilges or whatever, on this – this Voyage of the Damned?'

'Not quite,' Kyle said. 'I've a pretty good idea you won't need to. But to follow it up, we both need to be aboard.'

He felt a bit crestfallen when Hackman didn't even ask what his pretty good idea was. But then, Hackman was still fighting a rearguard action.

'But I'm not a bloody sailor.'

'Neither will the rest of the crowd be. Not if I know the criteria Jaggers applied to personnel selection. Cheap, cheaper, cheapest – seagoing qualifications optional.'

'I even get sick on a Channel ferry.' Hackman resorted to plaintive appeal.

'Then we'll take the train under it. After that you'll only have to worry about Biscay, the Med, the Red Sea and the Indian Ocean,' Kyle consoled him.

Hackman made his last desperate play. 'But her crew's already decided, Mister Kyle. You said it yourself – there's a list. I'm not even on it.'

'Half the maritime drop-outs who *are* won't turn up in Rotterdam because they'll still be stoned in some dockside bar or worse, trying to forget they volunteered. All you have to do is make sure the Mate – her chief officer – signs you on as a last-ditch replacement.'

'At my age? Without papers? Without any sea skills whatso-ever?' Hackman clutched at the tendered straw with childlike faith. 'No way. The guy's bound to tell me to get lost.'

'Oh, I won't turn you away, Hackman,' the former *Yuryi Rogov*'s chief officer-designate Kyle assured him gravely. 'I promise I won't.'

CHAPTER FIFTEEN

At first sight the ship appeared to share as much in common with Ted's widow as with Wanda of the several identities. Both old ladies now, the Motor Vessel *Centaur* and Mrs Williamson had nevertheless contrived to retain a fragile dignity which belied the hardships of their lives.

But that was only Kyle's initial impression gained when viewing her from a distance: an already familiar silhouette dwarfed by the maze of waterways and industrial complexes which make up the vast dock area of Europoort. As his cab drew closer, he began to make out the ravages that half a century of sea service had inflicted on the former *Yuryi Rogov*.

The Mercedes taxi that conveyed him from Rotterdam Central stopped well short of the accommodation ladder. A precautionary measure, he suspected: in case rust was infectious.

'*Tachtig guilder*,' the cabbie announced laconically. 'Eighty guilder.'

'Eighty guilders?' Kyle growled because he'd been travel-weary and in a fractious mood even before confirming his worst fears. 'Christ, I only wanted to hire the bloody motor, not buy it.'

'*Tachtig guilder*,' the cabbie repeated unimpressed while Kyle humped his seabags to the quayside. The Dutchman shrugged then: encompassing the wharf alongside numbers two and three hatches. 'Anyway, what you need more Mercedes for, Meineer? You already got plenty, ja?'

Kyle glowered. About thirty rather more battered clones of the cab he'd travelled in were still awaiting loading, *Djibouti* stickers displayed on dusty windscreens. Second-, even third-hand Rotterdam taxis obviously bound for proud purveyors of transport services in North Africa. Mind you, they did complement the *Centaur* at that, he reflected sardonically. Most of 'em looked as though they could have been more properly destined for Banji Beach, to be broken up with the rest of the bloody ship.

But this was the bottom end of the international shipping barrel: scouring the world for job-lots of general cargo in a trampship tradition practically gone. He didn't need to look at the cargo stowage plan – presupposing her previous mate had even been capable of preparing one to discourage her from capsizing *en voyage* from Narvik – to guess there was probably a fair quantity of third-grade Norwegian timber in her lower holds, and dried or canned fish products in the lower tween decks: all carried at cut-to-the-bone tonnage rates negotiated in desperation on the spot-charter market to help defray the cost of the *Centaur*'s last one-way voyage. To top off, the used vehicles would be craned into the hatch squares then rolled into her upper tween decks and lashed securely to prevent them taking charge should they run into heavy weather – he, personally, would make damn sure of that! The last event Kyle intended to preside over was a Panzer division of Mercedes Benz suddenly abandoning ship through her paper-thin sides and crash-diving into the depths of the Indian Ocean.

Closely followed by the *Centaur* herself.

. . . *and* him.

He stood for a moment frowning uneasily up at the ship now towering above. The subterranean throb of a generator transmitting though her scarred plating; the steady cascade of its outboard cooling discharge, punctuated by an occasional guttural shout from the stevedoring gang on the forward well deck affording the only evidence that at least something, and someone, was functioning aboard – apart from the corrosive onslaught of time, that was. The chemical process of oxidization never rests, never snatches a watch below. Streamers of rust, great lava-like excrescences of overlapping red scale, had formed below every opening in the *Centaur's* hull. Below the hawse pipes, the rims of portholes, under her freeing ports and bulwark cappings and rail stanchions.

Hefting his bags, Kyle climbed the rickety companion ladder, careful not to rely on the illusory assurance afforded by its frayed hand-ropes, immediately experiencing a resurgence of the trepidation he'd become familiar with during his last trip in a Singh-managed ship. Even the side ladder bounced and creaked and swayed, providing not so much a means of secure access to the upper deck as an adventure akin to playing Russian roulette, only, in this instance, it wasn't so much a case of which chamber held the bullet as which rotting tread would be the one to collapse and precipitate him into the flotsam-fouled dock water below.

The fair-haired young man who blocked his way at the head of the ladder wore no epaulettes to denote rank, but his khaki drills were relatively clean and pressed while the white hard-hat, tipped rakishly forward over clear blue eyes, suggested a seamanlike awareness of the hazards of working cargo in a ship, particularly one as decrepit as *Centaur*.

'Going somewhere, buddy?'

'Unfortunately, yes – the Mate's cabin!' Kyle snapped. 'Then on to bloody India should we be so lucky as to stay afloat. What's *your* name, laddie?'

'Shit!'

'Really?' Kyle asked.

163

'No, sorry – didn't realize you were the new Mate.' The young-ster went pink with embarrassment. 'Just joined myself an hour ago. Voorhoeve, sir. Wim Voorhoeve: Second Officer.'

Kyle already knew that. But he wasn't going to let on. 'Your name hardly tallies with your accent. You American?'

'Canadian. My parents were Dutch. Live in Vancouver now.'

'Kyle.' Kyle handed Voorhoeve one of his bags. 'You've been aboard an hour. Long enough to know your way around, Mister Voorhoeve. Pilot me topside.'

'Aye, aye, sir.'

The miasma of cooking and fuel oil, mouldering wood pan-elling and unwashed sailory assaulted him the moment he stepped across the coaming. *Dammit, it does smell like the Führer-bunker must have done, at that,* he thought gloomily as he followed the 2/O through the labyrinthine accommodation. *Except Hitler didn't have to endure the added and quite unique odour of rot-ting metal.*

The Mate's cabin turned out to be the most cramped, foetid, out-an'-out filthy hutch he'd ever found himself berthed in. Apart from the insanitary state of it, this was 1940s shipboard minimalism, a joy only to a maritime archaeologist. A single narrow bunk which offered all the ambience of a coffin awaiting its lid, flanked as it was by deep leeboards intended to prevent the sleeper from being propelled across the cabin as the ship gyrated. A wardrobe barely large enough to hang an old-fashioned oil-skin, three skewed drawers without handles under a dresser with a cracked mirror, and one of those pull-down stainless-steel washbasins well on the way to proving stainless steel isn't, judg-ing by the condition of it, which appeared permanently pulled down anyway.

Tentatively Kyle prodded the mildewed ragbag of bedding, involuntarily recoiling in revulsion as half a dozen cockroaches scattered from under to seek irritably clicking refuge down the sides of a mattress betraying the unspeakable traces of drink-incontinent first mates of previous voyages.

'Mine's worse,' Second Officer Voorhoeve remarked solemnly.

'The guy never flushed the en-suite heads.'

'I don't even *have* an en-suite heads,' Kyle complained, feeling disadvantaged.

'Neither do I,' Voorhoeve said enigmatically.

'Find two sailors, a hose that works, a five-gallon drum of disinfectant an' a match,' Kyle growled. 'I'll make sure we get sleeping bags if I have to pay for 'em my bloody self.'

In the hours before sailing, things would not get any better . . .

He knocked and a tremulous voice called, '*Entrar!*'

Kyle entered, frowning uncertainly. The curtains were drawn across the forward ports of the master's cabin situated below the starboard bridge wing. God knew it would've been gloomy enough in there, even if they hadn't been.

'*Que deseja?*'

'Kyle – Mike Kyle, Captain. The new Mate.'

The dimly discerned form seated at the corner desk moved fractionally. A *click* and a red-shaded desk lamp flared. Kyle found himself looking at the Devil. The underlighting revealed sprouting eyebrows crowning glittering eyes, a hooked nose and high cheekbones. The satanic first impression lost something in presentation when Kyle realized the captain of the *Centaur* was very old indeed, and still wearing crumpled pyjamas at two in the afternoon.

'*Fala Português?*'

'Not much. None to speak of.'

'*Inglês?*'

'*Si . . . sim* . . . er, yeah,' Kyle amended hurriedly.

The captain's brows knitted in sympathy. '*Não faz mal . . .* it does not matter. We will not speak much. I am Capitão Barrosa.'

'Sir.'

'You are good seaman, senhor?'

'I would hope so.'

'I no need to hope. You see before you a king among seamen,

Senhor Kyle, an emperor. At one time men would gaze in awe as my ship she passes. They would shout "Give way, Meester: give *way* to the command of Capitão Ferreiro Cavaco Barrosa!"'

The captain's suddenly not-so-fearsome brow creased and he plucked vaguely at his stained pyjamas. 'At one time. *Muito tempo* . . . a ver' long time ago. But now I, Barrosa, am *oitenta e quatro anos* – of eighty-four years – and reduced to . . .'

His voice faded. It didn't matter. Kyle had already seen what the once great master mariner was reduced to. And even that was to be taken from him soon.

The desk lamp flicked off and the squalid gloom of the Motor Vessel *Centaur* closed around its occupant. 'New crew will be arrive from the ship office, sign Articles in saloon at five this day. We sail at threes in tomorrow's morning, senhor – *zero três horas em*, ponto. Please, you will have my ship ready?'

It was more of an appeal than an order.

'Aye, aye, Capitão,' Kyle answered.

And gently closed the door.

The *Centaur*'s chief engineer proved to be a little more forthcoming if even less intelligible to Kyle, still desperately trying to get a grip on things.

'You see I will speak Eenglish very excellent, sair. I am supporter of your Tottingam 'Otspurs . . . offside, you bustard – fukkit the ref, yes?'

'I don't really follow football,' Kyle said faintly.

Searching the ship in vain for his predecessor, he'd finally run into the Chief as he materialized, spanner in hand, from the clattering bowels of the engine room. A Moroccan of giant proportions and with a seemingly permanent twinkle in his eye, Mohammad Ben Saaidi exuded sweat, diesel fuel and philo-sophical acceptance of the ways of superannuated trampships in equal measure. Despite the coincidence of his nationality, Kyle didn't see him as being remotely connected with Wanda.

166

Oily slipper-prints would've been left all over the carpet outside David's cupboard, for a start.

'You not get handover from las' Chief Mate, sair Kyle. Last Mate, he was a dog. He skip sheep soon as when head-rope go ashore. He ver' bad man. Heem and Second Officer, who go also. Both was from Congo without sustificate papers, sair. Both dogs, sair.'

The Chief grinned hugely then, displaying twin rows of chipped porcelain teeth of which he was obviously very proud, negotiated for a knock-down price from some pile 'em high, sell 'em cheap *souk* down the *Talaa Kebira*.

'My Second Engineer, he from Haiti. He try to rat out too, but I feex heem. I lock him in hees cabin before we come 'longside; he also dog but I myself, Mohammad Ben Saaidi, am too smart for Beaubrun. I keep heem in kennel wit' junior engineers and run generators myself untils we sail, yes?'

'We'll be ringing main engine to standby at zero two thirty, Chief,' Kyle said faintly, hoping he would understand. 'You can let him out then.'

The corpse floated almost directly below them. Almost certainly that of a male, it cruised face down, arms and legs splayed wide upon the black water: a once-human starfish rotating slowly in the propeller turbulence from the Rotterdam Police launch manoeuvring close to it.

Kyle had gone straight to the bridge following his encounter with Chief Engineer Saaidi. That's where he'd found the Second Mate hanging over the outboard wing, gazing down.

'Some guy went in from the dockside, they reckon. Maybe even last night,' Voorhoeve volunteered, unable to quite conceal a youthful preoccupation with the macabre. 'One of the stevedore gang saw it bobbing around and called the cops. I've never seen a dead body before,' he added in morbid fascination.

'Lean out any further, Mister, and you'll be seeing one a damn sight too close!' Kyle snapped. But then, repeated exposure to any experience dulls the appetite. That, if nothing else, he'd learned during the past week.

A boathook extended from the launch to snatch briefly at the victim's shirt before skidding off with a splash. Sluggishly the cadaver began to capsize: left arm first, lolling in a wavering arc, and then its face coming clear of the water. Kyle found himself gripping the scarred teak rail involuntarily as, just for a moment, he became seized by a terrible fear for Hackman. He hadn't seen his prospective voyage companion since they'd parted at the station, intending to arrive separately and discreetly. Surely *Hackman* couldn't have been . . . ?

The cadaver's face was black: whether by genetic predisposition, suffocation, or the onset of decomposition, Kyle couldn't tell. He was only expert at throat-cutting. But he was pretty sure it wasn't Hackman down there. It wasn't big enough. Quite small in fact. A little rat of a man, really.

'Think he could've been one of ours?' the 2/O speculated. 'The Bosun reckons four guys have taken it on the lam from the ship so far.'

Kyle didn't have a view – but he *did* appear to have an ever-expanding coincidence of corpses determined to follow in his wake. Not that he could lay this latest, and so-far peripheral, death at the door of Stollenberg's crypt: not without some proof – or could he? *Your paranoia again? Of course it bloody is, Mister!*

Yet his sense of foreboding wouldn't be stilled. Who *was* that once-man in the water? Might he just conceivably have died because of the Nefertiti?

He forced a casualness he didn't feel. 'Logical place to desert a rust bucket like this, about to embark on a voyage to nowhere. Last port of call in Northern Europe, with plenty of bolt holes for illegals till they find it's time to move on again.'

The launch listed precariously as two uniformed officers hauled the body inboard across the dipping gunwale. One raised a laconic hand in acknowledgement to their audience while the coxswain gunned his engines and headed for the dock entrance. The show was over. Kyle guessed they would be left none the wiser about who the dead man had been, given the short time remaining before sailing. Any dockland acts as a magnet for drunks and drug addicts, the incapable, the dispossessed and the hopeless. Many such grim recoveries are made from the Europoort waterways, a large proportion never identified at all.

'Time to start on your chart corrections, Mister Voorhoeve,' he grunted, turning away from the rail. 'If, by some remarkable chance, we happen to *have* any charts for the voyage, that is.'

Talking of the drunk, the incapable and the hopeless, the *Centaur's* saloon was full of them when Kyle went down at five to begin signing on.

Deserting a hard-case ship that won't pay or feed you properly is one thing. Surviving on the streets in a foreign country without papers once you've made it ashore is another. It was clear the word had gone out to the dockside bars. Seemingly every destitute seafarer in Europoort had heard she was sailing short of crew, and had turned up in the hope of keeping one step ahead of Rotterdam's thugs, pimps, procurers and constabulary.

'Get rid of 'em, Mister Chowdhury,' Kyle growled to the Third Officer, who'd turned out to be a diminutive Bangladeshi in his early twenties with long eyelashes, an earnest determination to be the next Marco Polo and a certificate in Bengali stating he was proficient at bridge watchkeeping and navigation issued, so far as Kyle could tell, by either the Ghana Praja Tantri Bangladesh Department of Shipping or the Chittagong High School Yacht Club. Whether Mister Chowdhury was as proficient at avoiding vessels proceeding on a collision course in the middle of the ocean remained to be proved, but the grim reality was that Kyle had stopped giving a damn any more. Driven to black-humoured distraction by then, he was rapidly embracing a fatalism that would've afforded a cutting-edge Islamic Fundamentalist grave concern for his future.

169

'Get rid of them . . . yes, sir,' the miniature Chowdhury swallowed, gazing uncertainly at the phalanx of unwashed humanity confronting him. 'Now, sir?'

'Now!' Kyle snarled. 'All but those with contract notes from Singh Shipping, an' the best of the rest.'

He caught sight of Hackman then, standing ill-humouredly aside from the throng, and felt a giant surge of relief. 'Him, Chowdhury – the big guy with the broken nose? The one who looks as if he's shaved during the past week? Keep him and a few more as interviewees for replacing the AWOLs. Throw the rest off the ship.'

The odds-on favourite for being thrown ashore first, a Slavonic giant of Neanderthal mien bellowing, 'I am Badzey Myasnikovich from Belarus. I bloddy hot-shit sailor mans. I loves every officers an' I keel any mate who sez I don',', picked up the Third Officer and sat him on the servery so's he – the aptly named Badzey Myasnikovich – could move within strangling distance of Kyle, seated at the deck officers' dining table, should he be disappointed in his application.

It was the time of Third Officer Chowdhury's testing.

Kyle double-checked that the heavy chain stopper he'd brought down was conveniently to hand by his chair, then prompted, '*Well*, Mister Chowdhury?'

For a moment the hubbub stilled. Whether they understood English or not, the message was clear – the long-defunct clock in the *Centaur*'s saloon was about to chime metaphorical High Noon. Tattered foc'sle-wise hard-cases from a dozen third- and a few fifth-world nations waited tensely for Deputy Sheriff Chowdhury to make his play.

But sadly, he wasn't up to the challenge. Not without a field gun to compensate for his lack of stature. Silently, avoiding every man's eye and particularly Kyle's, the little Bangladeshi climbed down from the servery and picked a non-confrontational, hangdog course through the milieu to retreat into the alleyway.

Kyle took another turn around his fist with the chain then started to rise unenthusiastically, disappointed with the boy's having made no attempt to be an officer the very first time the chips were down, yet angry with himself at having placed the obviously ill-equipped kid in such a position.

Third Officer Chowdhury diffidently reappeared at the saloon door.

'Sorry to disturb you, sir,' he called, studiously remaining aloof from the silent jeers directed at him. 'Several gentlemen are making their way from the gangway to inspect our manning documents. I believe they are from the Netherlands Immigration Service.'

They didn't need translation. Not his last three words.

He was smart, was young Chowdhury. Smart enough even to step aside in time to avoid a stampede of abandoning wannabe sailors headed by Badzey Myasnikovich from Belarus, from trampling his slim frame into the filthy deck.

'Those with letters from Singh Shipping – form an orderly line over there. The rest of you queue here,' Kyle growled to the very few who were left.

Then he winked approvingly at Mister Chowdhury who, though of tender years and possessing a tendency to lie, hadn't taken long to work out there are several ways to skin a ship's cat.

Hackman tugged a sardonic forelock when his turn came.

Kyle stared stonily up at him, betraying no hint of recognition.

'Seaman's papers?'

'Got none,' Hackman growled, seemingly playing hard to get.

'What was your last ship?'

'A trooper. Down to the Falklands.'

'They must have given you papers when they made you a seaman.'

'They gave me a bloody gun an' made me a sergeant!' Hackman retorted unhelpfully, challenging Kyle to reject him. It was obvious the Badzey Myasnikovich incident had been the last straw, convincing him finally that his first sight of the *Centaur* was also going to be his last, an' bugger the Nefertiti.

'Know how to peel a potato?' Kyle asked airily.

'I was in the British Army, for Christ's sake,' Hackman growled and turned away, impatient to be off.

'In that case you're more than qualified for catering aboard this ship,' Kyle assured him without needing to resort to sarcasm. 'Place him on Articles, Mister Chowdhury – rate him second cook.'

He breathed a secret sigh of relief when Hackman hesitated, opened his mouth to protest further – then picked up his bag to trudge unhappily from the saloon.

But that was because, to ensure the Nefertiti's recovery, he *needed* Hackman aboard. His voyage plan called for two pairs of eyes.

His Good Idea? The one he'd referred to over that very early breakfast?

'A ship's a complex structure,' he'd explained eventually, as soon as Hackman had exhausted his whingeing over being press-ganged into volunteering. 'The statuette's hiding-place could be anywhere – under plating in the shaft tunnel, in her double bottoms, her deep tanks – hopefully we can discount a lot of them by working out the probabilities.'

'Even so, you can forget it, Mister Kyle. Everyone knows vessels are examined regularly. It'll be long gone: locked down in the Kremlin vaults.'

'If it was, the New Russians would have made the world aware of it by now. They'd have sought to gain political leverage out of it.'

'All right: stashed in the attic of some shipping ministry official's dacha on the Volga then.'

'A solid gold artefact studded with jewels? Just kept as a souvenir by some civil servant who probably hasn't been paid for three months?' Kyle shook his head. 'Anyway, the Soviets

172

weren't exactly safety-conscious about their merchant vessels. Condition surveys they carried out tended to be cursory to say the least. There'll be voids no one will have inspected during the whole of the *Yuryi Rogov*'s service under the Hammer and Sickle – and believe me: none of her more recent owners will have spent a single avoidable dollar on checking to ensure she's stayed seaworthy. It's still aboard, I know it.'

'So despite my not knowing the difference between a bosun an' a boathook, you expect me to search her from top to bottom on my own while you just drive the bloody boat?'

'Would I ask a blind man to find a needle in a haystack?'

'Probably. You and the doctor shared a lot in common when it comes to stubborn. What *are* you saying, then?'

'That you won't need to search. Neither of us will. Not when there's at least one person out there who already knows the precise spot where Stollenberg hid the Nefertiti.'

'You mean the guy who . . . ?'

'. . . beat me to Singh's office last night,' Kyle nodded grimly.

'Ah, that's all right then,' Hackman said heavily. 'I'll ask around. There's only a few million people in London.'

'He – assuming we're looking for a "he" – won't be staying in London for long. He's running out of time and opportunity. He can't afford to.'

Hackman caught his drift. 'Meaning if he hopes to score he's got to get aboard this ship of yours.'

'Ours, Hackman.'

'Of *ours*,' Hackman gritted, 'before she leaves Rotterdam.'

'More than that. Europoort's no sleepy backwater. Shoreside security's tight. He can't just walk in then walk away with the statuette without taking the chance of being searched at the gates – and there'll be too many people aboard while she's loading to risk being surprised while recovering it. I suspect he's already anticipated having to make his move after the *Centaur* sails – and that he's taken steps to ensure he sails with her, Hackman.'

'What steps?'

'I think I can guess,' Kyle said grimly. 'We'll know if I'm right when he turns up.'

He'd hesitated then, biting his lip pensively. After all, he had arrived at the only logical conclusion, hadn't he? An exercise in reasoning that even Cox of Special Branch would have approved of. So why did he feel so uneasy about it?

'Given luck and a fair wind, with both of us aboard to keep watch on him during the voyage, he'll eventually lead us straight to it.'

Which explained why he felt no surprise when the key to the mystery finally turned up at the front of the queue for signing Articles.

No more than he felt on registering the new arrival's identity. And certainly not that he was able to present a contract, date-stamped the previous day by the office of the recently murdered Jagjivan Singh, guaranteeing him a deckhand's berth on the final voyage of the *Centaur*.

Kyle knew he would come – because he knew that the man who stepped forward and calmly appraised him with those cold and unsettlingly self-confident eyes had little alternative. Not if he hoped to recover the priceless Nefertiti before the ship reached its final destination on a wreckers' beach south of Srivardhan. Kyle was also gambling on the probability that the man wouldn't recognize him.

Why should he?

The only time they'd sighted each other previously was in a frail widow's flat in Battersea. Only briefly at that, and in an entirely different context. Kyle hadn't been in uniform then, and there'd been no mention of a seafaring connection.

Yet he still found great difficulty in keeping his voice level, and his hand clear of the heavy chain secreted below the table. But he somehow contrived to, because he'd made a dual commitment to that gentle man who'd been his brother in all but blood. The first had been to clear his name while restoring his academic reputation.

The chain would only have assisted in achieving the second.

'Name?'

'Lewis, sir,' David McDonald's killer confirmed with a clarity born of his military training. 'John Lewis!'

CHAPTER SIXTEEN

It was the oddest thing, particularly in the light – or should that more properly have been the gloom? – of Kyle's earlier introduction to his reticent captain.

At precisely five bells – two-thirty in the following morning – eighty-four-year-old Capitão Ferreiro Cavaco Barrosa arrived on the *Centaur*'s bridge wearing not the heavy jersey or salt-stained reefer normally favoured by trampship skippers, but the meticulously valeted, number one brass-bound uniform of a Portuguese master mariner.

Oh, the collar of his pristine white shirt was just a size too generous for a neck wasted by the process of ageing, and his white cap, resplendent with its trim of golden oak leaves around the peak, sat perhaps a little too low over the captain's skull now devoid of all but a few wisps of hair, but the eyebrows were still kings of eyebrows – *emperors* of eyebrows. Eyebrows that commanded – no, *demanded* respect! Brows that provided topsails for eyes which had once rooted recalcitrant sailors to the deck with their authority. Which had, from boy seaman to ancient mariner, looked upon a long life-span of marine wonders and reflected the joy and the hardship, the awe and, sometimes, the fear that the sea can engender.

Or had done once upon a time, anyway; as the captain himself had so pathetically conceded. *Muito tempo*. A very long time ago . . .

'*Bom dia*, Senhor Kyle.'

'Good morning, sir.'

A subterranean explosion as a starting cartridge fired, and a shudder ran through the deck while the main engine struggled to pick up. Chief Engineer Saaidi had indeed earned his splendid teeth. A moment later and the intermittent vibration settled to a steady, if slightly asthmatic, rumble. Like that of its master, the tired heart of the once-*Yuryi Rogov* continued to beat in the service of its trade. A final eight thousand miles of steaming lay ahead for both of them and then, jointly, they would cease to be: the superannuated Capitão Barrosa and his superannuated ship. Both destined, in the actuality as well as the metaphorical sense known by seamen, to end their careers 'On the Beach'.

'Crew on standby. Singled up to head and stern lines, Cap'n.' Now *that* had provided a salutary glimpse of the coming voyage in itself, Kyle reflected wryly: inexperienced hands fumbling with unfamiliar ropes on unfamiliar, dimly lit decks to orders issued in unfamiliar tongues. 'Both anchors and cables cleared.'

'You have made my ship secure for sea, senhor?'

Kyle hesitated. 'Secure' wasn't exactly the first term that sprang to mind when referring to the *Centaur*'s seaworthiness. More a professional euphemism, really, for making the best of an impossible task – but he knew what the Old Man meant: just as the Old Man knew what he, himself, had meant.

Oh, he'd personally checked the lashings on the vehicles in their tween decks stow, and – just to be sure, because Kyle didn't know the young man's abilities well enough yet – discreetly supervised Second Officer Voorhoeve supervising the sealing of the hatches. And the young Canadian had done a creditable job considering such procedures probably only figured as theory during his sea apprenticeship. No push-button, self-closing hatch covers for the creaking *Centaur*. It had been back to heavy wooden boards manhandled across transverse steel beams, with three fingernail-breaking layers of tarpaulin dragged over each hatch square to be secured around coamings by flat steel bars and wooden wedges driven hard home. Battening down the hatches in the traditional sense of the word.

'Ship secured for sea, Captain,' Kyle confirmed.

The Rotterdam harbour pilot arrived at the head of the starboard bridge ladder, gazing about him with some perplexity that such a vessel should venture as far as the port entrance, never mind to another continent. Or that there could be men so poor, so desperate, or so indifferent to their own well-being, prepared to risk making the passage.

It would have been within the powers of the Netherlands shipping inspectorate to have prevented the *Centaur* from sailing on the grounds that she was clearly unseaworthy. But there are considerations other than absolute safety, or very few ships past their prime would ever be allowed to sail from anywhere. And many of them wouldn't anyway, if called upon to spend money to buy their release. Impounded, they'll lie and moulder unacknowledged while crews remain unpaid and often unfed, and harbour dues continue to mount, whereas a commitment by their owners to have vital repairs effected at the next specified port of call can sometimes suggest one mutually satisfactory solution to resolve the impasse – and if the vessel just happens to be conveniently diverted from that specified port of call, or sails on past it without actually entering, then both legislative and commercial constraints are still appeased.

It began to sleet, the bitter November east wind driving wet flakes to haze the orange dockside lights, causing the ill-dressed, ragged Crowd on the exposed foc'slehead to seek miserable refuge in the scanty lee of the windlass.

'*Bom dia, Pilote,*' Barrosa greeted. He didn't seem to be aware of the inconvenience of the weather, and made no attempt to shelter in the wheelhouse. Kyle watched with mounting concern while instantly dissolving cotton wool buds soaked steadily into the serge of the captain's unprotected uniform.

'*Goede morgen, Kapitan*,' the Dutchman nodded civilly. Then cocked a faintly bemused eye at Kyle as if questioning his prudence in entrusting his life to such an obviously frail anachronism.

Kyle gazed stonily back.

Kyle would never be disrespectful of the captain.

Not before they'd cleared the English Channel and left Ushant astern, with the *Centaur*'s bow rising to the first swells of Biscay, did Kyle find time to take stock. Prior to that waypoint, the demands on him as First Mate had proved many, varied, and most of them damn near impossible: not least in attempting to fit unfitted men into watches and chivvy the ship into a semblance of a ... well, once again, 'routine' wasn't quite the word to use, as routine suggests familiarity with a previous procedure whereas fewer than half of the forty-odd crewmen recruited by Singh Shipping had experience of the jobs they'd been signed to do.

On the credit side, the main engine had kept going thus far, and the power failure which blacked out the *Centaur* just as she'd entered the fog-shrouded, south-bound traffic separation lane through the Dover Strait had soon been restored when the Chief shunted demand to the only other generator still functioning. As it turned out, the crisis caused little disruption to the ship's navigation aids because most of them didn't work anyway, and, apart from a hand-held yachtsman's GPS Third Officer Chowdhury had been given for his last birthday, none of the rest were reliable – probably hadn't been since printed electronic circuits replaced glass valves.

Good kid, Chowdhury. Resourceful. *And* Second Mate Voorhoeve. To afford him posthumous due, Jaggers Singh appeared to have provided Kyle with unexpectedly competent fellow bridge watchkeepers for the passage. Without confidence in his juniors, the need to oversee them while simultaneously attempting to pursue his own hidden agenda – that of colluding with an already disgruntled Second Cook Hackman to somehow uncover the statuette – would quickly prove unsustainable.

And the captain was unlikely to help ease that pressure. A foreign-going shipmaster does not normally stand a watch himself anyway, other than to oversee the eight-to-twelve junior watchkeeper – 3/O Chowdhury, in the *Centaur*'s pecking order – and to relieve for meals. Kyle suspected that was as much support as he could hope for from the clearly declining Barrosa who had already been forced to stumble below following the Dover Strait incident, his once-pristine uniform heavy with moisture and his face grey with fatigue, skin drawn parchment-thin over numbed cheekbones after spending the night hours stubbornly, and it seemed unnecessarily, scorning the shelter of the wheelhouse in solitary defiance of the elements out on the starboard wing.

It was as if the captain had deliberately pushed himself to the limit. But to what limit? To prove he was still as able as the young – or for some deeper, even more melancholy motive linked to the *Centaur* herself, now embarked upon her last-ever voyage? Kyle didn't relish such added complication, but he couldn't rid himself of a rising suspicion that Capitão Barrosa was hoping – no, *willing* this to be his final voyage, too; and in the broadest sense of the word.

The man was eighty-four years old. He could never hope to be offered another command, not even by managers such as Singh who depend on recruiting shipmasters who not only hold certificates that satisfy international requirements, but who are also vulnerable to pressure. Among them are skippers who, because they dread penurious retirement even more than risking their lives and those of their crew, will continue to take their vessel to sea despite knowing full well that, in protecting their investment, its owners have placed as much reliance on the strength of their ship's insurance policy as its structural ability to make the next port.

Kyle had problems aplenty without adding a wistfully suicidal

Old Man to his list of disasters waiting to happen. Having had more time to think it through, he'd come to appreciate his underlying voyage plan was already flawed enough in principle without allowing for the perverse.

His original notion, that he and Hackman could, between them, hope to continually monitor the movements of John Lewis until he made his move for the statuette, had been inspired as much by desperation as practicality. For a start he, Kyle, as four-to-eight navigating watchkeeper, would be committed to spending at least eight hours of every twenty-four confined to the bridge. Hackman, for his black-affronted part, had duties in the galley during daytime hours.

On the positive side, it seemed unlikely Lewis would risk broaching the Nefertiti's cache too prematurely – too far in advance of the *Centaur*'s arrival at whichever port of call he intended to jump ship. Which meant either Naples, where they were scheduled to offload some of their Narvik cargo and take aboard more used vehicles, Port Said, while they queued to enter the canal, or Djibouti. Kyle felt it safe to assume the former Marine-turned-mariner would consider their terminal destination of Banji Beach a passage unnecessarily far.

So not only were Lewis's windows of opportunity restricted, but also his timing had to be crucial. If he did recover the artefact too soon prior to arrival, where would he then conceal it as a temporary expedient? He shared a cabin next to Hackman's with three other seamen. They lived cheek by jowl in the cramped and outdated confines of the ratings' poop deck accommodation. Lewis couldn't even be sure of hiding his toothbrush, never mind a solid gold figurine, from prying eyes.

And Naples was still almost two thousand miles distant – nearly seven days' steaming assuming, by the grace of Allah and Chief Engineer Mohammad Ben Saaidi, that the wheezing *Centaur* maintained the semi-respectable twelve knots she'd managed so far. The last day, particularly the night hours before they entered Italian waters, would mark the first period of the voyage when he and Hackman should constantly monitor Lewis's movements.

Until then Kyle intended to restrict their quarry's own opportunity to range the ship free from observation by ensuring Lewis was allocated to the same watches as himself; the downside being, whenever they had cause to be together on duty, that Kyle would have to grimly determine to mask his ever-constant rage at what evils he knew the man to be responsible for.

It was a lousy prospect, not the least his being forced to show civility to the man who'd killed his closest friend, in order to avoid courting Lewis's suspicion – but what alternative did they have? The man, albeit unconsciously, commanded the initiative. And only he would decide at which port to exercise it. They must simply watch and wait until he chose to act as a conduit for the privileged information passed to him either by his own father or by old Ted Williamson, and led them to the Nefertiti. The chances of them discovering it unaided were virtually nonexistent.

Oh, as Kyle had tried to explain to Hackman in London, he could narrow down the extent of any search to some degree by discounting those likely areas surveyed during the *Centaur*'s years as the *Yuryi Rogov*. There were also parts of ship which must have been denied to Stollenberg's retreating escort on the grounds of immediacy. The colonel's decision to hide it could only have been taken as a last-minute act of desperation, therefore it was almost certainly concealed within a compartment his men could quickly fall back to – suggesting some part of her structure above main deck level: the *Centaur*'s centrecastle or poop housing? While, unless Stollenberg's group happened to include a Waffen-SS trooper with a bit of carefree time on his hands and equally expert with welding torch or Schmeisser, the Nefertiti was unlikely to be sealed within a steel void.

So didn't that point to its most likely hiding-place being behind some material as instantly workable as wood? Some panel or sheet that could have been eased from its frame within, say, a cabin or the saloon, the old officers' smoke-room or the former apprentices' half-deck, to mention only a few, then the statuette inserted before its covering had been quickly replaced?

That was where Kyle's logic ran out, and his frustration began. The cruelly dilapidated *Centaur* had nevertheless been a product of a craftsman's age despite the material shortages of war and the subsequent development of plastic facings. Many square metres of veneered panelling or quality timber lining graced her formerly elegant interiors: mildewed through neglect now, and mostly chipped and scratched and nicotine-stained by the disregard of the seamen who had sailed in her – and almost all of its vast coverage never disturbed since she'd lain in the fitting-out basin of the Bremerhavenschiffswerft.

But where did they start on such a mammoth search? And *how* . . . with a claw hammer and pinch bar? Methodically prising off panel after bulkhead panel to explore the rusted steel voids behind, while all the time hoping no one, particularly John Lewis, would notice their mid-ocean platform being broken up before she even reached the breakers of Banji Beach?

Even attempting to communicate discreetly with Hackman, never mind collude actively with him to dismantle the ship, carried an element of risk.

Any conversation between them – which, between the Mate of a hard-living tramp and a member of its catering department, generally tends to be one-sided, colourful and pithy anyway – had to be seen as work-related or it would invite ribald speculation, the last thing they could afford in the circumstances. A ship is a hive of gossip, albeit the *Centaur*'s gossip took longer to circulate, requiring laborious translation into several languages. Kyle was acutely aware that any mess-deck rumour of excessive familiarity between a senior officer and a member of the Crowd would eventually reach Lewis's ear, and could well alert him to be on his guard.

Not that he or Hackman had run risk of compromise so far. They'd hardly set eyes on each other since their brief post-Badzey Myasnikovich confrontation in the saloon. It was the second night out before Kyle felt he dared seek out his co-conspirator.

After handing the evening watch over to 3/O Chowdhury at eight he headed aft for the ratings' quarters – nothing suspicious about that. Simply the Mate undertaking a spontaneous round of the decks. He strolled enforcedly casual along the centrecastle's dim-lit, rain-spattered alleyways hoping, nevertheless, that his journey remained unobserved.

But *did* it?

Funny. How the mind plays tricks, endows the most innocent of actions with an element of unjustified guilt. Just for a moment Kyle could have sworn eyes were following his every movement as he descended the rusted ladder to the after well deck, tracked him as he made his way past numbers four and five hatches, canvas covers gleaming under a constantly replenished patina of hissing sea-spray. Every so often a white-crested wave more boisterous than its fellows would rear above the level of the bulwark to gurgle joyfully at him before falling away – mocking his self-conscious attempt at subterfuge, his quite unwarranted paranoia. After all, he had legitimate cause to be abroad. While who else aboard would wish to expose themselves to the elements to observe the Mate's movements, when they could be snuggled up in mess deck or cabin?

Happily he didn't have far to search. He found the reluctant chef hanging over the taffrail in miserable contemplation, oblivious to the chill nor'-westerly ripping at his waterproofs. Kyle drew him into the discreet shadow of the poop housing.

If he'd anticipated a euphoric reunion he'd've been disappointed.

'You never told me I'd be stuck without my mobile bloody phone!' was Hackman's opening salvo. 'The battery's flat already an' this ship's the wrong soddin' voltage to recharge it.'

Kyle had never given such landlubberly deprivation a moment's thought until then. The need to power electric toothbrushes and sailors' hairdryers had hardly been uppermost in the minds of

1940s ship designers being bombed by the RAF every night, while any alternative generating capacity the Soviets installed later to run their sophisticated electronic surveillance kit had long been stripped out of the *Centaur*, and sold off.

'She's 110 volts DC. They all were in those days.'

'So how do I contact my RMP mates in Frankfurt?'

'Why do you need to, Hackman?'

'Because I'm supposed to be here as an investigator, Mister Kyle, an' investigating is what investigators do – not frying what seemed like three hundred bloody eggs for bloody breakfast!'

As if to illustrate the underlying cause of his discomfiture a rogue sea caused the *Centaur* to porpoise sullenly through a thirty-degree arc, masts gyrating ponderously against the wind-torn sky. Hackman muttered a choked 'Excuse me,' and hurried back to the rail.

'My fried egg was a very nice egg,' Kyle called after him. 'All crispy burnt round the edges.'

When Hackman staggered erratically back, still battling to acquire his sea legs, he was wiping bloodless lips.

'They were to suss out GsG9 for me, remember? Follow up on the connection between Wanda an' young Gunther Stollenberg's former Entsagung cell? Or are you comfortable with ignoring the fact we've still got her murder to explain?'

'Of course I'm not.'

'An' neither am I, Mister Kyle. Not comfortable at all. Especially when her killing doesn't even begin to fit into your cascade scenario involving Williamson stroke Lewis Senior stroke Lewis Junior, currently our colleague aboard this Queen of the Seas.'

'Neither did my finding Jaggers Singh with his throat cut – until Lewis turned up cool as you like with a letter from his office!' Kyle countered with mounting asperity. 'Like it or not, Hackman, we've no choice but to assume Wanda's death was down to him too, unless you can prove differently.'

Which brought them back full circle to Hackman's original complaint.

'So how do I prove anything without being able to contact anybody?'

'Well, there's no way of getting in touch with the shore if that's what you mean, other than to place a marinelink call by radio.'

'And where's the radio?'

'On the bridge.'

'Oh, that's nice and discreet,' Hackman growled. 'If I whisper, only half the bloody crew'll be able to eavesdrop.'

'Then you'll have to wait until we berth in Naples. Make your call ashore, assuming it's necessary.'

'And what does that mean?'

'Lewis might have made his move by then. Which is one reason why I'm risking our being seen together, Hackman. We haven't even worked out how we're going to handle the situation when he does.'

'We don't. Particularly if he goes for gold before we get to Naples. Let him liberate the Nefertiti, step up our surveillance and radio ahead for the Carabinieri to meet us. It's a police matter, Mister Kyle. I'm not in the business of meting out summary justice.'

'Of course not,' Kyle agreed, not meaning a word of it. But David had only been another client to Hackman.

'We've still got some time. You plan to have a stab at finding the Queen for ourselves?' Hackman asked.

'I'll look around, see if I can figure which compartments Stollenberg's SS were most likely to have headed for when they retreated aboard. But I can do that on my own. No point in risking our both being compromised.'

'Meanwhile I'm best placed to keep a weather eye on Lewis –' Hackman broke off abruptly and walked to the corner of the deckhouse, peering forward into the wind. 'It's the damnedest thing,' he said.

Kyle moved cautiously to join him. 'You feel it too, Hackman?'

'Like we're being watched?' Hackman shivered involuntarily and Kyle got the impression it wasn't merely the cutting edge to

186

the wind. 'You get it sometimes when you're keeping obbo on a suspect. Auto-suggestion. You, the watcher, being watched.'

Kyle knew about auto-suggestion. It had featured very largely in his life since he'd got himself into this macabre web of intrigue.

For a moment they both scrutinized the after end of the centrecastle, but no sign of movement could be made out against the black-silhouetted midships structure. A few pale yellow rectangles – the open galley door, the boat deck entrance to the officers' accommodation, the engine room skylights shining vertical rays of harsh fluorescence to catch the round of the *Centaur*'s tall funnel describing lazy arcs to stir the clouds blowing from Portugal.

'She's still graceful,' Kyle said softly, because he was gazing at a relic of a maritime era almost forgotten but never surpassed. 'Eaten up with cancer and on her way to die, yet she's still beautiful when the night is kind to her.'

'To a sailor, maybe,' Hackman shivered again. 'It's your element, Mister Kyle, not mine. Everything about this floating crypt gives me the creeps.'

Odd, but Kyle couldn't sleep after that. Not even when he turned in knowing he'd be roused at one bell, quarter to four the next morning, to stand his watch.

It wasn't so much the term Hackman had used, but the way he'd voiced it. Not in the dry vocabulary of the seaman, but as an outsider looking in. And a pretty hard-bitten outsider at that. Nevertheless the unease in the former Redcap's throaty growl had been unmistakable.

A floating crypt, he'd called her ... with forty-odd men already in it.

CHAPTER SEVENTEEN

The late November sun was shining bright as they came down from Ponta del Camarinal. Shortly they would begin the major course alteration to port which would take them round Tarifa and into the Gibraltar Strait.

Lewis was duty helmsman. And a competent one. From what Kyle had observed so far the former Marine, despite his training having been more military than nautical, had fast become proficient at the sailor's basic skills. Wheel orders accepted with a crisp acknowledgement, always anticipating the swing of the ship's head, never oversteering as her laden hull laboured to settle on the next course leg. The kind of man who took pride in what he did, and who would never be so careless as to overlook the need to compel a shipping agent's head forward before cutting the chap's throat.

Lewis would get a lot more practice during the coming weeks – at steering, that was. The *Centaur*'s previously erratic autopilot had irreparably failed halfway across Biscay.

'Nice morning, Mister Kyle,' he commented without taking his eyes from the compass.

'It is indeed, Lewis,' Kyle responded levelly. 'A good day to be alive, in fact.'

'Did a few tours over there when I was in the Royals, sir,' Lewis offered, permitting himself a moment to gaze at the distant Rock coming into view to port. 'Good place for a run ashore.'

'Watch your heading or you'll have another one,' Kyle countered automatically – then felt ridiculously guilty because the caution had been unwarranted.

'Naples has its attractions too,' he added by way of apology. Which made making small talk with the man seem even more bizarre, knowing that, because of Lewis's actions, four other people were no longer able to endorse his, Kyle's, previous comment on the morale-boosting properties of sunlight.

'I might just try my luck there, then.' Lewis grinned – and looked Kyle straight in the eye.

'A few miles' steaming yet, Lewis, before you get the chance,' Kyle parried blandly.

'Nine hundred and seventy-nine,' Lewis said. 'Eighty-one and a half hours at twelve knots, once we've come abeam of Europa Point. I took the liberty of glancing at the chart when I was tidying up, sir.'

'You've done a bit of navigation then?' Kyle muttered, not quite knowing how to respond.

'A bit. Just yachting.'

'Ah,' Kyle nodded vaguely, hiding behind the deep-sea man's generally patronizing view of amateur sailors.

'Was selected to help crew the Royal Navy entry in a Round the World Race a few years ago. The South Atlantic winter leg, sir – Sydney to Rio.'

Kyle was still brooding over whether Lewis had implied any challenge related to their arrival in Naples, when Captain Barrosa arrived on the bridge.

This time the captain had to pull himself haltingly up the starboard ladder, and Kyle's heart went out to him. Even more so when he saw that, once again, Barrosa had donned his ornate uniform with its splendid brass-bound cap, making no more concession to the new warmth of the sun than he had to the sleet-laden chill of the Netherlands. Only occasionally had the aged recluse benefited the officer of the watch with his presence topside since they'd taken their Rotterdam departure, and usually then in the dark hours of the night.

Could it be, Kyle reflected sadly, that he feels bound to hide his years? That he fears that he, in common with his ship, can no longer bear close scrutiny? That only by presenting himself in featureless silhouette, or dressed in clothes to remind all who see him of his former status, can Capitão Ferreiro Barrosa hope to retain some shred of the dignity he once possessed?

On previous days, morning and evening, Kyle had seized the initiative and, cajoling the routinely oil-fouled Chief Engineer Saaidi into joining him, called at the master's quarters to report progress. Always the curtains of the Old Man's day cabin were drawn, always the lamp switched briefly on to reveal those eyebrows, the dishevelled pyjamas, the hollow features of a man undoubtedly aware that he was dying and who appeared to have determined to do little, beyond his necessary duty, to delay his departure on his next and greatest-ever voyage.

Their conversations had been polite but brief. Courtesy calls, really. Kyle had no ship's husbandry matters to discuss as no topside maintenance would be carried out during the *Centaur*'s final passage east. Any consumable deck stores she'd once carried were long gone, her Congolese owners having sold off everything that wasn't welded on or bolted down before she left Narvik. Not a single pot of paint or drum of grease, coil of mooring wire or length of rope remained in the dank, rusting interior of the Bosun's locker. Even the fire hoses left aboard had proved barely adequate to wash down filthy decks, never mind attack a conflagration, spraying, as they did, from everywhere but their nozzles through a multitude of rents while powered, via leaking hydrants, by pumps that barely pumped . . . which, considering their bilge suction was also vital to the *Centaur*'s ability to survive, boded ill should her wafer-thin hull spring a catastrophic leak.

The Chief, for his part, smiled his amiable porcelain smile and assured them both that 'Okay, so my engine, she is a dog. But den, my engineers: dey is dogs too, sairs. I go to their cabins where dey are sleepings an' say "Getton watch, Dog," so dey go mumpy-face mumpy-face downs to my engine room – an' what you tink dey do den? I tell you, sairs. Dey sleeps four more hour on the control platform. But not to worry, sairs: Allah, he stand watch wit' me. Allah will provide.'

Ah, but is He good on lifeboats? Kyle wondered, thinking about the pumps again while regressing into that protective black fatalism he'd come to adopt since he'd first set eyes on the *Centaur*. Even after cannibalizing the few working parts that still functioned, and the best – or least corroded – wire falls from davits that mostly leaned drunkenly askew, he'd only been able to salvage one scarred boat he would dare to risk lowering in an emergency – and then, ideally, while alongside a harbour wall on a flat calm day.

As for the alternatives of the life-rafts they may be called upon to entrust themselves to, should the worst very possibly happen? Kyle didn't even want to *think* about having to rely on the life-rafts.

A big Shell tanker was powering towards them through the shimmer of the west-bound traffic separation channel, heading to pass down their port side. The sun stroked her trim white superstructure, causing it to gleam like burnished gold while, in the background, the Rock of Gibraltar stood silent watch over the Strait. Inshore, between them and the North African coast, a fleet of gaily-painted fishing boats out of Ceuta trawled for their daily bread.

For a moment, Kyle forgot about murder unutterably foul, and about a relic that was priceless yet not worth a single human life. About long-dead Schutzstaffeln and David's missing Hoover, and a gallant old soldier's dream that had turned into his worst nightmare – particularly if old Ted had been able, in his last split second of comprehension, to glimpse the face behind the windscreen of the vehicle bearing down on him. Kyle even forgot about the psychopathic killer of many disciplines and undeniable charm who had also ended *his* dearest friendship, yet who now stood watch with him not ten feet away, immune, for the present, from retribution.

He simply leaned beside the Captain, forearms folded on the worn teak capping of the bridge front, and gazed about him, relishing the warm Mediterranean wind on his face and the gentle rise and fall of the scabrous deck below his feet, and felt thankful to be back at sea even aboard a ship such as this.

An officer in whites appeared on the wing of the tanker's bridge as she came abeam, and raised an arm briefly in salute. A thoughtful act – and a charitable one. By her condition the *Centaur* ex-*Yuryi Rogov* had forfeited the respect she might once have attracted in the days before that young man was born.

Barrosa stiffened, became fiercely erect and returned the courtesy. For some minutes after that he remained motionless, gazing astern at the superior ship's fast-fading counter. Kyle couldn't help but wonder at what emotions had been stirred, what cobwebs of nostalgia had briefly parted in the Old Man's gloom-filled mind.

'Give way, Meester! Give *way* to the command of Capitão Ferreiro Cavaco Barrosa,' perhaps?

But only once upon a time. *Muito tempo* . . . a very long time ago.

Third Officer Chowdhury relieved him at eight. Kyle waited until the young Bangladeshi had settled in then went below for what, aboard the *Centaur*, was euphemistically referred to as breakfast. Eggs again. Scrambled, this time.

Mess-deck rumour in translation had it that in Rotterdam, constrained by the parsimonious victualling allowance budgeted for by their owners, the Chief Cook, a brooding Hungarian called Bokros, had done a deal with a purveyor of ship's provisions he'd met in a bar – a shady man of Oriental origin called Fuk Yu – to purchase a large quantity of . . . well, eggs. Chinese eggs. Rather old, heavily discounted eggs. Two thousand of them. Which, between forty-two crewmen, worked out at 47.62 eggs per stomach.

They had the consistency of rubber. They tasted like rubber. They might just have afforded the nutritional value of rubber.

Tonight Bokros, given cause for concern by the stiletto which one of the Italian greasers had held to his throat, had promised the crew could look forward to a more varied menu. A menu of choice. *Oeufs Grand'Mère*: *Rissoles d'Oeufs*: *Oeufs sur le Plat à la Metternich* . . . or *Omelette Paysanne*.

The Second Mate was the only officer remaining in the dining saloon when Kyle arrived.

'The toast's okay, sir,' Voorhoeve grinned. 'They're good at toast.'

Hackman came through from the galley and slammed a plate of greyish scrambled-something before Kyle.

'Had to keep it hot in the oven,' he chastised: a purse-lipped wifely scold. 'Don't blame me if it's all dried up!'

'It was all dried up when it came out of the pan, Chef,' Voorhoeve pointed out.

'I only *said* I could peel potatoes!' Hackman's retort hung in the air as he disappeared, wiping washday hands on his filthy apron.

'Coffee, sir?'

'Black, two sugars, no milk.'

'Just as well.' The 2/O lifted his own cup and walked to the servery. 'We've run out of powdered already.'

'Even worse, we've run out of bloody cigarettes,' Kyle growled. 'I stopped smoking at seven-sixteen this morning, until we dock in Naples.'

He tentatively prodded his breakfast then pushed the crucified monochrome eggs aside and reached for the toast and margarine. It promised to be a long voyage. Stollenberg had a great deal to answer for.

'Not wishing to pry, sir, but what made you take on this . . . challenge?' Voorhoeve asked over his shoulder. 'Sure as hell it wasn't the chow or the wages.'

'It's a long story,' Kyle said. 'Anyway, I could ask you the same thing. I looked through your discharges. You're well qualified, Wim. Did your time in Canadian flag bulkers, worked the US cruise ship trade; didn't blot your copybook, as far as I could see. Yet now this?'

'Call it taking self-indulgent time out from the rat race for command. Allow myself the luxury of seeking a little adventure?'

'Adventure?'

'Okay, putting it another way – I guess I wanted to experience an era before it vanishes altogether.' The Second Mate grinned, slightly self-conscious. 'I guess it sounds trite, but my dad was at sea before he settled in Vancouver. Dutch ships mostly. Retired as master with the old Koninklijke Nederlandsche Line. Still joshes me about what he claims were his days of proper seagoing, before containerization and loading computers an' bridge decks stacked with electronics. Three-island ships – tramps, classic freighters like this. The carriage of general cargo in open stows, he called it.'

'There's not many *Centaurs* left, that's for sure,' Kyle affirmed gravely, respect for his younger colleague increasing even more. 'You were lucky to find a berth in her.'

'It wasn't too hard. Singh Shipping were advertising for officers.'

I'll bet they were, Kyle thought. *Jaggers must've reckoned it was his birthday when you applied, Mister Voorhoeve.*

'Decent guy, Mister Singh.'

No he wasn't. He was an exploitative little man who will not be sadly missed by our seagoing fraternity! But Kyle didn't express that view aloud either. Not even for the vicarious satisfaction of referring to Jagjivan Singh in the past tense – though he didn't really think like that deep down.

'Offered to reduce his advance commission against my salary to help out,' the 2/O added appreciatively.

See what I mean? Kyle endorsed his previous lack of charity. *Jaggers even collected from both ends. From the owners who paid him fees for crewing their ships and from the usually desperate sailors he signed on.*

But it didn't diminish a son's determination to show his father what he was made of, while Voorhoeve Senior's nostalgia was understandable, too. Kyle was aware that seamen tend to be a conservative breed, particularly those hailing from the western traditional seafaring nations. Some still pine for the 'good old days' although they probably weren't. Previous generations had bemoaned much the same sense of deprivation when iron superseded wood and, subsequently, sail gave way to steam.

Mind you, young Wim could finish up getting more adventure than he bargained for. But Kyle had no intention of deriding the Second Mate's thoroughly laudable motive although, having already sailed previously in one of Jagjivan Singh's 'classic freighters', he'd more than satisfied any nostalgia he'd ever harboured. Still, once Voorhoeve had this trip in his discharge book he'd make a better ship's officer for the experience.

Always assuming, that was, the *Centaur* managed to hold herself together for the next few thousand miles to Banji Beach.

Kyle was developing a sinister feeling about that. He'd now explored several compartments within her in his attempt to anticipate Lewis's plan to recover the Nefertiti, only to discover that the exercise had proved as much anxiety-provoking as of practical help.

Because the more his seaman's sixth sense became attuned to the *Centaur*'s increasingly weary movement in a seaway, compounded by what he'd seen of her fast deteriorating structural condition, the more Kyle had become concerned that yet another contest was being waged aboard in parallel with his own.

Bizarre fancy – standard-issue paranoia? Try as he would, Kyle couldn't rid himself of the conviction that they all stood to become losers in a race which, if it did reach its grim conclusion during the remainder of the voyage, promised to prove even more catastrophic in terms of human life than the one he'd been propelled into by David McDonald's murder.

A race in this instance – or perhaps another game of Russian roulette was a more appropriate description, considering the freighter's background – between the former *Yuryi Rogov* and her faltering captain.

To decide which of them – the Old Man or his ship – would succeed in pre-empting the other by . . . well – by *dying* first?

Spectres abounded on that last night before they entered Italian waters.

Their ETA Naples, engine willing, was scheduled for late afternoon on the following day. If John Lewis did intend to smuggle the statuette ashore there, then he would have to recover it during the dark hours while the ship was quiet and only the duty watch abroad – which meant, in order to avoid suspicion, he'd be forced to act between sunset and four a.m. before turning-to again for his early morning trick at the wheel.

Yet why did Kyle sense foreboding, rather than anticipation that justice might soon be done? Why, as they ploughed steadily through the lop of the Tyrrhenian Sea with Sardinia's Cap Spartivento safely astern, did the usually imperturbable Hackman appear to share his unease?

'We *are* being kept under obbo,' his co-conspirator muttered as soon as they met at the after end of the boat deck when darkness fell. 'I know it. I feel it in my water. Someone's watching us right now.'

'Lewis?'

'No – yeah, Christ, *I* dunno,' Hackman retorted. 'He'd just turned up in the crew mess after his watch when I had to leave to meet you. Bloody ships! All ladders an' corners. He could've followed me up here an' I'd be none the wiser.'

'Sure you're not just being paranoid?' Kyle asked, shamelessly disregarding the devils in his own head. 'You said it, not me – that the mind can play tricks when you're engaged in surveillance.'

'The mind can play tricks when you're trying to punch fog, too.'

'Your mobile being down?'

'I'll be happier when I know more. Hopefully that'll be after I've called Frankfurt from shore tomorrow. To be certain Lewis is our man we need to establish some link – no matter how tenuous – between him and Wanda Inadi. It could be more significant than you appreciate, Mister Kyle.'

'In what way?'

'Because I still say if Lewis didn't kill the *girl*, then . . . ?'

'Look, Hackman,' Kyle snapped irritably, 'we've been that route already. We've got no alternative suspect, and we don't have time to waste. Just get down aft and locate the guy, then, between us, we'll watch him like hawks till the morning.'

'Suit yourself,' Hackman grumbled. 'But we're wasting our time: trust me. I've been thinking it through while creating my epicurean egg delights. Even if you're right about Lewis, he won't make his move tonight anyway.'

'*Now* you come up with a theory,' Kyle snarled, getting ever more fractious as his own conviction that they were being observed by unseen eyes ran riot. 'Explain, Hackman!'

'Common sense. If you had the choice between running the gauntlet of Italian Customs backed up by the Carabinieri, or their Egyptian oppos in Port Said, which country would *you* choose as the soft target to smuggle gold ashore?'

Kyle hadn't thought about that. But he wasn't going to admit it.

'We still wait for Lewis to make his move.'

So they waited for Lewis to make his move. Or rather Hackman did, having legitimate, albeit grudging, reason to hang around aft. Kyle simply hovered in the region of the centrecastle accommodation until Second Officer Voorhoeve's middle watch ended and it was time for a weary chief officer to climb the ladders to the bridge.

Quartermaster Lewis appeared quite unperturbed, to say

nothing of fresh as a daisy, when he relieved the previous helmsman.

But that was because he'd spent the whole night in his bunk when he might have been abroad recovering the Nefertiti.

Hackman swore to that. Quite fluently.

The barometer began to drop at just about the time when the *Centaur*'s first head rope snaked ashore.

They would remain alongside for less than twenty-four hours before they sailed again. By then, according to the Eastern Mediterranean forecast, the storm would come.

CHAPTER EIGHTEEN

Kyle had to smile, despite his anxieties, as from the lofty height of the bridge wing he watched Hackman go ashore.

The reluctant cook almost ran down the rickety accommodation ladder the instant it was rigged, he was so evidently anxious to feel dry land under his feet. They'd arranged to meet later, in a trattoria Kyle knew of on the Piazza Santorini after the former Redcap had made his yearned-for telephone contact with his mates in Frankfurt. Kyle was quite looking forward to the unexpected break. Initially he himself had decided to forgo the luxury of a run ashore and the prospect of a decent meal, preferring to remain aboard in case Lewis harboured more devious intentions. But that sacrifice had been rendered unnecessary by events. Italian Immigration and the Naples Carabinieri had seen to that.

As soon as they'd docked, two officers had taken post at the bottom of the *Centaur*'s gangway, plainly charged with ensuring that none of her crew tried to slip into the country without papers, which, considering they were berthed in the irresistibly unsavoury port area of Mergellina, would deny roughly fifty per cent of her ragged complement a night on the Neapolitan tiles for a start. As it happened, John Lewis went ashore himself a little later anyway, in company with some of the more legitimate Crowd. More crucially for Kyle, the presence of the local constabulary meant that Lewis, even had he planned to, could dismiss any prospect of returning aboard later to try smuggling the statuette ashore in Italy.

Which went to support Hackman's theory that the ex-Marine would pick the softest entry point. Logic did indeed suggest that the most likely place for Lewis *et* Nefertiti to jump ship would be the more lax surrounds of Port Said harbour – or in Djibouti, of course. But even Stollenberg's original Waffen-SS hard men would have entertained some apprehension about escorting a solid gold Egyptian Queen through the mean streets of Djibouti.

No, the crunch would have to come in Port Said which, had Hackman only argued his case more forcefully instead of moaning about being denied the use of his mobile phone, would have saved Kyle a lot of nervous anxiety. Particularly as, in a fit of virtuosity, he'd suddenly resolved to give up smoking.

All said and done he was part way there already, having been left with little option but to endure the first, and worst, three days of deprivation after the *Centaur* ran out of bonded stores. Endured them so successfully in fact that, even after they'd docked, he'd managed to fight the temptation to rush ashore immediately and plead with the permanently smoke-hazed Carabinieri to sell him one.

His resolution was not destined to last.

Kyle shouldn't have done it.

He should never have taken off so recklessly across Spaccanapoli, the surrogate raceway that separates both the City of Naples and a significant number of its inhabitants into north and south. Especially as he'd only challenged the lethal divide to do the one thing he'd sworn to avoid doing in the first place. Like buy the pack of cigarettes he'd so far denied himself.

Not that Kyle's exercising greater self-discipline regarding his approach to shopping would have changed anything. What was to happen next went more to demonstrate the fickleness, the sheer perversity, the fundamental *injustice* of fate. Events were to prove that he, instead of having run grave risk of foreshortening his life, had unwittingly contrived to extend it.

At the time he'd considered his irresponsible action a perfectly valid response to the panic felt by any nicotine addict finding themselves under stress without a crutch to hand. Kyle had tried to fight it. Even when the taxi from the ship dropped him at the Piazza Santorini he was still in virtuous denial.

Or more or less, anyway. Okay, so admittedly he *had* planned to ask the cab driver to stop en route so's he could pick up a packet. Just in case. Merely for psychological back-up, knowing Hackman was bound to aggravate him by finding something to gloom about over supper – but he didn't intend to act- ually smoke them. Or maybe just one, or two at most? And only then if his roughly three-day, thirteen-hour and twenty- two-minute-old resolve to stay off the weed became, well, temporarily unsustainable with the euphoria of seeing Hackman again.

But by the time he'd checked that Second Officer Voorhoeve harboured no immediate plans to abandon ship, had handed over the deck to Third Officer Chowdhury and left him to get on with supervising the discharge of the Narvik consignment, then called in out of courtesy to tell the captain's eyebrows and pyjamas he was going ashore, he was late in leaving for his nine o'clock rendezvous. So he couldn't afford to delay the taxi further – which created a self-defeating cycle, because his not being able to buy cigarettes after he'd decided to caused precisely the kind of stress which would previously have made him light up in order to combat it.

Either way it meant that by the time he did finally meet up with Hackman, by then impatiently pacing the kerb fronting the

Trattoria Guzzanti, Kyle's hunger had become focused almost solely on the acquisition of tobacco rather than food.

Their subsequent battle to capture a vacant table in an animated sea of patrons diverted Kyle momentarily. It was only after they'd seated themselves next to a rather attractive girl wearing a white suit, and ordered a long-anticipated bottle of wine for starters, that he began to suffer the pangs of withdrawal again.

'You don't . . . ah, happen to have a cigarette on you, do you?'

'You know I don't smoke, Mister Kyle.'

'Quite right, too. Bloody foul habit.'

The negative-tar Hackman eyed him suspiciously. 'Last night you told me you'd given up completely. You mentioned it six times on the boat deck.'

'Oh, I have,' Kyle assured him. 'I have.' Then swivelled in his chair to peer anxiously across the dim-lit, traffic-congested Spaccanapoli, trying to pick out a neon-bright vendor's sign that promised Marlboro or Lucky Strike.

As he did so he caught the eye of the attractive woman at the adjoining table and, quite unexpectedly, she smiled at him. It took him completely unawares: it had been such a precocious, blatantly inviting smile.

'I think you'd be better to concentrate on me first,' Hackman said grimly. 'On what I have to tell you.'

'You managed to get in touch with Frankfurt then?'

'And just as well I did. You didn't get the whole story from your Special Branch man. Not his fault. He'd no reason to consider it relevant at the time.'

'You're not going to tell me two Stollenbergs make a coincidence after all, are you?'

'No. For once, sir, your tendency to jump to conclusions unsupported by fact was justified. Your late anarchist, Gunther, *was* the colonel's son all right. And he did have a love affair going with the girl Inadi before he lost his head rather more literally to German Special Forces.'

Kyle frowned. Thus far Hackman's opening amounted to confirmation, not revelation. So why did he look so tense? Typical of

Hackman. Surely any intelligence he'd gleaned had to be to their advantage, and they *were* here to briefly unwind as well, dammit. The omens for a good night ashore were positive. A bottle of wine on the table. A proper meal to relish without an egg in sight. An unusually balmy evening for winter despite his sensing, in its Judas caress, a forewarning of the coming storm; even the fact that doe-eyed, anonymous women had suddenly begun to smile at him. Really, all he wanted now was the pleasure of a single cigarette to complement it, though, to give Kyle his due, he still tried very hard to fight the urge.

'Does this new information concern Lewis?'

'Damn right it does.'

. . . only a couple of minutes, that's all it would take. To nip across the road and do business, so to speak, with the nearest tabaccaio.

'We've got a problem with Lewis – a major one –' Hackman broke off resignedly, surrendering to Kyle's chemical dependency. 'Look, Mister Kyle, just go an' buy some before I start, will you?'

'Some what?' Kyle contrived a look of innocent mystification.

'*Cigarettes*, for – !'

Kyle rose, feigning reluctance. 'Now you mention it, maybe I will. Just in case. Back in a tick.'

'Cross that bloody road without looking and you won't be back at all,' Hackman called cryptically after him. 'Sailing again tomorrow, even after what I've just found out, will be the least of your worries.'

Kyle nearly turned back there and then. What had Hackman learned from his Frankfurt connection that, by implication, suggested an increased threat when they returned aboard the *Centaur*? What, in particular, had he discovered that concerned John Lewis?

Yet he didn't turn back despite that parting shot from Hackman. Because he had an ominous feeling he was about to need a cigarette more than he'd ever done before; but he did cross the road much more hurriedly than he would under less stressful circumstances, and bought the bloody cigarettes. Had actually returned safely, albeit shakily with the discord of infuriated motor horns still ringing in his ears, to the trattoria kerbside when . . .

Well . . . *that* was the moment when the injustice he would brood upon so many times over the coming months decided to reveal itself.

The real irony was that Hackman, for his part, had probably been convinced that Kyle's two-pronged determination to kill himself – whether slowly by the repeated inhalation of noxious substances, or summarily by single impact with a motor car driven by an Italian – had been calculated to infuse Death with a sense of urgency. But Hackman could hardly have anticipated that Death's response would be so random. For a start, the statistical odds were stacked heavily in Hackman's favour. He'd proved himself to be a more prudent man by nature, who didn't take people at face value without seeing their credit card, who took exception to being aboard ships that threatened to sink, who probably looked both ways at every kerb, stoutly resisted jaywalking across arterial highways and didn't even smoke.

That was what made subsequent events fly in the face of logic.

When Hackman, rising with faintly bemused relief to make space for Kyle to squeeze back in his chair, abruptly diverted his gaze to the middle distance somewhere behind and to the right of Kyle – and looked utterly perplexed instead!

Just before the first bullet hit him.

Thus proving, beyond argument, that mortality statistics are only a guide to, and not an absolute guarantee of, longevity.

Kyle, engrossed in threading a zigzag, multi-apologetic return course between the closely packed tables, didn't even realize it *was* a bullet for a few moments. Or bullets. Altogether there must have been eight or nine squeezed off.

Come to that, Kyle never even registered anything sounding remotely like shots: only the staccato yammer of one of those two-stroke Vespa scooter things accelerating from the pavement fronting the trattoria to merge seamlessly with the exhaust-hazed traffic gauntlet he himself had just run.

He hadn't even turned to spare the wretched contrivance a glance. The sight of a scooter being employed as an aid to procuring suicide on the streets of Naples is hardly unique. The departure of what did, admittedly, seem a particularly noisy one was rendered even less notable when, for no evident reason, the suddenly sag-jawed waiter ahead of Kyle chose the moment to decant a plateful of *Tacchino in Carpione* on to an elderly diner's lap, a woman started screaming, and panic apparently became *de rigueur* on the Piazza Santorini.

'Bloody Italians!' Kyle reflected uncertainly. 'Typical Neapolitan overreaction to a waiter's clumsiness.'

Which wasn't really fair considering, by then, that Americans and Brits, Germans and Heaven knew what other nationalities were diving just as volubly for the illusory cover offered by overturning tables, flimsy chairs or, in the case of the more pragmatic, the prostrate bulk of whichever adjacent patron had been terrified enough to make it to pavement level before them.

Though Kyle might have been excused such racist misapprehension in the circumstances, because what was taking place around him *did* take a bit of hoisting in. It seemed that, within minutes of his catching up with his mentor in the art of skulduggery, a waiter had committed the ultimate professional sin; fifty-odd suppers had been brutally interrupted; Hackman had been catapulted backwards with two bullets in his chest, and that the one ally he felt he could trust implicitly had, while mirroring the hopelessness that assailed him on viewing David McDonald's body, ceased to be, well . . . anything at all.

The pretty woman at the next table may have been more Neapolitan streetwise than Hackman. She'd tried to make a run for it when she'd seen the Vespa draw up. Only she ran the wrong way. Now her body huddled very close to Hackman's. She wore delicately chased gold earrings, shell pink lipstick and that neat white suit – white apart from its underside, that was, where blood was still accumulating sluggishly, and in a second area oddly reminiscent of a flower motif where another round had entered just below her left breast.

Capillary action creating scalloped patterns again, of course. Kyle was becoming quite proficient at recognizing the blood absorption properties of various materials. The carpet around Wanda's cupboard and the crew list lying before Jaggers Singh had already afforded textbook examples for comparison.

'I know her,' the captain of the Squadra Mobile said. 'She comes here often. Usually others pay her bills.'

'Others?' Kyle muttered numbly.

'Men, signore. She is – was – a local *puttana*. A prostitute?'

'Why, for Christ's sake?' Kyle asked.

'Attractive. Good legs.' The Captain shrugged. 'Jobs are hard to find in Napoli.'

'I meant why would anyone ashore here want to kill *Hackman*?'

The Squadra Mobile officer eyed him more in forbearance than with the innate curiosity one might have expected from, say, a policeman like Cox – or Hackman himself. 'Two persons are dead, three seriously hurt. The others are all native Napolitani as far as we know. What makes you think your English *capitano* was the target, signore?'

'Cook,' Kyle corrected, slightly put out by the officer's assuming Hackman had been of superior rank to him but, more crucially, intuitively steering away from the question. Having been a merchant seaman all his adult life he'd learned not to say more than was absolutely necessary to foreign policemen, particularly when the mind is rendered sluggish by shock. 'Hackman was our Second Cook, not the captain.'

The fine difference was too subtle to attract more than another shrug.

'For that matter you were here too. The bullets must have

passed very close. Maybe you should feel lucky they didn't use a grenade, eh?'

Kyle didn't feel very lucky. He didn't miss the inference either.

'They?'

'Our world-famous Camorra.' The officer managed to inject a sardonic shrug. 'Or the NCO – the Nuova Camorra Organizatta, signore. For years they have been at each other's throats to control the drugs market, the extortion, the protection rackets.' He indicated the devastated piazza, the ambulances, the blue flashing lights of Squadra response cars still handbrake-parked at melodramatic angles to the kerb. 'We will investigate, but I suspect this will prove to have been a warning to other ristorante owners paying protection to the wrong side. Next week they will offer their dues to both families, and with renewed enthusiasm.'

Kyle wasn't so sure about that. While content to go along with the officer's assertion that this blood-bath had simply resulted from some local Mafia initiative to improve their cash flow, he knew instinctively that Hackman's death *hadn't* been caused as a result of criminal infighting, and that, if anyone was lucky, it was the Squadra Mobile captain himself. He'd never heard of SS-Standartenführer Stollenberg.

Or of a certain very able seaman, for that matter. Currently enjoying an unsupervised run ashore somewhere in this same city?

Although, once again, Lewis had proved he wasn't infallible. As with the gas trap that didn't quite explode in David's flat, he hadn't quite managed to achieve his objective this time either. Not only had he failed to take out both of his watchers but he'd failed to pre-empt his exposure as a serial psychopath – any lingering doubts Kyle had previously harboured about the ex-Marine had been dispelled by Hackman himself in the minutes before he died. Lewis had clearly been fingered by the Redcaps in Frankfurt as having some involvement with what lay hidden aboard. *Damn right it concerns Lewis*, Hackman had growled with what, at that moment, had seemed quite unjustified apprehension.

So even while he found himself labouring yet again to make headway through what had become a routine fog of disbelief, his initial resolve to give nothing away was firming – Kyle had no intention of bringing Lewis to the Carabinieri's notice. Justice Italian-style would be too civilized and take rather too long to implement. Much quicker, much more satisfying aboard ship where the nights were black and the sea discreet in its reception.

A Carabinieri helicopter arrived to flail, seemingly aimlessly, over the area trying to identify one rider on a scooter out of maybe a quarter of a million in the greater Neapolitan metropolis. It reminded Kyle of the house fly – the charnel house fly in the mortuary that had captured his attention when viewing David McDonald for the last time. *As ineffectual as that small creature, you are*, he thought bitterly, frowning aloft without really seeing. *As impotent as any insect hovering over dead animals.*

Hackman and the woman gazed up at the helicopter too, even more uncomprehendingly. On an impulse Kyle stooped to retrieve a table napkin fluttering in the increasingly blustery foretaste of the coming storm, laying it ever so gently over the once-precocious Lady In White's upturned face before turning to blink down upon Hackman's still faintly petulant expression while experiencing a sense of loss far greater than he could ever have imagined only a week or so ago. Slowly, reluctantly, he drew a second makeshift shroud to cover Hackman's features too.

'Can't you move them, for God's sake?' he snapped. 'At least cover them properly. Afford them *some* dignity?'

'Soon. Immediately the pictures are taken,' the Squadra captain promised awkwardly. As if on cue a photographer interrupted with a terse *'Per favore!'* and Kyle was shepherded aside to relive an Identikit scenario to that played out by Cox's scenes-of-crime team in David's flat. Piloted brusquely clear of bloodstains and left to watch as the Neapolitan police camera created a stroboscopic barrage of flashes bouncing from white stucco walls.

The captain, obviously feeling the pressure of playing macabre host, fumbled in a tunic pocket. 'Perhaps a cigarette, signore?'

Automatically reaching for one, Kyle suddenly remembered. Stayed his hand as the true irony of his deliverance dawned.

'Gave 'em up three days ago,' he heard himself explaining. Or more apologizing in a way, to Hackman – attempting to justify his inadvertent desertion of the killing ground only minutes before, when he'd excused himself briefly to play tag with Fiats while Hackman waited safely to get shot. 'Found I couldn't cope with being ashore without a pack handy. Just in case something *really* stressful happened?'

The captain appraised the contorted subjects of the lensman's art with a somewhat quizzical eye, lit a second one and passed it, butt-foremost, to Kyle. They stood side by side, Kyle drawing hard yet with strangely little satisfaction as a black van arrived to disgorge two sombre-suited undertakers.

Presumably contracted by some minor Carabinieri official on commission, Kyle reflected sourly, thoroughly disillusioned with Italy and Italian restaurants, *from the local Pompe Funebri who, in turn, pays the Camorra a level of protection geared to the increased volume of business they generate.*

He'd chain-smoked three cigarettes and tasted none before the now familiar shiny chrome-skeletoned stretchers miraculously expanded and green plastic body bags were unfolded with measured ceremony.

But then, the moon shone bright, while the boisterous precursors of the coming weather front were still pleasantly warm and – apart from the shooting at the Trattoria Guzzanti – it was a lovely night in which to appreciate Naples.

There was no hurry.

CHAPTER NINETEEN

Something else died on the Piazza Santorini that evening, in company with Hackman and the pretty woman.

Kyle's capacity for emotion.

He'd ceased to feel anything at all by the time the Italian police, after taking his witness statement, finally returned him to the crumbling *Centaur* in the early hours. No grief, no burning rage, no fear or even casual concern for his own survival – not even hatred for the man who had obviously intended to eliminate him too, along with Hackman, and who, having betrayed his hand, must seek any opportunity to try again during the coming voyage before being free to turn his attention to the statuette.

But Kyle himself wasn't entirely disadvantaged. Next time he would be waiting. Once the first shock subsided he'd had time to consider his new challenge. From now on he wouldn't be constrained by uncertainty, inhibited by what had proved to be a futile subterfuge to remain an anonymous observer.

Untrammelled now by emotion, Kyle simply harboured a flat resolve to see the nightmare through to what had to be its bloody conclusion, accepting as a matter of fact that one of them would never reach Port Said. He would make sure of that, even if Lewis didn't. Because the rules had changed. From now on he was more fitted to make it a straight duel between dispassionate equals.

The Obsessive versus the Psychopath.

Even so, there were many riddles unresolved, and many more raised by the events of the last few hours. As Kyle wearily climbed the swaying accommodation ladder while the Italian police talked in low tones below him, he was still wrestling with the questions raised by Hackman's callous assassination. A sort of time-and-motion analysis of a murder, albeit one that didn't quite fit.

How, for instance, had Lewis managed to achieve being in the right place at precisely the right instant? He couldn't have known they'd intended to meet at the Trattoria Guzzanti – or even guessed they'd intended to meet at all, for that matter. The ex-Marine had gone ashore with others of the crew after Hackman but *before* Kyle himself, yet he'd turned up, booted and spurred for killing so to speak, within minutes of Kyle's arrival in the taxi. So how, in that short space of time, had he contrived to acquire a Vespa scooter, a black-vizored rider's helmet and a machine pistol? Okay, he'd proved himself resourceful, his military training would have made him so. He could have stolen the wheels and the hat – but surely not the weapon? And he hadn't taken one ashore with him: the presence of the Carabinieri at the gangway would have precluded that. Every crewman leaving the *Centaur* during the previous evening had been searched to ensure they weren't carrying the basis of a survival kit that could facilitate their jumping ship in Italy.

The old inclined-to-act-on-impulse Kyle would have charged straight aft and challenged Lewis – had it out there and then with David's murderer, and one or the other of them would almost certainly have failed to survive the confrontation. But not the new Kyle, the coldly dispassionate Kyle. Because he wanted the Nefertiti more desperately than ever to extract some good from this catalogue of slaughter – to restore McDonald's reputation as a researcher in the eyes of his peers, if for no other reason. And to enable that sad ambition, he *had* to allow Lewis his head.

Or should that be enough rope. To hang himself?

Which would have been a splendid aspiration if it didn't take him back to square one – no, even further back than that. His whole strategy to find the statuette had been compromised, his hidden agenda in sailing as Mate exposed. The killings on the Piazza suggested that Lewis had known all along why the two of them were aboard – must, after all, have recognized Kyle from their previous brief meeting at Mrs Williamson's – and, stripped of anonymity and unsupported by Hackman, how could he hope to continue tracking the already prewarned AB's movements in the crucial days before their Egyptian landfall?

Suddenly Kyle felt very much alone.

Second Officer Voorhoeve was waiting for him at the head of the ladder, having relieved Chowdhury as cargo officer at midnight. As with the floating corpse in Rotterdam docks, the Canadian's expression revealed a mix of excitement at finding himself on the periphery of such an awful event, and evident regret for its victim.

'Hackman. The cops say it was Hackman,' he greeted wonderingly. 'Jesus, you couldn't help liking the guy for all his complaining.'

'Two bullets in his chest make it pretty bloody obvious *someone* didn't, Mister Voorhoeve!' Kyle snapped before he could stop himself, then felt angry with himself for all his determination to abandon sensitivity. The 2/O could hardly fail to be touched by the sudden death of one of their own as, it appeared, were others of the Crowd, though only Heaven knew why. The gravel-throated Hackman had fed them the lousiest scrambled eggs in maritime history, while totally ignoring one half of them to snarl ferociously at the rest – and they were hardly a close-knit complement anyway. Nevertheless Kyle could see many of those who would normally have been asleep, even some of Saaidi's engineers, gathered in a group on the after well deck, silently observing the constabulary comings and goings.

'Sorry, Wim, that was uncalled for,' he retracted. 'Anyway, the Carabinieri don't seem to think it had anything to do with who or what Hackman was. There were other casualties. A local woman was killed too.'

'Scuttlebutt has it the Mafia were involved.'

'Something like that.'

'And that you were there as well, sir. That you could have been taken out too?'

'I needed to buy cigarettes,' Kyle said as if that explained everything. Which it did, in a way. Only the fact that he'd been jinking around tables on his return had taken him clear of the line of fire. 'You got the gangway book there?'

'It's okay. They're all back aboard, those guys the cops allowed ashore. Three sheets in the wind, most of 'em. Only made it up the ladder on hands and knees.'

'I didn't ask you to interpret the damn thing,' Kyle snapped, teetering on the edge of volatility. 'I want to see it.'

'Sorry, sir.'

The book showed that Lewis had not only gone ashore at 18:45 in the company of two of the European seamen and the Chief Cook, Bokros, but he'd also returned with them, logged back aboard at 01:34. Hackman's death had occurred shortly after nine – plenty of time to consolidate a predictably reliable alibi in the interim, Kyle observed grimly – a preliminary spell of hard drinking in Mergellina's seedier tavernas and John Lewis's companions would've been seeing double or even treble shipmates anyway – belt and braces insurance in case the Carabinieri failed to swallow the gangster wars scenario. He didn't see any point in risking compromising himself further by questioning the others. The former Marine could have taken an hour or so out to go manhunting while they wouldn't have noticed anything out of place had Vesuvius itself erupted.

Hackman's signature had been hastily scrawled in the *Ashore* column at 18:20. The column beside it was still blank. It would always remain so.

'Guess I'd better report to the Old Man,' Kyle muttered, completely lost about what to do next. More the old Kyle than the new, really.

Voorhoeve's response was rather more circumspect this time. 'The police came to see the captain an hour ago, sir . . . I, ah – think he went back to his bunk right after.'

Kyle forced a smile. 'Which shows he's a pretty smart captain.'

Or a man gradually succumbing to the exhausting task of living. But he didn't say that to the second officer.

'Guess I'll leave explaining myself till morning then,' he decided, turning away. 'I'm going below. Any problems with the loading, shake me.'

'Aye, aye, sir.'

He'd stepped across the coaming into the lobby when Voorhoeve called hesitantly after him.

'Mister Kyle?'

'Yeah?'

'Glad you're okay, sir,' the 2/O said awkwardly.

Kyle swallowed with difficulty, and all the emotion he thought he'd forfeited until then welled up inside him. Oh, it wasn't Voorhoeve's engagingly naïve appreciation that got to him. Not even his tightly bottled-up sadness for Hackman. It was because, in the shadows etched by the halogen deck lights the Second had looked and sounded so much like David McDonald while offering that self-conscious declaration of camaraderie.

'Glad you're home,' had been the very last words ever spoken to him by the man he'd looked on as his brother.

Kyle had never forgotten smiling into the shipboard phone on that cold dark morning in London, feeling all happy and warm inside.

'See you later,' he'd promised.

Although, of course, he never did.

Not alive, anyway.

The breakfast eggs prepared by a hungover Bokros were marginally more palatable but infinitely less welcome than Hackman's offerings. Kyle ate them anyway. He had a feeling energy was going to demand a premium during the coming days, and for once his unease had nothing to do with the legacy of a Schutzstaffeln colonel.

The fluttering tablecloths of the Trattoria Guzzanti had been right. That morning's weather forecast for eastern Mediterranean waters was appalling – a massive winter depression centred over the Bulgarian mainland beginning to move slowly south through the Aegean. Early-edition Italian newspapers brought aboard by the stevedores bore front-page pictures of storm damage already caused to the islands of the Cyclades, and the west coast of Turkey. The weather pattern was as exceptional as was the *Centaur*'s ill-fittedness to meet it. If the front maintained its current course and speed, that event was due to take place somewhere between Cape Spartivento and the Libyan coast north of Marsa Susah.

Kyle didn't want to be aboard when they did. The Mediterranean in winter can be a terrible place for the best found of ships when the climatic processes run amok . . . not that he was surprised to learn they would be heading into a sea area where the isobars on the synoptic chart were practically leap-frogging to compete in emphasising the likely strength of the wind. So far everything else on the bloody voyage had gone pear-shaped for him!

And for Hackman, of course.

Especially for Hackman.

Any secret hope he'd cherished that the *Centaur*'s sailing might be delayed until the storm had passed was dashed soon after breakfast when the Carabinieri declared themselves satisfied the Piazza killings had been a commercially sponsored affair, a Camorra-inspired accident which, no doubt, some officers would pursue to the last lira. And anyway, if every vessel that lost a crewman by violence in a seaport like Naples were to be detained until the culprit was apprehended, then the oceans would be even more empty and the demand for lay-over berths impossible to cope with.

It meant Kyle now found himself faced with two competing priorities, both involving life-or-death courses of action. To hurriedly devise an alternative strategy to deceive Lewis into leading him to the Nefertiti's hiding-place despite the ex-Marine having ruthlessly proved himself aware that he, Kyle, *was* trying to trick him – which, without Hackman, hardly seemed possible – and, simultaneously, to exchange his avenger's helmet for his Mate's cap in order to prepare the decrepit *Centaur* to meet winds possibly gusting in excess of eighty knots.

The latter challenge being utterly impossible.

Not without replacing her frames, hull plating, upperworks, main engine and captain anyway.

It was during that lowest point of black deliberation that Kyle suddenly halted his growing inclination to surrender to the malign influences so patently marshalling against him, pack his seabag and ring down full ahead both legs for *l'Aeroporto di Napoli*.

Because it occurred to him that there *was* one last desperate initiative open to him that would, at least, restore the status quo in respect of Lewis, his only dilemma then being: did he have the moral right to pursue it? Could he be so calculating as to place yet another man's life at risk for his own now-obsessive pursuit of Stollenberg's bloodstained legacy?

He decided he would follow his instinct one last time. Okay, so his instinct had usually proved wrong so far, but there didn't seem a lot of point in being dispassionate if you weren't prepared to be, well . . . dispassionate?

And, anyway, looking again at the close-coupled isobars

building between them and Egypt, the bloody ship was still likely to kill more of her complement than any intrigue aboard her.

'*Jesus,*' Second Officer Voorhoeve muttered disbelievingly when Kyle ran out of breath.

'You said you wanted adventure,' Kyle pointed out.

'I'd kind of figured part of the deal would include living long enough to boast about it afterwards, sir.'

'You will if you're careful,' Kyle assured him, which was a pretty extravagant promise really, considering that, strictly speaking, it offered a guarantee against the worst that both John Lewis and the anticyclone could do. 'This time the element of surprise can only work against him. He won't even know you're backing me up till we've got him.'

'Jesus,' Voorhoeve said again. 'Lewis, huh? Of all the guys aboard you might expect to be capable of cutting a throat.'

Phrased rather more perceptively than Voorhoeve realized, Kyle thought uncomfortably, remembering the horrible manner by which Jaggers had met his end. Pressed for time to try and recruit the Second Mate, he'd only told him about David's subway death, how it broadly related to the statuette concealed aboard, and how Hackman's shocking demise from the plot had resulted from underestimating Lewis. He hadn't risked confusing the issue by bringing in Wanda or Old Ted, nor even Jagjivan Singh.

But recalling the scene of butchery in Jaggers' office suddenly made Kyle realize the enormity of what he was doing. By his own admission, the second officer had never been in closer proximity to death than audience to a flotsam cadaver in Rotterdam. He'd no real concept of what the most engaging of human beings could do to another when madness overcame compassion. And without awareness of the consequences, Voorhoeve could well prove fatally complacent.

'Look, Wim, on second thoughts I've no right to involve you.

If you'd rather forget it, then walk away. Lewis won't even know we've spoken.'

'Oh, I'm in.' Voorhoeve grinned, the youthful excitement in his eyes a bit too gung-ho already for Kyle's liking. 'Between us we'll watch the guy like hawks, Mister Kyle.'

'More to the point,' Kyle cautioned anxiously, 'make damn sure Lewis doesn't watch *you* like a hawk. And don't even think about tackling him yourself. Any move we make, we make together. Believe me, he's animal cunning – and he's a killer!'

'Watch and report: take no action. Aye, aye, sir. But like you said, it'll still be an awfully big adventure.'

Kyle forced a grin. 'That's too British for a Canadian to make up. You've read *Peter Pan* too.'

'Avidly. At ten years old he was my hero.'

Kyle's grin switched off the moment the younger officer turned away.

Not avidly enough, it seemed.

To die will be an awfully big adventure, was what Peter actually said.

Even while ensuring that the fore-end cargo had been made secure against anything the weather could throw at them, Kyle continued to feel guilty at having exposed Voorhoeve to a level of risk that belied the guarantee he'd given. But he sensed it was too late to retract his appeal for help now. He'd have to shoot the ebullient wannabe adventurer before he could stop him.

Jesus, he wished he hadn't picked that particular analogy!

The existing brigade of Djibouti-bound Mercedes in the forward tween decks was being reinforced by the last of a battalion of battered Fiats when he finally arrived on the after well deck. From what Kyle had seen so far, the 2/O and Chowdhury between them had done a creditable job, aided by the somewhat mixed seaman skills of the Bosun's gang, including – Kyle forced himself to observe with equanimity – AB Lewis. Dammit, Lewis even glanced up at him through the open hatch square on cue, and smiled acknowledgement, almost as if letting Kyle know how aware of being watched he was. That he'd sensed he was back under surveillance.

Kyle nodded curtly. Even knowing he had the advantage of the man again, he couldn't bring himself to smile back.

Come to that, smiling was hardly at the top of his agenda despite noting that, already, everything not close-stowed in the partly filled holds, any deck item that threatened to move in a violent seaway – even the massive kedge anchor secured under the break of the poop – had been doubly lashed with extra wire cannibalized from the redundant derrick topping lifts.

The trouble is, Kyle thought uneasily, craning over the coaming of number five to peer down, *that the ringbolts and eyes themselves, and even the supporting pillars they've been lashed to, have corroded to a fraction of their original design strength.*

'We will survive the storm, Senhor Kyle,' the voice behind him said quietly. Only to confute the assurance somewhat by qualifying, '*Se Deus quiser.*'

If God wills it?

Kyle turned. The captain was observing his concern with . . . was that a faintly quizzical eye under the sprouting brow? If so it was the first sign of normality Barrosa had revealed since passing Gibraltar. Kyle's reporting to the Old Man earlier on the circumstances surrounding the loss of a ship's cook had generated little more than a shrug of the pyjamas, a '*Não há remédio,*' and the switching off of the light.

An economical requiem for a man's life. *Não há remédio.* 'It can't be helped.'

Yet now, less than an hour later, Barrosa was up and about, shaved and spruce and even dressed more appropriately as a working shipmaster in black trousers and slightly rumpled shirt, albeit he still wore – not that Kyle would have denied him such a hard-earned privilege – his most splendid cap of golden leaves.

'I'd still feel easier strengthening His hand with good seamanship, sir.'

'You are frightened, senhor?'

The question was matter-of-factly put. It was not meant as an insult.

Frightened? Bloody right I'm frightened! Kyle thought. *Oh, not simply by the weather, which is an accepted hazard of my trade, but by what I feel in my bones is going to happen in the next few days or even hours, when all the terrible portents surrounding this voyage come to pass. The end of Hackman's life has already come about. There are five options left for Death to choose from. John Lewis's or my own or – God forbid – the rather too naïve Voorhoeve's now. Yours, Capitão Barrosa, as you have seemingly willed despite your occasional confused rally into youth – or your ship's. And should that latter event be precipitated with the exquisitely cruel whimsy I witnessed on the Piazza Santorini, then all of us are lost. All of us stand to die – and most of us shall.*

Se Deus quiser?

'I'm . . . apprehensive of what the forecast holds for us.'

'Good. I would not wish a chief officer who is – ah . . . *complacente*?'

Complacent – me? Kyle reflected grimly as Barrosa suddenly swayed, and stretched to grasp the coaming for support. *Rest assured, Capitão: with you in such distress, a crew composed of lubberly misfits, a co-conspirator whose role model appears to be Peter Pan, and a homicidal maniac running loose aboard, complacent is what I am not!*

Particularly when, as if to justify his silent observation, a flake of rust the length of a boathook broke away from the edge of the weather-protective coaming under the slight pressure of the Captain's faltering hand, to shatter like glass across the equally corroded deck.

In addition to the psychological jousting aboard, there now began a game of meteorological cat and mouse.

Which tends, by definition, to bode ill for the mouse.

They sailed with the depression chasing them all the way down to the toe of Italy and through the Straits of Messina. When, during the latter part of the middle watch the *Centaur* wallowed through an easterly arc to shape a new course to pass Crete, so did the periphery of the low. Despite their still skirting only the edge of the storm, that first night out was as black as tar while the frayed signal halyards above the bridge began to thrum like guitar strings under the pluck of the wind the moment they cleared Melito di Porto Salvo to lose what scant shelter the Italian mainland had provided.

As Kyle's morale continued to fall, so did the barometer.

When dawn broke, all colour had been lost to the world.

It was hard to avoid concluding that the cat was preparing to pounce.

The question was – which cat?

CHAPTER TWENTY

Kyle remained on the bridge after Third Officer Chowdhury came up to relieve him at eight. He felt he had little choice. The still inexperienced youngster was obviously nervous, as much, Kyle suspected, because of the responsibility he was about to assume on behalf of others as for any perceived threat to his own life.

The Old Man, for his increasingly ineffectual part, hadn't been seen since Messina but, so far, the ship herself had coped well. Although the easterly wind had increased to a full gale, with the wave lengths becoming longer and the faces steeper and the crests beginning to break into streamers of white foam, only occasionally did the *Centaur* bury her head into the dark grey rollers bearing down on her through the lowering visibility.

It went to confirm Kyle's earlier view that the old lady's sea-keeping qualities presented little threat. For over four decades as the *Yuryi Rogov* she'd proved herself eminently capable of riding out the weather's excesses on her Cold War journeys around the oceans. She would have been overwhelmed years ago had her hull design been in question. And Kyle had doubly satisfied himself that the distribution of her current cargo complemented her inherent stability. No, the *Centaur*'s continuing to live long enough to meet death by cutting torch, as opposed to death by catastrophic ingress of water, would only be determined by what little remained of her structural integrity.

And luck.

Maybe you should feel lucky, signore, the Squadra Mobile captain had said.

Thinking of the speed with which the barometer continued to plummet, signalling that the predicted hazard to the ship was becoming ever more imminent, and of Lewis now free to wander below with only the worryingly vulnerable Voorhoeve to monitor his movements while duty increasingly compelled Kyle to assume command in all but name: remain topsides as the captain preoccupied himself with dying . . .

He should feel *lucky*?

Kyle really couldn't, for the life of him, imagine why.

He found himself still tied to the bridge as noon approached. That made it doubly ironic that, of all the sailors aboard, the one man he would dearly have liked to keep him company was John Lewis.

But in the last hour the wind had climbed clear through Beaufort Scale Nine and was nudging Storm Force Ten. Now the troughs were ten metres deep with the waves carrying long overhanging crests and the foam streaming down their black-fluid faces as dense white rivers with minds of their own while, every so often, a rogue tumbler as big as a two-storey house would rear out of the surface spray to port or starboard of the bow and hang – a thousand tons of malice – before collapsing with a roar over the foc'slehead, rumbling and exploding across the antiquated hatch covers of numbers one and two until the ship could shake itself free from the medium that was trying to kill her. Each time she'd shied away, rolling and porpoising, and each time the eight-to-twelve watch quartermasters brought her back on course, but they'd been struggling.

It was for that reason only that Kyle wished for Lewis at the wheel. Because he was the best helmsman in the ship and he had the knack of anticipation. Just as he'd proved he could out-think Kyle and Hackman, so he offered the best chance to out-think the sea. There's a way to steer into a wave that softens the blow. It's not so much experience as a gift and seldom, in a well-found vessel, is it tested past destruction. But in an old ship like the *Centaur*, where every frame is already weary from the onslaught of a billion waves before, and every hull plate as fragile as the carapace of a crab, the skill to placate a monster rather than confront it head-on can prove a skill as precious as the lives that depend on it.

Kyle stayed his hand from calling Lewis nevertheless, and it had nothing to do with the Nefertiti or the savage hatred he felt for the man. He knew from the still falling glass that they weren't even in the worst quadrant of the storm yet and that, when they did suffer its full force, it would be John Lewis's time to take the wheel while he had the energy to stay there for what promised to be a very demanding spell indeed.

Three things happened simultaneously as the hands of the chartroom clock moved to twelve midday to signal the change of watch. The first was an inevitable event, the second a most feared event and the third was a . . . well – a sort of *non*-event?

Firstly came the arrival of the lowest and – please God? – the last of the low pressure fronts, announcing its entrance with a wall of torrential rain and screeching wind and an undulating blanket of continuous spray ripped from the tops of the waves.

The second was the arrival of a particularly malevolent sea. The *Centaur* hesitated, reared before its onslaught and, as her forefoot plunged down into the trough with the near-solid lumps of water flying back to explode against the wheelhouse windows themselves, gave a great, tired shudder while a dull, boom-ing tremor like a distant peal of thunder transmitted through her deck.

Which should have provided more than enough crises without the third and final event that occurred on that stroke of noon.

Or rather, that *didn't* occur.

When Second Officer Voorhoeve, who – while he may well have felt it his extracurricular duty to keep a hawk-like eye on Lewis during his watch below, should *still* have reported to relieve the exhausted Third Officer Chowdhury topside – simply failed to arrive at all!

Strangely it was Barrosa's abrogation of responsibility that drew the fire of Kyle's resentment in that frightening moment when everything that hadn't already gone wrong started to go wrong.

I knew it: I bloody knew it – he's going to die on us! he thought numbly, furious with the captain. *He's down there glooming in his cabin, working towards his end-game and going to bloody die an' win his race against the ship even though, judging by the way that glass is falling, such bizarre determination promises to finish up a damn close-run thing!*

But Kyle couldn't be blamed for thinking like that, because it did make sense in a nonsensical kind of way, even if only to the mind of a very tired and fractious Mate and the increasingly frustrating target of his ire. The more Kyle had thought about the Old Man's eccentric behaviour, the more he'd come to realize that the only thing left to Capitão Ferreiro Cavaco Barrosa was his past – his pride in having been a master mariner. But a master mariner who loses his ship other than by an act of war also loses his reputation. There are always those, particularly those unqualified to pass judgement, who will say he should have steered this course instead of that, he should have anticipated even the most exceptional hazard, been more prudent when exercising the arts of seamanship.

Whereas if the sequence is rearranged – if the ship loses its captain *before* the captain loses his ship then those who would criticize might find their criticism blunted. 'Ah,' they would be more charitably inclined to say. 'I remember Barrosa. A fine seaman. Had God not taken him just as he prepared to face his greatest test, then perhaps his ship would not have foundered after all.'

Well, the Old Man wasn't going to get away with it. No way was he going to be allowed to die merely to contrive a satisfactory last paragraph in his obituary. He would have to be dragged from his refuge if necessary, to take charge of the bridge and allow Kyle opportunity to explore below – because he, *Kyle*, had a hidden agenda as well, dammit! Although his had more to do with statuettes and corpses and fulfilling his promise to David, it had suddenly become desperately pressing now when linked to Voorhoeve's otherwise inexplicable failure to report for watch.

Apart from which he had to be given freedom to pursue his day job and try to identify the source of the tremor that had run through the ship. Because judging by the sound of it, everything else could well prove academic.

'Can you look out for us up here while I go and check nothing's come adrift, Mister Chowdhury?' he shouted above the banshee wail of the storm. 'Can you manage on your own for a while, lad?'

'Yessir!' Chowdhury said, drawing himself up and managing a smile.

'I'll have the Captain come up.' Even then Kyle, a stickler for place, would not bring himself to criticize the Old Man to a junior. 'The helmsman's doing well. Just let him keep her head to the weather and stay by his shoulder to keep his spirits up.'

The ship fell off another mountain.

The thunder boomed again.

The Third Mate gave up trying to smile bravely.

Kyle gave up being reassuring.

He snarled 'Ohhhh, SHIT!' and began to run for the cork-screwing internal stairway to the officers' accommodation.

She felt different.

Only subtly so. But enough for him to sense the reluctance in her to rise to the next sea. Weary, she felt. Half a century and more weary. A momentary pause before her fore end lifted, and a fractionally longer pause before it expressed downwards again to bring up violently into the next trough.

As if she also knew the end game had begun between her and Barrosa. As if Kyle's resentment at the captain's ploy to divest himself of blame was duplicated by the *Centaur* herself – and why not? So far as Kyle was concerned, the concept that she might feel such outrage didn't seem at all odd. As far as he was concerned, anyone who considers a ship merely to be an inanimate fusion of steel and wood contrived by man without the inclusion of a soul – anyone who thinks like *that* has no more knowledge of ships than those who . . . well, than those who, while they desperately love their pets, still can't bring themselves to believe that dogs and cats go to Heaven.

So of course the *Centaur* was hurt and angry and resentful. She'd come thus far towards her place of execution as docile as a lamb, hadn't she? And wasn't Capitão Ferreiro Cavaco Barrosa the man who had been charged with the task of taking her there with dignity? Who should have recognized that she deserved a good last voyage because she had done *her* duty with stout heart for generations of masters before him? Yet who now, because he was old and unhappy and it suited him, was prepared to turn his back on her during this, the time of her own greatest test?

The rumble came again, but punctuated by another sound clearly detectable to Kyle insulated from the cry of the wind. A metronomic banging: roll to port – *clatter*! Shudder to starboard – *crash*!

A cabin door near the foot of the stairway – the outer door to the Master's quarters. It had been left ajar but freed from its cabin hook to close, to swing open, to slam closed! Yet what kind of man could compose himself to die, and forget to close the door?

Despite being desperately concerned by then with a subterranean threat promising to be a thousand times more destructive than any unsecured fitting, Kyle couldn't prevent himself from lunging to stay the heavy door's momentum as it began to swing again. But in that moment of automatic response his gaze encompassed the cabin's interior just as the captain's permanently drawn curtains swung briefly away from the scuttles, permitting a fleeting grey beam to fall across the corner desk. Then the ship rolled back to port – even more sluggishly, this time – and the storm-light was instantly quenched. But not the scene that Kyle had registered in that macabre moment.

That still remained imprinted on his consciousness.

Not indelibly imprinted, which would be to overly dramatize the incident. But certainly for long enough to make the hairs on his neck begin to stand on end.

The next time she rolled to port she hung for rather a long time indeed. So much so that Kyle feared for a terrible moment that he would lose his fingers. He found himself actually trying to walk uphill into the cabin with the heavy, still-unsecured door tilted over him and threatening to slam down and against him, which, considering his right hand was gripping the frame knuckle-white to restrain him from tumbling helplessly backwards down the length of the athwartships corridor, would have severed all four fingers with surgical precision, just above their second distal joints.

Happily for his future well-being – if, indeed, he had any to look forward to now because the *Centaur* was showing every indication of preparing to sink – she came back up again to an even keel and he managed to hook the door back before proceeding into the master's day room, compulsively drawn to confirm what he thought he had seen.

Only to discover that he really had.

The below-decks ventilation trunking that ran vertically behind the captain's desk had subsequently been panelled over by her German builders when the *Yuryi Rogov* was being fitted out in the Bremerhavenschiffswerft in 1945. Because several such runs of galvanized ducting had been incorporated into the ship at that section – all of it now rusted and discoloured by age – they had framed across the entire span of the bulkhead leaving voids between each run; voids which, in depth, roughly accommodated the span of a man's fingers, always assuming, that is, he still *had* fingers after passing through the door they'd fitted at much the same time.

Or alternatively, could accommodate the base span of – say – a priceless three-thousand-year-old golden statuette?

Kyle glimpsed all that in the instant the curtains swung as the ship rolled again. Took it all in before the near-darkness closed around him once more. He knew it because someone had levered one section of mahogany panelling from its frame to expose the detail behind, although the bit about affording space for a statuette was still only presumption – if the Nefertiti ever *had* been concealed in there it was gone now. All that was left was the splintered panel itself: casually propped against the captain's leg . . .

The captain's *leg*? As in the leg of Capitão Ferreiro Cavaco Barrosa?

Oh, he was there as well. Sitting in his chair before the desk as he'd done throughout practically the whole of the voyage so far. And very smart he looked too, with his brass-buttoned reefer and his broad rings of gold braid and the magnificent eyebrows complemented by that absolutely splendid oak-leafed cap, tilted forward at a more jaunty angle than ever before.

Almost as if he'd been preparing himself to leave his cabin for the bridge, to reassume command of his ship. To shepherd her through her last great struggle. Just before . . . ?

Kyle couldn't be angry with the captain any more. Because he could see, now, how wrong he'd been in his cruel assessment, and that it hadn't been the Old Man's wish to die that had kept him down here in this sombre place of refuge for a grievously ill man. Because when it came to the pinch, and he'd realized his ship was in dire distress, he'd obviously tried very hard to come to her aid.

Only he hadn't been permitted to.

It seemed the reason for Barrosa wearing his cap at such a dashing angle was because someone had forced the old seaman's head violently forward and down to his chest.

In the instant prior to cutting his throat.

CHAPTER TWENTY-ONE

Kyle didn't have the slightest doubt about what had taken place within the last few minutes. And what hadn't.

For a start, Barrosa hadn't killed himself.

But then Kyle, being well versed in that particular aspect of criminal pathology, knew all about how to prevent the main arteries of the neck from retreating to seek anterior refuge behind the protection of a victim's windpipe. It was the kind of technique any dedicated psychopath would very quickly learn to adopt after having fluffed, say, their first attempt at serial killing. Because clumsily ramming a boning knife up and under a raven-haired Arab girl's throat must have precipitated quite a sharp learning curve – trying to keep Wanda quiet to avoid attracting the nearby Ringtree residents' attention during her death-throes.

Not that they'd have paid any bloody attention, mind you. Kyle still felt aggrieved at the way David's neighbours had totally disregarded his saving their lives, even though all he'd done was to turn off a gas tap and smash a window.

Still, silencing her must have entailed dragging her naked, perhaps still flailing and plucking at the skewer in her throat, from the bedroom where, according to the theory of Cox of Special Branch, she'd expected only to make love, heightened no doubt – because they must have been very sick lovers – by the adrenaline of risking discovery after one or other of them had killed David McDonald, then forcing her into the doubly soundproof cupboard.

Suddenly it all made sense to Kyle.

Or more or less, anyway.

Because it still didn't explain *why* she had been killed. No more than how John Lewis had come to be associated with Inadi or Abdeljalil or Whoever in the first place. Because hadn't Wanda's association with Stollenberg been through the colonel's son, Gunther – a connection severed years ago when GsG9 disconnected Gunther at source? Or could Hackman have discovered, through his Frankfurt contact, that some link between the girl terrorist and Lewis had also existed at that time? Certainly he'd intended to tell Kyle *something* about the former Marine immediately before the Piazza attack. *Damn right it concerns Lewis*, he'd growled in that sadly missed gravel voice of his.

Jesus – was that a muffled *shout*? Carrying through the open and, hopefully, safely hooked-back door to the master's adjacent night quarters?

Kyle snapped out of his frozen deliberations which, while they may have appeared a luxury in circumstances where a minute's delay could mean the difference between survival and dying, could only have taken seconds of real time to flash through his mind because the *Centaur* hadn't even recovered from her last sluggish roll yet. Always assuming, of course, she was ever going to.

Silly, really: the consequences of shock. How Kyle found himself muttering a polite 'Excuse me,' to Capitão Barrosa as he eased past the dead mariner before striding hastily down the still starboard-sloping deck to the open door – at which point he halted again.

In even deeper shock.

*   *   *

232

Two men were fighting in the gloomy confines of the captain's sleeping compartment, or more wrestling, really, grunting and locked together while both tried to gain possession of what appeared to be a gun.

One of the contestants in that obviously life or death struggle was Second Officer Voorhoeve; the other, Able Seaman Lewis. And Lewis was undoubtedly winning – already he had firm grasp of the gun butt, a Glock machine pistol Kyle vaguely remembered from pictures he'd seen, though he was better informed on throat-cutting than shooting people – and was gradually twisting it against the Second Mate's desperate counter-grip to turn the muzzle under Voorhoeve's chin.

Rather in the manner he'd killed Wanda. Much of a muchness, really. A boning knife, a Glock machine pistol . . . both ruthlessly efficient and both a damn sight more dangerous than those buttercups Kyle and David used to hold under little girls' chins to see if they loved them.

The ship remained as she was, lying over to starboard with a good ten-degree list. And the two men remained locked in combat as the barrel veered nearer and nearer to the point where even a gentle squeeze would blow the top of the suddenly not-so-gung-ho Second Mate's head off. And Kyle, for his part, remained transfixed in the doorway, unable in that fateful instant to move – not even to save young Voorhoeve.

Simply staring into the cabin at the glittering artefact protruding through the neck of what appeared a very old, waxed-canvas bag now casually discarded on the captain's bunk.

But then, rather like SS-Standartenführer Stollenberg must have felt in the Führerbunker half a century before him – it *was* the most exquisite man-made object that Kyle had ever seen.

The explosions catapulted Kyle back to reality, deafening in the confined space. The gun must have been set to automatic because more than one bullet was fired. The burst buried itself in the deckhead leaving a livid velocity burn up the side of the 2/O's cheek.

'For Christ's SAKE!' Wim Voorhoeve appealed to him, hand trembling under the strain of fighting for a few more seconds of life.

'Stay away!' Lewis shouted. 'Keep *out* of this, Kyle!'

'It's a bit bloody late for that!' Kyle roared back, all the hate, all the anger he felt for the man who had destroyed David McDonald welling to the surface.

He lost control then. Lunged to grasp the bag containing the Nefertiti and swung on Lewis with a red, murderous haze enveloping him, a terrible rage for what might have been. Lewis saw it coming – now *his* eyes were wide as Voorhoeve's as he tried to draw back. '*No,* Kyle. You don't understand!'

But Kyle did. Only too well. A multiplicity of corpses, an agony of tightly bottled grief had led him to.

The statuette was heavy. Much heavier than Kyle had anticipated. And the ship didn't help much either, corkscrewing and plunging as she was. When he swung the Nefertiti at Lewis's skull the bag tended to flail rather than describe a precise arc. The resultant imbalance contrived to deflect his aim slightly, the initial and most satisfying impact absorbed by the former Marine's shoulder before catching him on the side of the head – but it was enough.

Lewis went down in a heap with Voorhoeve on top of him while the machine pistol skittered into a corner. Kyle was dimly aware of raising the Nefertiti to strike again, but then the red haze faded to pink, and a wave of revulsion swamped him and he knew he couldn't emulate Lewis and simply kill a man in cold blood. And he felt rather glad to have made that discovery.

He peeled the canvas back to expose again the golden treasure still clutched in his hand, and thought how truly beautiful it was. And how utterly valueless. Because it hadn't been worth a single one of the lives it had cost so far. He tossed the bag back on the berth.

The ship thundered down below again, and lay over another two or three degrees with no sign of recovery. Either she was taking in water or there had been a massive shift of cargo. Whichever it was, they were still making way, which suggested all was not lost and that, even if there had been a hull failure, the sea hadn't yet reached the engine bed plates. There was still a chance the pumps could cope but Kyle knew he had to get back to the bridge because she was his command now and she needed all the help he could give her.

He helped Voorhoeve to his feet and said, 'Sorry, Wim, I have to go,' then frowned at the unconscious Lewis, not quite certain of what to do with him now it was all over. 'Maybe you should find something to tie his hands, huh?'

He picked up the Glock, found the firing mode selector, slipped it to safety, then handed it to the dazed Second Mate. No point in taking chances. It was an awkward shape; he was damned if he could figure how Lewis had managed to smuggle it ashore then back aboard again, in Naples.

'Just in case he wakes up before you do,' he offered dryly.

The Second Mate took the gun and stared at it wonderingly.

'You do know how to use it?' Kyle added anxiously.

'I think so,' Voorhoeve nodded.

'Good man.'

Kyle walked uphill past the captain and retrieved the key from the inner face of the day room door, reinserted it on the corridor side to ensure the lock worked, then went back to Voorhoeve. He'd done as much as he could to help the 2/O, who was obviously still shaken: Peter Pan meets Psycho.

'Lock the bastard in here to make doubly sure,' Kyle said. 'That door's solid mahogany under the paint. No way will he break through it even if he's in any condition to try. We only let him out if things get worse.'

The *Centaur* shuddered then, and the ever-present vibration transmitted through the deck by the plunging screw died away while the steady hum of the cabin blowers faded. It became very quiet.

The main engine had stopped.

'Bugger it,' Kyle supplemented, trying to act cool in case the Second Mate panicked. 'Things just have.'

Voorhoeve gingerly explored the powder burn on the side of his cheek.

'Not for me, they haven't.'

Kyle wasn't entirely convinced of that, not even in the short term. Not judging by the way the eggshell-plated *Centaur* was already beginning to wallow and pound as forward motion came off her.

'All the same, come up to the bridge fast as you can,' he confined himself to saying. 'As soon as you've finished down here.'

'That won't take long,' Voorhoeve said calmly.

Then he thumbed the Glock's fire selector catch from safety through single to automatic again.

The ship sighed even further to starboard. The free-swinging curtains, usefully substituting as makeshift inclinometers, indicated she was now carrying a good fifteen degree list, and Kyle suddenly became very nervous indeed. But not about the prospect of drowning. Not any longer.

More about the prospect of not being permitted time to.

Before he'd even begun to react to what, seemingly, was turning out to be the first correct conclusion he'd bloody well drawn since he'd come aboard, the Second Mate raised the barrel of the machine pistol in line with Kyle's chest.

It was surprising really, how philosophical Kyle became. Maybe because it was ended. Maybe because he was sick and tired of seeing people die, and having to debate the insoluble over and over again.

'You killed McDonald, didn't you, Wim?'

'Doctor McDonald,' Voorhoeve quite properly corrected, obviously feeling better.

'And Hackman. It was you at the trattoria, wasn't it?'

Not that Kyle needed to ask. He'd worked it out by then, given one more piece of the puzzle. It had all been a matter of rank. How the gun had been smuggled ashore and brought back aboard again without discovery.

'The Carabinieri didn't search you either, Mister Kyle, only the sailors. Guess they didn't think it appropriate to frisk any officer going shoreside.'

'While you could risk not signing the gangway log because you'd be the duty mate charged with checking it anyway?'

'I *was* only ashore for just over an hour,' the Second Mate submitted in mitigation. 'I made a special point of getting back in time to relieve Chowdhury.'

Lewis groaned and started to come round. Voorhoeve got a little jumpy then and the gun barrel wavered dangerously between them. Hurriedly Kyle blurted the first thing that came into his head, silly as it was.

'Your dad's hardly going to be proud of you, Wim.'

'Oh, I don't know,' the 2/O mused. 'Military men tend to take a more understanding line when killing has to be done. Not that he's ever likely to learn about this, I mean – who's going to tell him, sir?'

Kyle purposefully avoided the implication. And anyway, he'd just been given other cause to frown. 'Thought he was a merchant service master?'

'Who?'

'Your *father*, for Chri—!'

'Oh, shit, I forgot.' Voorhoeve grinned then. An apologetic, boyish grin. But so chilling – so unutterably mad it scared whatever the hell was left in Kyle clean out of him.

'Sorry, but that was a lie. The retired Vancouver sea-dog stuff? My real old man died a long time ago – not that I gave a damn. I'd cleared out as soon as I was old enough.'

Gradually it was coming together. What Hackman had been prevented from warning him of. The last and, frankly, overlooked factor. Oh, sure: the information the former Redcap had received from his contact with GsG9 *had* concerned Lewis – but only in a negative way. Essentially advising that Kyle had mis-read every clue, had been watching and waiting for the wrong crewman to make his bid for the Nefertiti.

Painfully, Lewis began to haul himself upright, sagging back against the captain's berth. Blood plastered his hair but otherwise he seemed okay. He didn't look all that pleased, though.

Voorhoeve jerked the gun Kyle had so obligingly returned to him, and suggested considerately, 'It was hardly worth your standing up, Lewis.'

Ever so diplomatically Kyle tried to change the subject. It recommended itself as the most prudent course of action in the circumstances, even mindful that the ship promised to sink at any moment. His nails were digging into his palms with the effort of it, though.

'Tell me about your father, Wim.'

'A stiff, resentful man from what I remember, sir,' young Voorhoeve said with a frown. 'Never forgot what he'd been. Always proud of it. A lot of them were like that. A lot of his generation, despite what they did.'

'What he'd been?'

Not that Kyle needed to ask. Not any longer. He looked down the barrel of the gun, and listened to the ship labouring, and waited to die one way or another while thinking how unnecess-ary it had been for the fair-haired young man to adopt a Dutch surname to explain his accent after he'd run away to sea. The North American drawl had become flawless through serving his apprenticeship in Canadian ships.

The second officer's German proved just as impeccable. Not entirely surprising, considering he'd been born one.

Probably a little bit later than his brother, Gunther. But just as crazy.

'A colonel in the SS,' Wilhelm Stollenberg confirmed, finger almost casually caressing the trigger. 'Waffen-Schutzstaffeln Standartenführer Manfred Stollenberg, sir. Sekunde Regiment, SS-Polizei-Panzer-Grenadier-Division.'

CHAPTER TWENTY-TWO

If Kyle temporarily disregarded the certainty that Stollenberg the Younger was about to shoot them, it was the courtesy that he continued to show that was so menacing. The polite deference. The engaging smile that warmed you to him but which, once you'd looked hard enough, betrayed not a shred of human emotion.

A worthwhile recommendation to include in any learned work on criminal pathology in fact, he mused. *First consider the amiable assassin. It makes it so much easier to manoeuvre into a position to cut a person's throat once you've persuaded them to think they like, and trust, you.*

Admittedly the quality would have proved superfluous in David's case. Just an impersonal push from a fellow traveller had been all that was needed. Similarly the deaths of Hackman and Old Ted had been distanced from personal involvement – you aren't required to form a trusting relationship with every vehicle that approaches before it can kill you – but Wanda had certainly taken to him on the rebound from brother Gunther. Too damn right she had!

And Jagjivan Singh. Who must have seen such a sea-wise volunteer as a gift from the god of shipping agents when Wim turned up at Shipskull Lane that night. Knowing how Jaggers operated, he could very well have tried to negotiate an extra commission instead of being a benefactor as previously claimed. Might even have tried playing the long game, insisted he'd already committed the second officer's berth to some other unfortunate sailor, self-servingly hoping to reserve the eminently hireable Voorhoeve for rather longer-term exploitation than a one-way voyage to Banji Beach. Either way he'd made a big mistake. The kind a chief executive officer only makes once. Otherwise Wim wouldn't have felt the need to kill him to facilitate substituting his own adopted name, supported by his own genuine documentation, on the *Centaur*'s crew list.

Or maybe he would have killed Jaggers anyway, simply because Stollenberg was a homicidal psychopath who felt no sense of moral responsibility, no guilt for anything he did, and eliminating one more human being in his pursuit of his father's legacy hadn't meant anything more to him than squashing a particularly irritating fly. Afforded positive benefit in fact, if it helped bloody the investigative waters further.

Odd though. How the originally selected 2/O had failed to join in Rotterdam. But then again – was it really so curious? Considering the man would have been expected to report aboard not long before that waterlogged corpse had been recovered from the dock.

A sea exploded under the *Centaur*'s bow. Kyle sensed the shock transmitting through her length as she reeled and groaned, and his heart went out to her for the agony she was being forced to endure. And to young Chowdhury, left alone up there on the bridge without his support.

'She's not got long,' Voorhoe . . . *Stollenberg*! – said, and picked up the Nefertiti. It was awkward, feeling sideways to pick up the bag, but he managed one-handed without allowing the barrel of the Glock to waver one millimetre.

He still looked as agreeable as ever. There wasn't an ounce of malice in the young man. Or any other form of emotion.

As he backed carefully up the incline to the night cabin door Kyle could actually see his finger whiten: absorb first pressure on the trigger.

'Guess it's time to go, huh?' the youngest – and, in Kyle's increasingly jaundiced view, hopefully the last of the Stollenbergs said quite matter-of-factly.

Well, that did it. That *really* did it for Kyle – gun or no bloody gun! All the stress, all the frustration, all the pent-up rage exploded in him because there were still too many questions, too many loose ends.

Apart from which, no bloody way was he going to put up with such summary dismissal by a junior!

'Don't you *dare* walk out on me, Mister!' Chief Officer Kyle erupted uncontrollably. 'I haven't bloody finished with you yet!'

You could have cut the stunned silence that ensued with a boning knife.

Even Lewis blinked apprehensively at the fury of Kyle's response, whereas Stollenberg positively froze before the verbal assault.

'Sir?' he blurted, visibly stiffening in shock, cheeks suddenly ashen.

Not, perhaps, that such a reaction was as surprising as it first seemed. Wilhelm Stollenberg may well have held the Teutonic disciplines in contempt but he was still genetically programmed to respond to them. In addition, all the youngster's shipboard experience had trained him to respect authority, particularly the authority of those seafarers with more gold rings than he.

In short, for a second mate to shoot his chief officer while in full flow calls for a quantum change in attitude, and that's hard for any psychopath to achieve when, by definition, they don't have an attitude in the first place.

'You owe me explanations, Mister,' Kyle roared, absolutely spitting mad by then. 'You'd be dead by now if it wasn't for me, laddie. You . . . you wouldn't even have that bloody *gun* if it hadn't been for me, dammit!'

'Calm down, Kyle, for Christ's sake,' the still groggy Lewis opined anxiously. 'It's my luck you're pushing, too.'

'An' you can jus' stay *quiet*, Lewis!' Kyle rounded on the former Royal, evenhanded in his volatility if nothing else. 'You've caused enough bloody trouble on this trip already.'

He did swing back to Stollenberg rather more judiciously though, appreciating he really had to try and get a grip, constrain himself from going right over the top and dying without ever knowing.

'Go on then. Tell me why you killed the girl,' he snarled. 'Why kill Wanda Inadi or whoever she was, an' – as much to the bloody point, Mister – why leave her in my cupboard?'

The 2/O's face cleared. Was *that* all? He seemed relieved that a perfectly logical explanation appeared all that would be needed to get him off the disciplinary hook.

'Because she wouldn't change her mind, sir,' he offered as though it was the most reasonable motive in the world for murder. 'And besides, I wasn't to know it was your closet, was I, Mister Kyle? You hadn't actually come on the scene then, if you'll remember?'

Another massive sea took the ship and smashed her briefly upright. They could hear the distant thunder of green water cascading off her decks, followed by the unmistakable scream of rending steel.

Lewis muttered a shaky '*Jesus!*' but Stollenberg didn't even appear concerned. He was even crazier than Kyle had thought. Anyone with a glimmer of sanity would've squeezed the trigger in that moment and launched into an Olympic sprint towards the nearest life-raft before his and Lewis's bodies hit the deck – but Kyle was damned if *he* was going to point that out.

'What do you mean – she wouldn't change her mind?'

'About Gunther.'

'Your brother? What about him?'

'I liked Gunther, you know. Even after running out on the old man I never lost touch with him.'

Not till he got his head blown off by GsG9, you bloody didn't, Kyle

242

eflected savagely, *because he was a menace to the German State and every citizen of it, persisting, as he did, in the Stollenberg family tradition of killing innocents.*

But sensing he was winning, if such all-too-temporary triumphalism could be applied to his current situation, all he actually said was, 'Yeah, I'm sure you were very fond of him – so what wouldn't Wanda change her mind about?'

And that's when it all poured out, in a flood of crippled logic positively begging Kyle's approbation. Or was young Stollenberg's tormented submission as close to a plea for absolution as any mind devoid of guilt could get?

Whichever it was, time itself appeared to become suspended for the fair-haired killer. While the deck canted further as the bones of the surely-breaking-up ship grated together and it became more and more evident that they were making water; and while steel plate screeled against corroded steel plate as the fracture they could now hear clearly in her belly lengthened even more; and while Kyle and Lewis endured what could only prove a very short reprieve with hard eyes and even harder hearts because they had both lost a loved one to the monster, Stollenberg didn't hurry in the least; seemed anxious only to placate his chief officer's wrath by explaining how such terrible recent events had been brought about.

Which only went to prove that the secret of the second Nefertiti hadn't been the only inheritance Manfred Stollenberg left to his sons – or rather to big brother Gunther in the first instance, being the only son who remained.

A terrible madness had been his real legacy. The genes of an insanity which, ironically, the colonel himself appeared to have evaded, for whatever atrocities the gallant Standartenführer may have committed in the name of the Führer, his only proven crime, it seemed, had been a misplaced devotion to duty.

Though he must have paid doubly for that in the end. A man of his pride? Watching his sons turn their backs on the ordered world of Nazism he'd fought so hard to bring about.

*   *   *

It had begun with a dream, according to the amiable confessional of Wilhelm. A dream shared by the anti-establishment lovers Gunther and Wanda soon after the *Yuryi Rogov* forfeited the protection of the Iron Curtain.

They dreamed that recovery of the Nefertiti could achieve what all the bombings and shootings and kidnappings they'd committed in their pursuit of anarchy had so far failed to do. Because the violent pair saw the artefact, not as a thing of wonder to be cherished but simply as a political instrument. Were they to hold one of Germany's greatest ever pre-war treasures to ransom under threat of destruction, then the ideological pressure they could exert on the State would be much more effective than any bomb they might plant in the Bundesbank.

Which was actually sound thinking on their part, although others may have viewed the statuette's potential a little differently. As a bargaining counter for criminal extortion, for instance? Because one doesn't have to be a political fanatic or an academic to be attracted by the challenge of resurrecting such a priceless possession. David McDonald would undoubtedly have been conscious of the wider threat that option posed. It helped explain why he'd been nervous, and justifiably so. Especially if he'd discovered rather more about the Stollenbergs than his abruptly terminated call to Kyle had allowed him time to tell.

Like the existence of a younger brother, Wilhelm – deep sort of chap, ran off to sea when he was a kid, disappeared from sight long before the rest of the Stollenbergs passed away – who only later learned of the existence of the artefact when Gunther shared Dad's legacy in a moment of togetherness.

Wilhelm hadn't thought much about it at first. More intent on pursuing his first love of being a seaman, he'd had little time for Gunther's political fanaticism, although he'd retained a deep affection for his brother despite thinking him a bit unstable – a real wild card – until the madness in him began to take hold as well. Didn't even think it odd that Gunther appeared to feel no guilt, no responsibility for those he'd killed and mutilated in his revolutionary zeal. Ultimately Wilhelm, too, reached a stage where it had only required a push to send him over that same line that separates the psychopathic from the homicidal.

And that point came when the lovers' dream ended before it could be realized; because, once Gunther had been officially blown away, Wanda had found herself left with a secret but not the knowledge to capitalize on it. Being a hairdresser in the Fulham Road or a terrorist with a mediocre track record hardly qualifies you to know much about ships. She was aware that the *Yuryi Rogov* was still afloat but not how to exploit the fact.

But happily there *was* one person she was familiar with – had been overly familiar with, in fact, on a couple of earlier occasions while Gunther was out blowing people up – who was not only eminently suited to help, but was bound to be sympathetic to Gunther's ideals.

So Wanda contacted Brother Wilhelm – or Wim as he was popularly known by then among his shipmates, having become a Canadian of ostensibly Dutch extraction – and suggested an alliance between his sea-wise abilities and her subversive skills.

One of the first things Wim Stollenberg, being a prudent seaman, had done when he met up with Wanda in London had been to evaluate the risk of his prospective voyage into intrigue. He'd visited the Imperial War Museum. Oh, not to research his father's myth – he knew all about that already – but more to research the researchers: discover who else, if anyone, had shown recent interest in the Stollenberg convoy that might compromise his own immediate plans. As Kyle had suspected, it was through the IWM that he'd learned about David and followed him on that last morning of his life from the address he'd been so helpfully provided with, to Lancaster Gate underground station.

Resolving their conflicting interests in the Nefertiti hadn't presented a moral dimension at all. One coldly deliberate push had been enough to send David over the edge of the platform, and Second Officer Wilhelm Stollenberg over the edge of sanity.

It had been fairly straightforward after that. Aided by Wanda to gain discreet entry, he'd then searched Ringtree Gardens in the hope of discovering just what information David *had* so far gleaned. McDonald's trusting nature had helped a lot there. Unprotected by any security code, the data on his computer had led Wim straight to Battersea and ex-Commando Sergeant Williamson that same morning – and subsequently, to the office of Jaggers Singh. Why stow away aboard in the middle of a night when the simple cutting of a throat would arrange his legitimate appointment to the *Centaur?* What better opportunity, in fact, to extend his day-job experience while he chose the time to make his move?

Wanda had stayed on in the flat, of course; but he'd had to kill her too, don't you see? Because she simply wouldn't change her mind. No matter how much Wim had tried to persuade her – and to be scrupulously fair, he *had* tried very hard, as later evinced by the trail of blood from the bedroom – she'd remained fanatically adamant that, once they'd recovered the Nefertiti, she intended to negotiate political rather than fiscal concessions from the German government: resolutely loyal to brother Gunther's anarchistic but unprofitable ideology.

Second Officer Voorhoe . . . *Stollenberg* had looked genuinely uncomfortable at that point. An unfortunate necessity, severing his relationship with Inadi, so to speak, then rigging the doctor's apartment to blow in order to gain time to contrive proof for the police, at least at first sight, that McDonald was indeed a madman and had only been fantasizing about the last unsolved riddle posed by the Stollenberg convoy.

While, as he'd already explained, there'd been absolutely no intention to kill *you*, Mister Kyle, sir – or not at that point. Only later. After I'd made the connection between your name in the doctor's computer address book, and your turning up to join in Rotterdam; you'll understand, I'm sure.

A fulsome apology indeed.

Made infinitely more chilling by the sincerity of its delivery.

*   *   *

A stunned silence ensued on the part of Kyle and Lewis. Not that taking time out to mull over young Stollenberg's arguments helped very much in the end.

Kyle could still only think of one response.

'You're crazy, Mister,' he decided. 'Mad as a bloody hatter.'

'Ohhhh *shit*!' Lewis groaned, and tensed.

The second officer stopped looking amiable. He didn't say anything, didn't take offence and begin shouting hysterically, or foaming at the mouth like a proper lunatic might have done. Didn't look particularly resentful even.

But the alacrity with which the Glock came in line with Kyle's chest again *did* indicate that not only had Kyle's hostility disappointed him, but that Kyle had just helped achieve the quantum leap needed for a second mate to shoot his Chief Officer.

'*Go*, Kyle!' Lewis roared unexpectedly.

'Pardon?' Kyle asked uncertainly.

Lewis launched himself hopelessly at the gun. Hopelessly because Lewis had been a Royal Marine. Apart from having been trained to keep his mouth shut if he couldn't think of anything prudent to say to a psychopath holding a gun, he could estimate to the millisecond how much longer it would take him to reach 2/O Stollenberg than Stollenberg would take to fire.

And he was right.

He'd hardly made it halfway across the confined cabin before Kyle, who hadn't actually got round to moving at all, saw the Glock twist fractionally as Stollenberg squeezed the trigger.

It was hardly Kyle's fault that he so singularly failed to back Lewis up.

Well, *he* wasn't a bloody ex-Royal, was he? *He* hadn't been educated in the fundamentals of hand-to-hand combat, had he? Where a concerted move by two men could buy those vital micro-moments of living time. The closest he normally got to that sort of thing was when confronted by a bevy of drunken sailors, whose malice was usually more verbal than physical anyway. Never by a chap with a gun.

Except for one occasion. Back on the Piazza Santorini?

It was only when Lewis kept on going – had actually reached the Second Officer and begun to grapple with him yet again – that Kyle realized something was missing. The sound of the gunshot, of the whole burst in fact, because he'd definitely watched Stollenberg thumb the safety forward through single to automatic.

Magazine jam? Misfire?

He'd hardly launched himself at the struggling pair before Stollenberg smashed the gun against Lewis's shoulder where Kyle had also recently, albeit with the best of intentions, struck him with the full weight of a golden statuette. But that had hardly been *his* fault either, he reflected savagely, considering!

Lewis yelled and recoiled in agony. Kyle somehow managed to collide with him while still off balance and slammed him back into Stollenberg, knocking the machine pistol from the 2/O's hand. The gun went skittering across the deck while Stollenberg, still clutching the Nefertiti, took off in the direction of the door from the day room. Kyle snarled 'Sorry!' to Lewis and kept on going, the rage black in him as he frantically attempted to overtake the fleeing Canadian.

A massive jolt – the *Centaur* reeled from the assault by yet another sea mountain – Jesus, she was falling even further over to starboard now, all the time thundering down below like a great submarine kettledrum while the deck canted and the floral-patterned inclinometers kept leaning further and further!

Capitão Barrosa slid limply from his chair with the shock of the sea blow whereupon Kyle, focused only on making a last furious lunge, tripped clean over the Old Man to sprawl full length just as Stollenberg gained a handhold on the alleyway door frame, instantly feeling to release the cabin hook retaining the inward-opening door.

Only then did the 2/O hesitate, bracing himself against the list of the ship and reaching down for the handle. But for hardly longer than a heartbeat: only time enough to smile ever so triumphantly downhill at Kyle.

'Guess I should ask formally, huh? Permission to abandon ship, sir?'

'Bugger off, Mister!' Kyle roared, not really meaning it.

'Aye, aye, sir,' Stollenberg acknowledged, smart as a brush.

He'd've been a damn good man to turn to in a crisis, Kyle reflected numbly. *The archetypal seaman officer in fact. If he hadn't been crazy.*

His excellent, albeit fundamentally flawed protégé gripped the handle and, ever so deliberately, hauled the heavy door shut against the pull of gravity. The door Kyle had already assured him was solid mahogany under the paint – the door there wasn't a hope in hell of breaking through.

Kyle knew from the way of the ship that he and Lewis were lost then. Knew exactly how David must have felt in that terrible instant between platform and rail – knew precisely what it felt like to be murdered.

He knew all that the moment he heard the snap of the key turning in the lock.

The key Kyle himself had already inserted on the other side. To save Second Officer Voorhoeve the trouble.

CHAPTER TWENTY-THREE

Kyle couldn't help but think how Samuel Johnson might well have had the *Centaur* in mind, and how sagacious the Doctor had been.

Being in a ship, he'd written a century and a half before, *is being in a jail, with the chance of being drowned.*

Hackman would have appreciated that. In fact, with Hackman's literary leanings it was a wonder he hadn't thought to remind Kyle of it. He'd've taken a certain wry satisfaction from quoting the subsequent line too: *A man in a jail has more room, better food, and commonly better company.*

Unarguably so, Doctor Johnson. Particularly if your shipboard alternative included Hackman as cook. And Stollenberg as part of the company.

Kyle tried the door handle to confirm beyond doubt that the second officer *had* locked it. He'd learned his lesson at last: he wasn't going to die because of yet another overhasty assumption on his part – even braced a foot against the angled frame and gave the handle an extra hard yank. Just to make doubly sure.

The handle came off in his hand. Fifty bloody years of usage an' all it did was prove Samuel Johnson overly optimistic. Chance didn't enter the equation, in this particular jail. Kyle's drowning in convoy with Lewis within the next few minutes had just been guaranteed.

Unless . . . ?

He felt an overpowering surge of relief. They *did* still have one option left!

Lewis appeared at the night cabin door as if on cue, leaning gingerly against its frame for support. Although he'd tucked his left arm into his shirt the shoulder still dipped slightly. It looked as if Kyle had managed to break his collar bone with the Nefertiti. But the machine pistol he held in his right hand was of greater interest right then.

'Show me how to clear the jam, Lewis. We can shoot the lock off.'

'Go to the movies a lot, do you?' Lewis asked.

'Say again?'

'Magazine's empty.' Lewis tossed the Glock carelessly aside. 'Since that first burst he'd been holding us up with an empty weapon.'

'Bloody useless gun!' Kyle snarled, airily disregarding the corollary that, if it hadn't been, they'd both be dead already.

The curtains swung even further and the grey storm light brightened in the cabin, causing the Capitão's braid – the cuff rings of which Barrosa had been so proud – to glint softly. Gold they were, but soiled by blood; just like the damned Nefertiti.

The *Centaur* gathered herself uncertainly, debating whether to capsize now or fight a little longer.

'We could try the scuttles?' Lewis suggested.

'This isn't a warship, Lewis. In the Merchant Navy we call 'em ports,' Kyle growled, nit-picking fractious. '*Port* holes, an' the ones in the night cabin are too small to wriggle through.'

While the forward-facing ones – the rectangular windows looking out over the well deck, against which near-solid water already thundered – were fixed panes of armoured glass. They'd

251

been designed to keep oceans out. Or those such as the percipient Doctor Johnson had in mind, in.

'I want you to know before we die, Kyle,' Lewis said, 'that I hated your guts from the moment I saw you at Nanny Williamson's flat and figured you for being after the Nefertiti – an' that you've done bugger all in the last few minutes to make me change my mind.'

'Careful, Able Seaman. I'm still the Mate. I could have you logged for insolence.' Kyle smiled weakly. There didn't seem much point in panicking when they'd nowhere to panic to. 'Anyway, if you thought I'd killed Sergeant Williamson, why didn't you turn me in there and then?'

'Because I intended to square the account for Ted myself.' Lewis shrugged. Not a good idea because he winced. 'But I wasn't a hundred per cent sure and I don't act on hunches without proof.'

'Of course not,' Kyle muttered uncomfortably.

'Which was why I fixed things with Singh Shipping to sign me on. I reckoned whoever wanted the statuette had to be aboard for this last trip.'

'Yet you *still* jumped to the wrong conclusion when you found me sailing as Mate,' Kyle summarized shamelessly. 'Not too smart, huh? Spending the whole passage to Naples watching the wrong suspect.'

'You're lucky I did, Kyle,' Lewis countered grimly. 'Hackman's being aboard saved you from going over the wall first night out. Couldn't make up my mind where he fitted in. Decided to wait until one or other of you made your play, then . . . '

Lewis didn't risk another shrug, but Kyle got the message. Before frowning uncertainly as a further, rather unsettling thought struck him. Especially as he was locked in with the guy.

'That contract of appointment you produced, Lewis. *You* didn't kill Jaggers, did you?'

'Didn't even know he was dead until Stollenberg admitted to it – though I could have, quite happily. He was banking on my needing to leave the country fast: demanded a hundred quid for helping out.'

'At least he never got to spend it,' Kyle said consolingly.

'Mary could have done with it. Especially now.' Lewis's expression grew hard. 'It's them I feel for. Mary and the kids, and Nan Williamson.'

It was Kyle's turn to shrug. He felt more inclined towards self-pity, right then, than sympathy. 'Presumably you were a Royal when you married. Mary must have known it wasn't the safest career in the world.'

'She was the factor that persuaded me to come out. Only I hadn't reckoned on meeting up with a lunatic in civvy street.'

'You got unlucky with Stollenberg.'

'I wasn't thinking of Stollenberg,' Lewis said, eyeing Kyle pointedly.

Hurriedly Kyle avoided pursuing that vein of conversation by stepping over the captain to frown hard at the ventilation ducting in the cavity where the Nefertiti had lain concealed for so long. Anything rather than hang around waiting helplessly and saying all the wrong things anyway. The corroded ducts were too narrow to even think of attempting to escape to deck level through them. The smallest child would've found it impossible.

Apart from which, the prospect of the ship going down while trapped in one of those made dying in the Old Man's cabin an infinitely preferable alternative.

Disconsolately he walked uphill to the door and pushed at it vaguely, then tried to look through the keyhole without success. It was blocked from the other side. By the key he'd inserted. And the lock was solid brass bolted through mahogany. Even given proper tools it would take longer to chip out than the ship would afford them.

It reminded him of the door to Shipskull Lane. Double-panelled, once proudly varnished, no doubt, but now covered by layers of poorly applied paint, the last peeling coat probably twenty years old. The Russians never did look after their ships properly.

Kyle shoved at the upper panel again – it would have withstood a battering ram. Bloody German shipyards. You'd've thought with the war going badly and the shortage of raw materials at the time, they would have cut back a bit on the quality they built into their vessels! Mind you, that *was* why the *Yuryi Rogov* had lasted long enough to take himself and Lewis down with her, and kill David and the others before that. He stood back and glowered at the damn door, trying desperately to think.

'You're not going to suggest I put my shoulder to it, are you?' Lewis called anxiously.

The lettering under the peeling layers of paint on the lower panel was only faintly detectable. Applied way back, and now only visible as barely raised characters under the pallid side-lighting. Russian? German? Didn't *look* like Cyrillic characters? *Die Füllu . . . Die Füllung mit dem . . .*

'Christ, it's just struck me,' Kyle muttered as tentative realization dawned. 'She was built during the *war*, Lewis!'

'I'll try not to forget that, Kyle,' Lewis promised.

'It meant she ran the risk – a high risk at the time she was built – of being torpedoed. An' sometimes, when a ship's torpedoed she deforms; sometimes the explosion can jam doors – trap crewmen inside . . . '

Die Füllung mit dem . . . Fusse STOSSEN!

'. . . so they fitted World War II allied merchantmen's compartment doors with kick-out PANELS, dammit!'

The panel with the foot to PUSH?

Kyle prayed his elementary German was about to prove the Nazis had done the same. He kicked the lower panel as if – well, as if his life depended on it.

It fell out.

'I still think, Able Seaman Lewis,' Kyle said, 'we should leave now.'

CHAPTER TWENTY-FOUR

Kyle did wonder, for one terrifying moment after they'd raced up the steeply inclined internal stairway to reach the deserted bridge, whether escape had benefited them much.

Viewed through the streaming wheelhouse windows the *Centaur* now listed a good twenty degrees, with the forward well-deck scuppers under and sea creaming clear over the maelstrom line of her submerged starboard bulwark to explode against the hatch coamings in fragmenting, wind-snatched cliffs of spray. Every new roller caused her to shy anew, her angled foremast to describe a further, drunkenly erratic arc against a low overcast still leaden with malice.

But at least he could *see* sky and – when he half-staggered, half-slid out to the starboard wing to gaze outboard and down – feel the wind, deliciously heavy with the taste and feel of salt, snatching at his hair. All of a sudden dying, to Kyle, seemed an infinitely less squalid business. An awfully great adventure indeed, if it had to be.

Lewis joined him, pointing. 'Someone wouldn't even qualify for a job as village idiot.'

A twenty-man life-raft had been taken by the storm in the moment it inflated. Now, still empty of occupants to stabilize it, it bowled sideways downwind and away from the ship, skipping and bouncing on edge from wave crest to sighing wave crest like a great orange and black Catherine wheel heading for the coast of North Africa. Some ill-trained and panicking sailor must have let go of the painter before thinking to get into it.

Mayday Centaur, Centaur, Centaur!

The ancient VHF crackled to life from the wheelhouse – you beaut, Chowdhury! You got a Mayday out before you took the decision to abandon – or before the bloody crew took it for you!

This is Italian warship Leonardo da Vinci. We now have you ahead on radar, sir, at one mile to windward.

A second life-raft, mercifully with men in it this time, drifted away from the ship's side. Its orange canopy flopped aimlessly, still deflated. Kyle could make out Chief Engineer Mohammad Ben Saaidi in the group of survivors packing the raft's entry port; as he watched, the Chief removed his splendid porcelain teeth and, gazing up at Kyle above him with a huge gapped grin, flourished them triumphantly before carefully placing them in his oil-soaked boiler suit pocket.

Kyle waved nonchalantly back, glad the indefatigable Chief had made it. So far.

A third life-raft barely inflated at all: only a pathetic, barely seen balloon still protruding from its split fibreglass container. And a fourth. Almost empty.

But not quite.

Jesus! Third Officer Chowdhury – Chief Cook Bokros and the utterly useless Haitian Second Engineer, Beaubrun? All clinging terrified to the ratlines, as well they might be. Only one of the buoyancy sections in the neoprene last chance that had been permitted to overrun its service period by months if not years had fully inflated.

The raft swooped crazily down into a black sucking trough, then expressed vertically as the next sea curled in below. Down again – then UP! Pirouetting uncontrollably now upon a great swelling of rumbling water. A fairground ride – a *fear*-ground ride! The manic waltzer – the death slide!

Kyle's hands convulsed, gripped the scarred teak rail before him as he watched in horror. The following crest began to fragment: boiling, then breaking to overwhelm Chowdhury's flotsam haven. The leading, unbuoyed section of the raft hinged back and rolled over the three men, trapping them within its clammy embrace before capsizing in a flailing tumble of orange and black.

'*Look!*' Lewis shouted.

The low, rakish silhouette of the Italian warship appeared briefly through the scudding sea-haze. She was turning now and slowing, presenting her broadside to the stricken *Centaur* to afford catchment to the rafts blowing to leeward. Then the visibility closed in and the wind increased to a scream while the rescue vessel disappeared as if it had never been.

The *Centaur* reeled before the press of the near-hurricane as Kyle launched himself towards the wheelhouse, lunging for the spluttering VHF handset with one eye hypnotized by the glint of the inclinometer – the proper inclinometer! The deck canted further – twenty-two . . . twenty-three . . . twenty-*five* degrees!

'Mayday Warship – this is *Centaur*!'

Mayday standing by, sir!

'I have men in the water – forty-two crew. We're abandoning . . . !'

Centaur – Warship. We will make a lee starboard side. Boarding nets already rigged. Good luck, sir.

Twenty-six – twenty-bloody-*seven* degrees! Kyle could detect the keening whistle of compressed air ejecting from a nearby ventilator, forcing from the holds where the sea was taking charge.

Lewis must have been ferreting about in the chartroom because he came out with two mould-stained lifejackets and handed one to Kyle.

257

'*Now* can we go, Mate?' he said.

'Bugger that,' Kyle snarled, though he didn't resent the suggestion. After all, Lewis *had* observed protocol, and asked permission. 'We still haven't found Stollenberg.'

Lewis just grinned wanly as Kyle helped him slip his lifejacket over his head and tie the tapes. He had guts, what with his damaged wing and the lifejackets about as useful as a salt oar, and being about to drown and everything. Not that Kyle would have expected anything less from a Royal Marine.

Lewis's perplexingly cryptic retort did give him cause to frown a bit irritably, though.

'Don't get too close to him if we do,' his companion in hazard advised thought-provokingly. 'And for Christ's sake, Kyle – even if you get the chance, *don't* hit the bastard with the bloody Nefertiti like you did me!'

They saw Second Officer Voorhoe . . . *Stollenberg* as soon as they ran out to the wing again, gazing searchingly aft this time, albeit forced to cling to the rail to prevent themselves skating clean down the streaming planking and out over the bridge end.

He was struggling desperately to man-handle a life-raft container to the side of the ship from its rack in the after boat deck stowage. It was heavy and cumbersome but he was managing. Whether his efforts were worthwhile or not remained to be seen. Only when the nylon painter was jerked, and the pressurized gas cylinders triggered, would anyone know if it would give the lie to its undoubtedly long passed service-due-by date.

Either way it was the last raft left on the ship. And in that wind-lashed maelstrom where the sea has been whipped to aerated foam between water and sky, a man in a lifejacket, with his mouth and nose only just supported above what used to be the surface, will very quickly drown no matter how many sea-survival courses he's attended.

The raft came free and Stollenberg, still smart despite his khaki drills being black with spray, levered the heavy canister to the very edge of the cliff, ready to jettison it.

Kyle snarled 'Come on!' and lunged for the ladder, not caring whether Lewis was following or not. Stollenberg must have seen the movement because he spun round then, and froze. Psychopath or not, he was evidently capable of feeling surprise – his incredulity was evident even at that distance. Capitão Ferreiro Cavaco Barrosa must have displayed much the same expression of disbelief when one of his most trusted officers unexpectedly stepped in behind his chair and placed his hand upon the Old Man's splendid cap.

Except that Stollenberg lived through his moment of astonishment. Then calmly placed his foot on the teetering canister. An appropriate move in the circumstances, Stollenberg. Kyle could even translate the native words as they spun through the young man's mind.

Die Füllung mit dem Fusse STOSSEN!

Except this time it's *das Rettungs-floss*, Wilhelm. The life-raft *mit dem* foot to push. The *last* bloody *Rettungs-floss* on the ship! Running flat-out as he was for Stollenberg, and all the while trying to keep his footing on the angled deck, Kyle couldn't for the life – or death – of him remember the German for 'last'.

The Second Officer pushed with his foot and the heavy canister rolled over the side. The 2/O yanked the painter and even above the screech of the wind Kyle heard the gas bottles evacuating below. He was grateful that Stollenberg was a seaman – and a damn good one. Having inflated the raft *he* wouldn't be foolish enough to let the thing go before he'd boarded.

He saw the bag then, lying on the deck – the waxed canvas bag containing the Nefertiti – but only for a fleeting moment before Stollenberg snatched it up and leaned over the boat deck rail with arm extended. Jesus he was cool – no, chilling in his calculated determination. He wasn't going to risk the chance of jumping and missing the raft from that height, albeit it was rapidly growing less as the list increased. He calmly intended to board from the next deck down, the promenade deck.

Ten yards to run – nearly *on* Stollenberg – until the *Centaur* gave a great lurch and fell even further! Kyle veered helplessly off course and cannoned violently into a ventilator, sinking dazed and sickened to his knees for the most crucial few seconds of his pursuit because it allowed the 2/O to climb astride the rail and poise himself to jump.

From the prom deck it would only be a moment to recover his footing, then transfer to the raft now bumping and soaring alongside before cutting the painter with its ready-attached safety knife – and allowing the wind to carry it down to the waiting warship, leaving Kyle and Lewis stranded on a ten-thousand-ton millstone.

Stollenberg looked back then, almost casually, straight at Kyle with his arm still outstretched and the Nefertiti poised to drop far beyond Kyle's reach, and smiled a terrible smile of triumph. Only the smile wasn't engaging any more. Or even human. Because when Kyle stared into the second officer's eyes he saw twin pools of undiluted evil. He saw what David must have seen in that last frantic scream of his life.

And Kyle knew he was looking at the true Stollenberg Legacy.

He still tried. He lunged from his crouch and launched himself furiously to grasp Stollenberg – his fingers even brushed the khaki shirt, almost pushing his quarry off balance. Caught by surprise, the 2/O hastily swivelled on the rail, literally threw the bag to the deck below, then clumsily vaulted after it.

Kyle realized he had a chance then. Slamming against the rail and staring wildly down he could see Stollenberg had landed heavily – still sprawling helplessly with the Nefertiti under him and, Kyle prayed, probably two or three ribs smashed by the impact of falling on the artefact.

He heard someone shouting from a distance as he, too, climbed the rail and, berserk now, prepared to launch himself feet-first on top of the helpless man.

'*No*, Kyle – *stay* there, for God's sake!'

A hand grasped his collar and yanked him unceremoniously backwards, clean off the rail. Arms flailing, he crashed to the deck to find himself staring up through a red, confused haze at Able bloody Seaman bloody LEWIS!

'You don't understand, Kyle,' Lewis was yelling at him. Which was curious. Because it was precisely the phrase Lewis had tried to utter the *last* time Kyle had hit him under a misapprehension.

With the Nefertiti?

It was the oddest thing.

How Second Officer Wilhelm Stollenberg began to go black within thirty seconds.

In less than a minute the eyes that had so shocked Kyle had begun to dilate and a clear fluid to ooze from them. Even on the deck above they could hear his lungs screeching for air; blood erupted from the corner of his mouth and the once-fair hair seemed to go like wire as they watched. Foul yellow pustules appeared to form under the livid black and his face, already tortured beyond imagination, became deformed.

He couldn't scream. His head had arched back, his teeth glistened white in a last rictal smile, his windpipe compressed with the agony of whatever enormity had stricken him. And then, within two minutes at most, the tortured writhing became spasmodic, and then ceased altogether; and Second Officer Wilhelm Stollenberg was dead.

'*Jesus*,' Kyle whispered as he cautiously drew back from the lip of the upper deck, numb with the horror of what he had witnessed. 'What killed him?'

'Stoff Three Eight One,' Lewis said.

CHAPTER TWENTY-FIVE

They made it to the last life-raft with bare seconds to spare. Even as they leapt from the canting boat deck, the two minutes Stollenberg took to die – which was still longer than he'd afforded most of those he'd murdered – had reduced the height they were forced to jump.

In the end a sea swept in and, while it rumbled and exploded across the after well deck, tearing the hatch cover clean from number five to vortex monstrously into the hold itself, ripping Fiat motor cars and packing cases of cheap tinned fish and balks of Norwegian timber from already suspect lashings to a cacophony of rending steel, the same sea also raised the raft almost to deck level.

'GO!' Kyle roared and took Lewis's good arm to reassure him, then the two of them leapt together for the gyrating entry port as it pirouetted past them.

They landed in a foot of water under the orange canopy. Kyle ignored Lewis's muffled cry of pain, concerned only to scramble for the safety knife attached to the painter. He slashed it and it parted, and for that Kyle was desperately grateful because, while life-raft painters are fitted with hydrostatic releases to free them under water, there's no guarantee that they will always work and, even if they do, the raft would still have been dragged metres deep by its umbilical.

And then they were scudding downwind, but *still* with the *Centaur* looming over them, and Kyle stared helplessly up as the mainmast stays came guillotining down towards them like thrumming giant cheese wires as the ship began to capsize, whereupon tons of white water that had previously raced across the well deck to explode against the port bulwarks came avalanching back, carrying splintered hatch boards and shreds of canvas covers and detritus from the breached hold itself along with fifty years of accumulated filth and anything else lying loose on the decks.

Kyle yelled, '*Geddown*, Lewis!' somewhat unnecessarily, then shielded his own head in terror as the lethal flood smashed down on a neoprene canopy offering not the slightest protection. It only needed a heavy shackle, never mind a balk of spruce or a Fiat motor car, to penetrate and kill.

The deluge exploded through the entry port, swamping the already half-filled space and hurling Kyle in a tangle with Lewis, who simply clung there and swore in a continuous, seemingly never-ending monotone. A rending sound as something heavy ripped through as predicted, and then a larger object, soft and yielding, slammed into the raft from above while the wire stays of the mainmast zipped alongside them, aerating the already frenzied sea into foam.

The deluge became intermittent, then stopped altogether, and Kyle could see through the narrow slit that they really were drifting clear, although he couldn't quite understand why he was blinking at a *plan* view of the decks: the kind of aspect only a seaman clinging to the mainmast truck would normally expect to see if he dared to look down at all; or a seagull, of course. Flying above the ship.

Until he realized he was viewing the *Centaur* – no, the *Yuryi*

Rogov, for that's who she'd been most of her life, and was still the name she was entitled to bear with a certain pride as she went to her grave – but now she was lying on her side, still awesome as she blotted out the storm with her elegant funnel smashing flat on the sea and her rusted topsides revolving faster and faster while her derricks tumbled from their crutches.

Then she came bottom-up, with gouts of white spray bursting through the rent in her hull. Until her inverted bow dipped and her rudder and propeller rose to the sky, and she began to slide, almost hesitantly at first as if frightened of what awaited her, and then faster as she realized she was about to go to a far more fitting place than some beach south of Srivardhan, fouled with the rusted bones of a hundred no longer wanted ships before her.

And then she was gone.

Kyle half floated in the waterlogged raft and blinked a little, as any seaman would over the death of his vessel. And then looked up at the now-concave canopy still collapsed under the weight of the object that had struck them. It was already torn when the shackle had crashed through. Now, with the violent motion of the raft it was beginning to rip further. He unlashed the paddles and bailer and, kneeling with difficulty, prodded tentatively aloft at the neoprene-bouncing supercargo, trying to dislodge it.

It slipped sullenly, unresistingly sideways to lodge, dangling, over the entry port.

Lewis blurted 'Jesus Christ!' and involuntarily recoiled in shock.

'What the hell's wrong with you now, Lewis?' Kyle snapped irritably, still piqued at being yanked off the rail by an able seaman.

He swivelled to see what Lewis was staring at – and yelped 'Jesus *Christ*!'

The black-swollen face of Second Officer Stollenberg hung upside down from the canopy, staring in at their place of

ragile refuge through bulbous eyes, with the once-fair hair
dank and dangling and his limply swinging arms swollen to
errible proportions.

'Don't TOUCH him, Kyle!' Lewis shouted. 'Don't even put a
fingertip on him!'

'I wasn't bloody *planning* to,' Kyle snarled back, trying not to
be sick.

Revulsed, he gingerly poked the blade of the paddle under
– above? – Stollenberg's chin and shoved. The second officer
slithered unresistingly from the canopy and entered the water
with hardly a splash. *Lucky he wasn't wearing a lifejacket*, Kyle
thought macabrely, *or he'd be following in our bloody wake all the
way to the warship*.

'Now throw the paddle in after him,' Lewis snapped urgently.

'We need it, Lewis.'

'We don't. I can promise you we don't, Kyle.'

There were more paddles in the stow so, just to keep the peace,
Kyle threw the paddle clear of the raft then wearily picked up
the bailer.

Kyle just had to make his point.

'Back there on the boat deck? Were you seriously trying to tell
me, Lewis, that Stollenberg was killed by *washing* powder?'

'Don't be silly, Kyle!' Lewis growled, understandably fractious
now with the pain of his broken shoulder.

'You said it was Stoff Three Eight-something.'

'One. Three Eight One.'

Kyle frowned. 'Well, Rushby said that was washing powder.'

No, come to think of it, Rushby hadn't actually *said* it was
washing powder. But he'd definitely mentioned washing powder. Kyle wished, then, he'd paid a little more attention to the
professor.

'I don't know who the hell Rushby is, but he obviously didn't
do a classified chemical warfare course. He was thinking of
Trilon One Four Six – that was a generic code name based

on a detergent common in Germany at the time. They always picked code names that were as innocuous as the weapon they represented was devilish.'

'So what was it that killed Stollenberg?'

'A super-derivative of Stoff One Four Six – the specific cipher reference for Sarin nerve gas, Kyle. Hundred per cent kill factor and fast-acting. The Nazis developed small quantities of it at Dyhernfurth just before the end of World War II. Thank God they didn't produce it in family size. You saw what it could do to a man – chances were Stollenberg only got a drop small as a pinhead on his skin when the flask finally disintegrated.'

Kyle was glad he'd listened to Lewis for once, and thrown the paddle away.

'What flask?'

'It was in the bag with the Nefertiti. Only being steel, and not gold, it had corroded to hell over fifty years in a salt atmosphere. Ted Williamson warned me about it, just as Gunther must've warned Wilhelm. The old battler realized it was bloody dangerous, though he didn't know why. Just saw the chemical Death's Head with what he called a *Verboten Nicht Touchen* legend on it, and thought it would make a damn good booby trap if anyone found the Nefertiti before he and his troop returned to the ship to heist it. And believe me, they would have done if she hadn't been passed to the Soviets. They were very tough soldiers, Ted and my dad.'

It still didn't make sense to Kyle. The Second Officer had always been so meticulous. Okay, he'd made a few mistakes, but in general he never took unnecessary chances.

'But if Stollenberg knew the flask was lethal, an' probably in a dangerous condition, why did he risk leaving it in the bag? He wasn't that crazy, Lewis – hell, he even *dropped* it on to a steel deck before jumping after it.'

'He didn't.' Lewis smiled tightly then. 'When I surprised him in Barrosa's cabin he'd already removed it and carefully laid it aside on the Old Man's berth. Must have taken guts to touch it. For all he knew, the super-Sarin could have been leaching out for years.'

'So?'

'I put it back while you were yelling at him. You were bloody pompous, you know – all that *I'm the Mate: Right Hand of God* stuff? If I'd been Stollenberg I'd've shot you there an' then.'

'He was too good a seaman, conditioned to think like a second officer. He wouldn't have dared,' Kyle retorted, not even convincing himself.

The bailer hit something metallic submerged under the dirty water swilling in the bottom of the raft: the shackle or whatever that had nearly brained him when it ripped through the canopy, swept overboard by the same flood that had aided Stollenberg in abandoning too – damn dangerous, sliding around unsecured.

Kyle leaned forward, feeling to recover it. It was glinting softly even before he'd lifted it clear of the surface.

Not gunmetal. Brass?

No. Not brass either. Kyle gazed hypnotically at the heavy lump of jetsam clutched firmly in his hand. Without a shadow of doubt it was the most exquisite man-made object he'd ever seen.

'It may have been decontaminated by immersion,' Lewis said almost conversationally. 'I'll tell you in roughly thirty seconds.'

It wasn't only Commando Sergeant Williamson and Corporal Lewis who'd been hard as nails.

Kyle wished Lewis had been more reassuring, had said it *would* be decontaminated by now. The Able Seaman's uncertainty made the next half-minute seem a very long time.

The motion of the raft became calmer as the Italian warship allowed the windblown raft to pass ahead of her, then moved to place it under her lee.

'Little William's got his birthday party in a fortnight,' Lewis said. 'You can come if you want to.'

Kyle, the confirmed bachelor, wasn't sure about that. Most of the guests would be six years old. One psychopath running amok had been enough. He didn't know if he had the courage to handle a room full of them.

267

Mind you, he probably should return to the UK to clear up a few misconceptions before looking for another ship. Apart from which, he still had to track down McDonald's missing Hoover – and it *would* be nice to feel a part of a family again.

The Nefertiti – the once-mythical Nefertiti – gazed up at him enigmatically.

David would be so pleased.